HER STAND-IN COWBOY

HER STAND-IN ROMANCE SERIES
BOOK ONE

Crystal Walton

Impact Editions, LLC
Chesapeake, VA

Impact Editions, LLC
www.crystal-walton.com

This is a work of fiction. Names, characters, places, and incidents are a product of the author's imagination. Locales and public names are sometimes used for atmospheric purposes. Any resemblance to actual people, living or dead, or to businesses, companies, events, institutions, or locales is completely coincidental.

Book Layout ©2013 BookDesignTemplates.com

Cover Design ©2019 Josephine Blake of Covers and Cupcakes

Author Photo by Charity Mack

Her Stand-in Cowboy/ Crystal Walton

ISBN 978-1-7328162-2-0

Library of Congress Control Number: 2019916936

To all my fellow boy moms, solidarity, friend. Solidarity.

And to each of us who needs this tender reminder: You are seen, you are known, you are loved. When it's hard. When it makes no sense. Through the questions that rage and the aches that taunt. Even after loss, love continues to pursue your heart. Right now and always.

Chapter One

Only in Ainsley Jamison's life would her own letdown find a way to shoot her in the face as retribution for oversleeping. On a positive note, the morning's power outage had eliminated the chance of anyone seeing her stumbling around her dark room like a vertigo-ridden showgirl. She should celebrate the wins, right?

Her almost-laugh petered into a sigh. Why today? She couldn't miss another appointment.

After a whirlwind rush through her normal routine, Ainsley kissed her baby boy goodbye, thanked her younger sister Kate for watching him, and whipped her hair into a ponytail on her way out the door.

The damp wind soaring from the mountains took full advantage of her thirty-second run to the van. Even in North Carolina, the cotton dress she'd grabbed off the mounds of clothes she'd tripped over in her scramble to get ready wasn't exactly November material. At least she didn't have to worry about mismatched socks. Her underwear, on the other hand, felt... odd.

She eyed her hot-mess-of-a-mama self in the rearview mirror before backing out of the long driveway. Thankfully, she'd be facedown for her chiropractic appointment. Not that Dr. Southerland would pay her lack of makeup any mind. He'd seen her through worse—nine months of it.

Another swing of emotions rocked her on her way down the country road she'd traveled nearly every day of her life. She glanced from the empty passenger seat to her son's car seat and grasped at the reminder that she shouldn't feel alone.

Still, as the wipers smeared watercolors of memories across the windshield, questions she couldn't answer only beat stronger. Why did the rain choose to wash some memories away and not others?

A ring from inside her purse rerouted her dead-end thoughts. Until she saw the name on the screen.

She almost didn't answer but gave in as always. She'd make it quick this time. "Hey, Mama. Can I call you back? I'm driving—"

"Riding? What in heaven's name would you be riding this time of day?"

A merry-go-round of insanity? "Not riding, Mama. *Driving.*"

"Oh. So, you have time to talk then. Perfect. Listen, punkin', I was thinking about our Thanksgiving plans—"

"Our *canceled* plans." Was the woman trying to give her a heart attack? "I thought you decided to stay in Florida with Aunt Jean for Thanksgiving."

"You know how things can change, sugar bunches. I was at the farmers market yesterday, and you'll never guess who showed up like the perfect gentleman at the exact moment I needed help."

Instead of the response Mama's dangling pause of suspense begged for, impending dread rose in Ainsley's throat. She swallowed it back down and adjusted her seat belt for the fifth time since buckling it. Not that either move made her the least bit more comfortable. And for crying out loud, why did her underwear's waistband feel like it was bumping into her bra?

"Ainsley, baby, did you hear me?"

She took a sip from her water bottle and uttered more of a grunt than an answer.

"Well, if you're not going to guess, I'll just have to tell you," she said, as if that wasn't exactly what she'd wanted to do all along. "Stephen Jewels."

Ainsley's foot slipped off the pedal. *Set-up Steve?* The woman truly *was* trying to kill her today. She yanked her water bottle out of the cup holder again and downed a third of it.

"I'm telling you, punkin', it was a divine encounter. We got to talking about you, Thanksgiving, and, well, it'd just all be so perfect. Oooh," she gushed. "I knew right then, I had to bring him with me."

Water spewed all over her steering wheel. "With you?" The prospect of her coming alone was daunting enough, but *with* Steve Jewels? No, this wasn't happening.

Ainsley regained control of the now-wet wheel and any semblance of a non-freaking-out tone. "Mama, we already talked about this. We agreed pulling together a big family Thanksgiving would be too hard on everyone, remember? Not to mention the expenses, the traveling." The endless harping, the awkward family tension, the noose she'd be obliged to test out before it was all over with.

"Fiddlesticks. You just don't want everyone over to that blessed farm you never should've taken on by yourself."

Here we go 'round the mulberry bush, the mulberry bush, the mulberry bush. Here we go 'round the mulberry bush so early in the morning.

"And Stephen isn't able to fly out to see his family for the holiday. You know darn well I couldn't leave him uninvited. He'll be coming, and that's the end of it."

Ainsley made a sharp turn toward Common Grounds. If she was going to come up with a way out of this nightmare-waiting-to-happen, she needed caffeine. And maybe a brownie. Or five. "Mama, I should really go. I'm already rushing to get to my appointment, and I don't want to wreck on my way for coffee."

"A hysterectomy? Oh, honey, are you sure that's what you want to do? I mean, given your situation, getting your tubes tied certainly isn't a bad idea, but—"

"Coffee, Mama. I'm getting *my coff-ee.*" With a side of cochlear implants for her mom if she could afford them.

Ainsley circled into a parking spot. "I just pulled up, so we'll talk later, 'kay?"

"But Ainsley—"

"Bye." She tossed her phone into her purse, tipped her head against the headrest, and waited for the rain clambering against the hood to beat the conversation and all its implications out of her mind.

Like that was happening.

Set-up Steve? Her matchmaking mom? The combination would be a disaster in the best of scenarios. Never mind having to avoid relationship advances *and* nonstop digs about the farm she wasn't entirely convinced her mom was wrong about.

She massaged her temples. Lordy, she might have to get a double shot today.

With a resigned sigh, Ainsley fished behind her seat for the umbrella she kept in the van and stepped into a blast of wind soaring up her dress. If she'd had half a molecule of brain power this morning, she would've at least opted to throw on some leggings.

She cleared the café's door without bulldozing anyone over in the parking lot and started for the two-person line. At least this would be quick.

Or it would've been if Mr. World's Most Complicated Order Ever weren't at the front of the line.

Ainsley stood on her tiptoes in search of the café's owner somewhere in the back. Knowing Mia, she had a solid reason for leaving the three younger workers Ainsley didn't know very well to man the counter alone. Still, unless that reason came with a free extra-large Irish cream coffee, Mia was going to owe her one.

She checked her cell while waiting on the baristas to figure out Mr. Dress Coat's order. Ten minutes until her appointment. She bounced on the balls of her feet, about to hop the counter to make the coffee herself. But when the three girls flat-out smacked into each other in a frantic spin, amusement overran her impatience.

Three blind mice. Three blind mice. See how they run. See how they run.

For once, the nursery rhymes permanently stuck in her head had her laughing out loud.

In a tailored rain jacket and dress shoes he probably got at Nordstrom, the guy ahead of her turned to seek out the source of her untimely display of delirium.

Ainsley cut a glance from his entertained green eyes to the scuffed black and white tiles and waited to move until she caught a peek of him strolling toward the condiment bar. Finally.

The three blind mice thankfully managed to breeze through the next woman's order as well as Ainsley's Irish coffee.

"Ainsley, hon'?"

She looked up from her cup in time to avert a collision with a girl coming in the opposite direction. Of all people, Hula Hoop Heather stood smack in front of her donning a pastel colored shirt that could've used five extra layers of thickness at minimum.

Ainsley tugged on her ear to avoid staring. She liked Heather. She did. But there were certain unspoken bonds women shared—understandings that all women agreed up-on. Like the undeniable fact that pantyhose were made by the devil, for instance. That the makers of the underwire previously worked in torture chambers. And that sometimes a girl simply needed to breathe.

Ainsley got that. Truly. Those sacred understandings were as grounded in friendships as the inherent pledge not to stare at or comment on each other's bodies. But when a girl looked like she hula hooped without wearing a bra for the past two decades, how were you supposed to pretend not to notice?

"Great day, I thought that was you." Heather pulled her into one of those awkward pat-hug embraces. The kind where one of the people felt like a wet noodle in the ravenous arms of a pasta fiend.

After the endurable length of time, Ainsley pulled back with her coffee cup held out to thwart a spill. "It's nice to see you, Heather, but I'm afraid I can't chat. I'm gonna be late to an appointment if I don't—"

"Ha." Heather slapped her thigh, sending her inner-tube duo ping-ponging across her stomach. "And here I'd almost thought you'd come into town for a little R and R for a change. Should've known you wouldn't tear yourself away from your place unless you had to."

"I've never been one much for hanging around." Despite Ainsley's vigilant attempt to veer her focus neck up, it somehow kept drifting south. "I prefer to lay low most of the time. Not stretch my limits." Was this conversation seriously happening?

She picked at the lid to her cup. "I was just swinging by for a little pick-me-up. Even this early, I was already starting to sag—*drag!*" Heaven help her. Nodding excessively, she gulped down her coffee, not even caring that it was black and hotter than Georgia asphalt. At this rate, she could use the jolt to shock her mouth into hushing up already.

"Well, you just be sure to get out for some fun every now and then. Let yourself loose sometimes. It's good to be free, honey."

Except in cases where elastic served a sacred purpose.

"Loose. Free. Yeah, that, um, definitely seems to work for you. So listen," Ainsley rambled toward the ceiling. "I should really go. You know how busy life gets with everything pulling at you." Appointments, bills... gravity.

With a thumb aimed behind her, Ainsley forced quick eye contact followed up with a genuine smile. "We'll touch base another time?"

"Sure thing, hon'. You take care of that little man of yours, now, you hear?"

"Always." Ainsley waved her cup at Heather while turning and let out an exhale once she was fully facing the opposite direction. Until another sight stopped her short—again.

You've got to be kidding me.

Chapter Two

Mr. Nordstrom Model was still at the café, taking his sweet time hogging up the condiment bar. He opened the bottom cabinets, withdrew a container of sugar, and proceeded to refill the empty jar up top. All while... whistling?

No one should be that chipper *before* drinking their coffee. And who openly pillaged through a supply cabinet unless they were an employee?

Ainsley checked the time on her cell once more. Five minutes left before she'd be late for her appointment. She faced the trusty ceiling again and exhaled slowly.

Once the guy completed his concerto, he swirled the sugar into his cup. And swirled. And swirled. Holy crow, was he going to eat his drink, or what?

An unceremonious snort escaped before she could stop it.

Mr. Sugar Rush turned. "Something funny?"

Oh, so many things she could say to that. Ainsley scratched her eyebrow like it would do a darn thing for the reply leaving her mouth without permission. "You mean aside from the Candy Land board game you just turned your coffee into?"

A ridiculously attractive dimple sank into his smooth cheek. "Not a fan of sugar?"

"I generally prefer to taste my coffee."

He graced her with a nod of concession and motioned for her to have a turn at the bar, to which she gladly exaggerated her single—and far more respectable—spoonful of sugar.

She withdrew a baggie from a side pocket in her purse containing a plastic spoon and a dozen cup stoppers. If she stirred herself into the next millennium, maybe she could ignore that grin following her every move.

"You bring your own supplies to the coffee shop?"

"When I can. You shouldn't be wasteful. It's bad for the planet." And now she was giving the guy a lecture on the environment. Glorious.

Grinning even wider, he raised his cup as if toasting her noble speech.

Meanwhile, Ainsley just stood there, unsure whether to toast back like a blithering moron, hide the sugar jar from him, or simply make a beeline for her car and forget this little interaction had happened at all.

Before she could decide, the toy she'd shoved into her purse the last time she and Josiah had run to the Post Office turned on. She cringed from head to toe. Once that sorry thing got started playing, there was no end to it. She would have chucked it in the trash ages ago if she had more than a sucker's chance of hoping her mom would forget she'd given it to Josiah when she last visited.

The toy's dying batteries created a horror-movie-sounding theme song that droned on endlessly. Somehow, it never seemed so fitting and yet, so unbelievably embarrassing.

Ainsley casually adjusted her purse strap on her shoulder. "That's, um…" Definitely her cue to leave.

When Mr. Dimple Quirker Extraordinaire's eyes didn't veer from hers, she didn't attempt to say more. Just turned, stopped at the door—because evidently, she couldn't help herself from toasting her cup in the air like an idiot anyway—and finagled her umbrella open one-handed.

She shouldn't have bothered. It flipped inside out the second she stepped through the door. Streaks of rain ran down her hair, her neck, her arms.

Just perfect.

Running through puddles, Ainsley tried to tame her dress from making headlines while masterfully dodging stares from patrons who probably had a wager going on to see who could keep a straight face the longest. Who could blame them? Between juggling her purse, cardboard cup, and useless umbrella, she looked like a bona fide circus act.

As if it couldn't get any worse, a gust of wind stormed up her legs until her dress matched the irreparable umbrella still flying upside down.

There went keeping her showgirl routine confined to her bedroom. Forget small-time. She was officially pulling out all the stops on a full-blown Marilyn Monroe scene for the entire world's viewing pleasure.

She dropped the traitorous umbrella and scrambled to cover her thighs but not before she caught a glimpse of the reason her britches had felt uncomfortable all morning. Granny panties. Like, actual full-size, boxy Fruit of the Loom underwear nearly covering the full length of her stomach.

Gah, she was going to kill Kate for dumping that package Mama had sent last week in her room. Stupid power outage. Stupid pile of clothes she had to dig through in the dark. Stupid... dimples closing in on her.

Have mercy, why did life hate her today?

Sheltered by a cooperating umbrella, Mr. Sugar Rush whisked her off to her van with perfect Mama-approved chivalry. He tented the black shield above them both as she opened the driver's side door, never more eager to gun away from a coffee shop in all her life.

"Any chance you didn't see that?" she asked pathetically.

"Which part?"

Ugh. It didn't even matter. The only thing that did right then was putting an end to what her mom surely would've deemed another divine encounter.

Ainsley mumbled her thanks while closing the door, pulled out of a parking lot she'd never be able to grace again, and avoided the rearview mirror with everything in her. She didn't bother turning on the heat to dry herself off. Her hot cheeks were bound to accomplish the job in half the time.

Sighing all the way through her seat, she bumped up the wipers and focused on the road to the chiropractor. But even after she'd parked in front of the glorious sign her body looked forward to seeing every month, she doubted Dr. Southerland could do enough cracking to shake that scene out of her head.

Marylin Monroe in granny panties? For land's sake, getting assaulted by her own breastmilk was less awkward.

Her cell rang as she made a dash inside with her Irish cream. A few sips of coffee hadn't come close to prompting a plan—*any* plan—to unravel Mama's set-up scheme. She reluctantly answered anyway. "Hey, Mama. I'm about to walk into my appointment, so…"

"I know when you're trying to avoid me, Ainsley Grace, and I'm not havin' it. It's been too long since we've all been together. Do you not want to see me?"

And the guilt trip begins.

"Of course I do." She stopped herself from pointing out her mom was the one who'd hardly made two licks of effort to come back to visit the home she'd chosen to leave in Whispering Pines three years ago.

The unresolved wound twisted and burned as it always did when she gave it room to fester. She slipped a business card off the front counter lest she shred her coffee cup instead. With her cell pinned between her ear and shoulder, she bent the card back and forth. "You know I want the family together. It's just that the farm—"

"Is too much for a single woman to manage. Not to mention it's no place to raise a baby."

Ainsley balled the card under her fingers. "It was fine enough when you raised us there."

"That's not the same thing."

Of course it wasn't. Ainsley blocked a dozen retorts with the longest sip of coffee humanly possible.

"You need to move in with Aunt Jean and me."

Coffee everywhere.

"What?"

"It's either us or Stephen. You can't keep living on your own."

Ainsley wiped her mouth. "I'm not on my own. Kate—"

"Has her own life to live, punkin'. You can't rely on her forever. Daphne neither."

Ainsley swallowed hard. Though postpartum life lent a hefty upsurge of untimely emotions most days, the truth of depending on her sister and cousin's help extended much deeper than fleeting hormones.

Something about the sound of the over-the-door bell dinging behind her caused her to snap. "You don't have to worry about Kate or Daphne or even Josiah, for that matter, because I'm not on my own." She wriggled up her shoulders, determined to get her mom off her back—even if it took a little fiction telling. "I've been seeing someone for a while now, and it's pretty serious, so…"

Oh, this could come back to bite her on so many levels.

"That rancher you met online from Montana? I thought he dumped you."

"Technically, *I* broke it off." One of the many benefits of having made-up boyfriends. She never had to get hurt.

"Good riddance. If you ask me, the man thought the sun came up just to hear him crow." Mama tsked. "All that talk, and he probably couldn't jump over a nickel to save a dime."

Okay, so maybe Convenient Colin's story wasn't Ainsley's best work, but wow. She didn't know whether to be insulted or impressed that she could create a make-believe person worthy of such abhorrence.

"Don't you think you're being a little rash? You never even met him."

"Exactly. What kind of man comes up with every excuse under the sun to avoid meeting his girlfriend's family? I'll tell you what kind. One with something to hide. And honestly, baby, do I need to send you another article on the homicidal maniacs out there preying on unsuspecting women who—?"

"Oh my gosh, Mama. Colin wasn't a homicidal maniac."

"Well, I'm sure he didn't advertise that on his online profile."

For the love of all things good and merciful.

Ainsley squeezed her forehead. "You don't have to worry about that this time. I didn't meet this new guy online. We met… through a friend."

"He's from Whispering Pines?"

Ainsley stifled a yeah-right snort. Aside from there being absolutely zero eligible bachelors in their country town, she'd never get away with making up a local who wasn't tied to a family Mama knew. "No, we met while he was visiting. He travels a lot. Business." That would provide ample reasons for why he wasn't around.

"Ainsley, if you're repeating history—"

"I'm not." And never would again. "He's different." She ran the crumpled business card along the edge of the counter, losing her thoughts to the heroes she'd fallen in love with on page after page of every novel she'd ever read. "He's strong and compassionate, brave and protective. Loves his family the way a man should." Everything her ex-husband hadn't been.

"Then why on earth is the man traveling so much?"

"Because he actually cares about others more than himself," she whipped off with legitimate defensiveness before remembering he wasn't real. "He's... a doctor."

"A traveling doctor?"

Why did her hearing suddenly have to improve? "Yeah. You know, the whole doctors without borders kind of thing. Like I said, sacrificial."

Mama's delayed response needled through the line. "Since when are you into the highfalutin doctor type?"

Crud. She squeezed her eyes shut in search of a back door. "He's a vet, actually."

A vet? She bit her lip. That's what she got for binge-watching the latest season of *Heartland* last month. "A very rustic, down-to-earth, cowboy type of vet." Who traveled all over creation on wildlife rescue missions? She banged her cup to her forehead. She needed to quit while she was ahead.

"A cowboy vet. Why am I not surprised? And does this young man have a name?"

Abort. Abort. "Um…" A fast and furious glance at the doctors' names mounted on the wall behind the counter provided no options. Mama would recognize each one. Stalling, she unclenched the mauled business card in her hand and zeroed in on the one name she didn't recognize shining in red font. "Connor."

Whoever that was. Must've been a new hire.

"Does Connor have a last name?"

Ainsley didn't have time to hesitate without it sounding suspicious. A quick glance at the card again ended in a tentative, "Allen. Dr. Connor Allen."

"Allen." Mama mulled over the name as if waiting for it to register. "And you're happy with this fella?"

With the make-believe boyfriend her family would never know apart from a borrowed name? "Yep. *Very* happy." She stared at her too-small cup, needing a gallon of coffee to wash down her guilt.

"Well then," she finally said. "I can't wait to meet him at Thanksgiving."

The business card fell beside her hasty plan with enough holes in it to sink a tank. "Oh. Yeah, no, coming for Thanksgiving probably isn't going to work out. Like I said, he travels a lot, and I'm sure he'd—"

"Love to," someone said from behind her with a lilt capable of throwing her entire equilibrium off balance.

Ainsley forced her stiff legs to inch around.

Her phone, her cup, her dignity—it all dropped to the floor as Mr. Dimple Quirker Extraordinaire extended a hand.

"Connor Allen. Pleasure."

Sweet mercy on high.

Chapter Three

It took everything in Connor to maintain a straight face as the anti-sugar girl from the café bounded around the compact treatment room like a bird trapped in the subway. Ainsley Grace Jamison, according to her file. A year younger than him, single, and the first person he'd met since moving here who wasn't afraid to ditch the obligatory southern pretenses in favor of saying what she really thought.

"Absolutely not." She whirled around. "It's a ridiculous idea. I mean, I don't know you from Adam. And what are you even doing in Dr. Southerland's practice?"

Connor rubbed a hand over his mouth to shield the grin the spitfire brunette had a way of coaxing out of him. "On a normal day, I'd say I'm doing my job." But considering today had veered off normal from the second he'd met her, he wasn't entirely sure what he was doing. Or what he was getting himself into. All he really knew was, in a town as small as Whispering Pines, North Carolina, it didn't seem fair to only be meeting her now.

She stared at the closed door like she was claustrophobic.

"If it puts your mind at ease, you'll go back to seeing Dr. Southerland in December. I'll be leaving on the seventh."

"That was short-lived," she said rather matter-of-factly.

Yep, no problem whatsoever saying what she thought.

Connor gave up wrestling the corners of his mouth. "I've been here two months, actually. One more to fulfill our arrangement, then I'll be heading on to work with my next client."

"Client?" She studied him. "Are you a traveling consultant, or something?"

"Something like that. Owners temporarily bring me on board long enough to get the inside look I need to make some evaluations."

"Wow." She made an impressed face. "An in-demand chiropractic consultant. I didn't know that was a thing. If I should know who you are, I'm gonna apologize right now. I've been out of touch with pretty much the entire world since having…" Whatever she was about to say took a back seat behind the wave of panic climbing her face.

"Since, what?"

"Nothing." Ainsley swayed in place while scouring all four corners of the ceiling. "So, I take it you're some kind of expert?"

"I don't know about that." He scratched his jaw. "Some people think my father is though. He owns one of the leading practices in the nation."

"So, why isn't he the one doing the consulting?"

"And leave the city?" Connor snorted. "Nah, my old man's too comfortable in his own kingdom to descend from his throne."

Maybe she had some of that southern politeness in her after all, because there was no way she missed the jaded tone strangling his words. Yet instead of trying to pick apart what he left unsaid, she leaned against the wall adjacent to him and nonchalantly tried to adjust the high waistband under her dress. "So, you're a bigwig consultant with an empire behind him." Amusement nibbled at her lips. "And here I thought you worked at Common Grounds."

"Because I grabbed a coffee before coming into the office?"

"Because you were going through the supply cabinets like you owned the joint."

"The sugar jar was empty. Now it's full. Problem solved." He shrugged. "It's kind of what I do, I guess."

"Fix other people's problems, you mean?"

When he didn't deny it, she matched his raised shoulders with a raised brow. "You don't think that's a little... *presumptuous* on your part?"

Before he could answer, her antsy pacing kicked back into gear, now accompanied by a string of mumbles he doubted she meant for him to hear. "Expert consultant. No wonder he's on the haughty side. Impertinent is more like it. Assuming..."

Connor tugged on his ear. "Does that mean I'm playing Mr. Darcy or Mr. Knightley for Thanksgiving?"

The comment drew her feet to a stop and her cheeks into a war with a smile he would've paid good money to keep watching. Her hands strayed to her hips. "How about Mr. Collins?"

He didn't have to be too well acquainted with Jane Austen's characters to know he'd just been playfully insulted.

Her grin finally won—for five seconds, maybe, but he'd take it.

"Listen, Doctor Allen, I appreciate the offer to help me with the mess I've gotten myself into. Truly. But I assure you, it'd end up being disastrous for us both. You don't know my family."

True. For all he knew, he'd blindly offered to walk into a potential catastrophe. Yet, for a reason he couldn't decipher, the girl carried a draw about her. And whether it made sense or not, he needed to find out why.

"So, thank you again," she continued. "But can we simply carry on with today's adjustment and erase the first half of this entire morning from both our memories?"

The adjustment was one thing. Forget meeting her? Not possible.

Tipping a nod at her adamancy, Connor motioned to the adjusting bench.

She tugged down on her dress before lying on her stomach, and Connor couldn't decide what intrigued him more: her girl-next-door modesty or her guns-blazing spunk.

He carefully felt along her back. He could tell from looking at her that she was as hardworking as she was determined. Yet underneath, her musculoskeletal structure told an invisible story. The girl had enough tension and strain railing through her to pop a gasket.

Connor situated his hands over her L2 vertebrae. "Breathe out."

Amazingly, she obliged, as did her stiff joints. A series of pops echoed through the room, and the instant gratification nearly melted her through the bench. She might not like him yet, but at least she trusted him with her spine. Maybe she wasn't as hard to crack as she put on.

"I know I only heard one side of the conversation," he dared. "But it sounded to me like that tight corner you've backed yourself into doesn't have an easy way out without my help."

Ainsley whipped around on the bench.

He would've laughed at her pitiful glare if the waves of hair falling out of her barely-together-ponytail weren't distracting him. What he'd assumed was a simple brown turned into strands of auburn highlights only outnumbered by the intricate strands of blues in her eyes.

"You really are presumptuous, aren't you?"

He chuckled. "You can thank my New York City upbringing for that, but I prefer bold."

She seemed to grant him the exchange. "New York City, huh? Of all the places you could go to consult, what on earth lured you all the way out to Whispering Pines?"

"Fate, I suppose. My first lead fell through last minute. Dr. Southerland contacted me with an open door, so… here I am."

A skeptical look trailed over him. "Here you are," she said after a minute. "Running away from something in New York?"

He dragged a knuckle along the crease of his mouth, more amused by her brazenness than anything. "I like to think of it as running *to* something. Exploration. Discovery." Connor sat on the rolling stool. "Lots of names for it." None of which his father approved. "Guess you could say I was looking for a change of pace." He would spare her the full details he didn't want to get into anyway.

Her eyes flicked away from his. "Then I'm afraid you've come to the wrong place. Not much here but farmland, meddling families, and antiquated values."

He angled to catch her gaze. "I've only just met you, Ainsley Grace Jamison, and I can assure you. You've already proved that wrong."

A shade of pink made the smatter of freckles along her cheeks even cuter, but it didn't take long for the reaction to fade. "Trust me. You haven't known me very long."

Truth be told, he didn't know her at all, and yet… "Being your date to Thanksgiving dinner could change that."

She jerked halfway up, shrieked, and flopped backward again. "Ow."

Connor rounded the corner of the bench to find a loose section of her hair tangled around one of the bolts securing the headpiece in place. He bent to one knee for a closer look and offered another shriek-inducing attempt to free her. Fighting a laugh, he scrubbed a hand down his chin. "Well, this is a first."

"My specialty." Full-on blushing this time, she gave the ceiling tiles another solid examination, and that was all it took. Ainsley Grace had officially done him in.

Connor pushed off the bench to stand. "Give me a minute."

"Don't you dare come back with scissors," she called as he slipped out of the room.

Once he was hidden in the supply closet, his laughter came freely. She was something else all right. He was probably walking into more trouble than he needed during his short stay in North Carolina. But based on what he'd seen today, playing her pretend boyfriend would be worth every ounce of it. He just had to convince her of the same.

Connor came back in to the horrid sound of some creepy thing that clearly needed to be put to death.

"I'm sorry. I tried to reach for my purse and accidentally bumped this stupid to—" She cut herself off again. "...Thing," she modified. "I'll take care of it." Restricted from moving, she tapped her head against the bench and sighed. "As soon as I'm not tied down by my own hair."

Though Connor sensed she kept deeper secrets than could be stashed in the bottom of a purse, he let it go and waved the wrench he'd brought in at her. "I'm on it."

With the dismantled headpiece in hand, he gingerly uncoiled Ainsley's hair and motioned to her freedom. "My lady."

"Thank you." A look teetering near chagrin fanned her eyes his way as she sat up. "Sorry about all this. I don't usually—"

An incoming call added an extra melody to their background horror tunes. Ainsley rifled through her purse in the corner chair and whipped her cell to her ear. "Hey, Kate. Please don't tell me Mama called you too—" She clasped her head. "The Haygoods? Wait... They said *what?*"

Chapter Four

It usually took a lot to burn Ainsley's biscuits. Today, they were on fire.

She dumped the last of the soiled hay into the wheelbarrow, pushed her hair off her sticky forehead with her arm, and scanned the empty barn stall.

In need of repairs? Not mucked out enough? Underworked horses? The Haygoods' excuses for terminating their boarding agreement still felt like pointed accusations. Ainsley had never promoted her services as anything but a partial board. They knew that coming in and had greatly appreciated the price break that came with it. Just because they weren't the type of horse owners who wanted to get their hands dirty with responsibility didn't mean they needed to criticize her facility.

She yanked the wheelbarrow up by both handles but didn't make it out of the barn before the partial truth in their comments bonked her in the head—literally. She dusted the fallen wood shavings from her hair and squinted toward a spot in the old rafters that evidently had started to rot.

An overwhelmed sigh backed her beside tack gear she hadn't brought herself to move for the last three years. She traced the worn leather bearing familiar scents she wanted nothing more than to be a staple of her son's childhood, the same way it had been for hers.

But as a gust of wind waved her father's favorite halter against the wall, doubt shook against her heart. What if Mama was right about the farm being too much for her to handle?

The reminder of her mom's call spurred flashes of the disastrous morning. Not the least of which was making a complete fool of herself in front of Connor. Seriously, who else in the world would get their hair tangled in an adjusting bench of all things? Of all moments? She couldn't have staged a more awkward damsel-in-distress scene if she'd tried.

Ainsley smiled in spite of herself, picturing her knight in shining armor brandishing that silly dismantled headpiece like it was a slayed dragon. She bit her lip. Mr. Collins, indeed.

A ding from the baby monitor app on her phone signaled Josiah had awoken from his nap. With one last glance around the barn in need of work she'd never be able to finish before Thanksgiving, Ainsley tucked all thoughts of the morning away and hustled up to the farmhouse.

She unbuttoned her work shirt on her way down the hall, flung it into her room as she passed it, and hurried toward the whimpers coming from the middle bedroom.

Her dark-haired seven-month-old sat up in his crib with wide blue eyes caught between love and need, both of which undid Ainsley every time she saw them.

"Hi, sweet boy." She lifted him out and breathed in the source of the deepest exhaustion and greatest joy she'd ever known in her life. "Did you have a good nap?"

Josiah walked up her stomach, already itching to move.

"Hang on, sweetie. You know the routine." Such as it was these days.

Gusty winds rapped against the side of the house. The loud sound could've been a fishing line hooked onto Josiah's bottom lip. Tears ensued.

"It's okay." She settled him with her in the rocker. "I'll always keep you safe." She swept his hair back, kissed his soft baby skin, and prayed the promise was one she could keep.

She refused to watch the clock while nursing. She savored bonding with her son. Savored the time and peace it lent her. Usually. Today, however, was in a class of its own.

Even though the storm had mostly died down, her thoughts kept whipping across the property. A month until Thanksgiving. A month to get things in order if she was going to prove to Mama she'd made the right choice for her and Josiah both.

He squirmed as though sensing her stress, and Ainsley hated the whole predicament even more.

She propped him up against her shoulder to burp him. "It's going to be all right, baby." Somehow.

A solid pat to his back launched a flow of spit-up along her neck and down the inside of her camisole. Lovely.

The sound of the doorbell ringing prompted a series of barks from their dog, Matty, followed by Kate's rushed footsteps. Josiah spun toward the commotion and nearly climbed off Ainsley's shoulder to find out the source. His little feet kept walking up her torso, squishing the spit-up now pooling in the cups of her bra.

"Ainsley," Kate called with a little too much inflection. "You have a guest."

Now? "Um… just a minute." After finally pinning Josiah to her hip, she scanned the room for a burp cloth. *Why* was there never one in reach when she needed it? She grabbed a baby washcloth instead.

"Might want to hurry," Kate called again.

"All right, already." Ainsley stuffed the washcloth into her bra to soak up the spit-up and hurried down the hall. "What's the—?"

As soon as her feet breached the living room carpet, her whole body braked to a halt, skidded over two dimple-sized potholes, and sent any ounce of decorum she had left into a pile-up of emotions on the verge of spontaneously combusting.

Squatting on the hardwoods, Connor rubbed their Blue Heeler's ears, who was having as much trouble sitting still as Josiah was.

Ainsley glared at Matty's in-heaven puppy eyes. *Traitor*.

"What are you doing here?" In. Her. Living. Room.

Connor rustled his windblown hair as he stood. "Hello to you too."

He obviously missed the decorum-in-flames thing. Ainsley tried to straighten her off-kilter stance while swaying Josiah side to side. "How'd you find my house?" Her files at the chiropractor's office soared to mind before she got the words out, but she wasn't about to backpedal now.

Connor took in the sight of her home, either to stave off the grin that was sure to follow or to appraise her living quarters. "One of the things I love about small towns…" He ruffled Matty's ears again. "It's not hard to find out where people live."

What about where people were buried?

Ainsley grasped Josiah's squirmy legs tighter. She'd wanted to keep her son out of the picture completely. His vulnerable heart didn't need any more confusion at such a young age.

Then again, it might not have been a bad thing for Connor to find out she was a single mom. If he had any doubts about pretending to be her boyfriend, seeing Josiah had likely skyrocketed them enough to run him off. If not, her spit-up perfume would surely do the trick.

She studied his expression. Waiting. Yet unlike the escape route most guys furiously searched for at this point, Connor seemed only to search for a way forward.

"We didn't get to finish talking about our…" He glanced at Kate and back. "Arrangement."

He *still* wanted to go through with it?

She willed herself to ignore the way he looked at Josiah like he was a sweet gift instead of an added complication. Before the emotion could get the better of her, a glop of spit-up leaked from under her bra, ran a rivulet of slime down to her belly button, and soaked into the top of her underwear.

Don't cringe. Don't you dare cringe.

Ainsley strained to shift as casually as possible.

"You all right?" Connor asked.

She looked away from the dimples apparently tied to some kind of X-ray vision. "Perfect. I'm just…"

Josiah climbed up her front again, stretching her shirt farther downward with each hasty step.

"Be still. Will you stop? No—" Ainsley nearly fumbled him trying to spare Kate and Connor a glimpse of her soaked undergarments, but it was too late.

In slow motion, the baby washcloth tumbled out and landed onto the floor like a wad of tissues a preteen girl had stuffed in her bra before her first date.

She should've tried to catch it or, at the very least, the gasp of horror leaving her mouth. Instead, she stood there with noodle arms and the only thing she could think of reciting through her head. *London Bridge is falling down, falling down, falling down.*

No one moved. Every creak and draft in the house jumped up five decibels as their three-person circle stood in awkward silence. The kind that should only be allowed to happen in a dream you could wake up from.

Of course, she wouldn't be that lucky. Matty approached the cloth like he thought the thing might be alive and sniffed with gusto. Evidently deciding it was a chew toy, he flopped onto his back and began mauling it between his teeth and paw.

Connor's lips twitched, and it was official. Ainsley had full-on died of mortification right then and there. She looked at Kate with half a notion to tell her to add some spit-up to her headstone, lest she dare go a moment without being covered in it even in the grave.

Kate stole the incriminating evidence from Matty and motioned to the mud room. "I'm gonna go do some laundry." Ever the angel Ainsley depended on, her sister took Josiah and bounced him on her hip. "Want to help Auntie Kate, buddy?" She tickled his pudgy thigh when he reached for her dark curls.

As giggles trailed toward the back of the house, Matty looked from them to Connor, clearly torn on whether to stay or follow.

Seriously? He just met the guy.

Ainsley patted her thigh, and her dog quickly sat at attention by her side. Wise choice. Something told her she wouldn't make it through this conversation on her own.

She rubbed Matty's head and looked everywhere but at the New York City chiropractor standing in her foyer as if he belonged there. "So, that wasn't... what it... looked like."

Green eyes she could get lost in looked up from the floor. "Like I said. You've already proved you're an interesting girl, Ainsley Grace."

It killed her when he said her name like that. The accent, the familiarity. She wasn't sure what it was, only that the sound held an indulgent, warm brownie feel it'd take a dozen salads to counteract. She gripped Matty's collar. Why did chocolate have to be such an addictive vise?

"I, um…" *Am an intelligent woman who knows how to form words*. Ainsley drew herself out of the gooey lure and crossed her arms. "I really don't have time to train you." She needed to find a new boarder, get necessary repairs done, and figure out how in the world to foil Mama's Set-up Steve ploy.

"Train?"

"It'd never work otherwise. You're all wrong for the part."

"You really know how to dole out the compliments, don't you?"

"You can thank my country upbringing for that, but I prefer honest."

Connor laughed. "And I *assume* that honesty covers your imaginary boyfriend?"

Her scrunched lips relented. He had her, but that was all the compliment he was getting, or her honesty would land her in deeper hot water than any tangled lie could. "You're right. I shouldn't have made him—*you*—whatever, up." She backed against the Lazy Boy and sat on the chair arm. "If you knew my mom, you'd understand, but still. It's all a mess now."

"Not necessarily." He sidled up beside her, not needing to say more.

What was with this guy's persistence? She eyed his profile. He wasn't the rugged type you found in these parts but handsome nonetheless. "Why do you want to do this?"

A shrug. "Maybe I'm just a good-natured guy."

"Uh-huh."

He laughed again. "Okay, maybe I kind of like that it bothers you."

Ainsley shoved him away from the chair.

"Kidding." His smile bounced him right back like a rubber band. "No, seriously, I'd like to help you out. I know I'm only here another month, but I'd like to get to know some more people before I go too." A husky laugh at the feel of Matty's tongue on his hand drew him down to the floorboards again. "And maybe a few of the animals. I could use a friend who knows the ropes around here."

Not if the way Matty was turning to putty in his hands was any indication. Ainsley highly doubted a guy as confident as Connor needed any assistance making friends, four-legged or two.

When she didn't recant her wary stare, he gave Matty one last pat and pushed to his feet. "Think of it as a mutually beneficial arrangement. No ulterior motives, no charity help. I'll even pitch in around the place to earn my keep."

She practically jumped off the chair in hopes an increased height would improve her hearing. "I'm sorry. Are you saying you want to *stay* here?"

An amused look sized up her defensive pose. "That's kind of a bold advance coming from an honest country girl."

Her cheeks burned. "I'm not asking you to move in with me. *You're* the one who said—"

His grin cut off her pointless rambling.

"You enjoy that, don't you?"

"What?"

She motioned to all that encompassed Connor Allen. "Pushing my buttons."

"Maybe a little."

And *maybe* she'd kick him *a little* out of her house.

"Truth is, I just found out a pipe burst in the condo I'm renting. My landlord doesn't know how long it'll take to repair the water damage. So, I'm kind of homeless at the moment."

She stared him down until he laughed.

"I'm not making this up. I swear. Believe me, I thought it was a joke at first too, but who knows. Maybe it's providence."

"Providence?" Wow. Presumptuous didn't begin to cover it.

"If we're gonna make a fake relationship fly, it probably won't hurt if I'm around more anyway, right?"

Won't hurt who?

Ainsley bit her knuckle, kicking herself for entertaining the crazy idea for even a second. "No." She straightened. "It'll never work. Bottom line, we don't have time to pull this off. *My* Connor's supposed to be a country vet— cowboy hat, boots, southern demeanor, the works. And you're..." She waved over his profile again. "*Not.* Have you ever even stepped foot in a barn?"

"I might surprise you."

She headed for the door. "I'll take that as a no."

"So, we'll train."

"A whole year wouldn't be enough time to transform you into a cowboy."

"I bet you're underestimating yourself."

"Better than overestimating," she countered.

Why she expected to find anything other than an impish expression meeting her when she turned, she'd never know.

"We only have to make it through Thanksgiving weekend, right?"

Along with every second of looking at him without singing "Hot Cross Buns" out loud.

Connor started toward her. Slowly. Confidently. Each swaggering footstep raised the heat in Ainsley's cheeks. She stared at the floorboards, never envying a carpenter bee more for its ability to burrow itself into the wood.

"One month," he said a few feet away. "No complications or attachments." One foot away. "I can go into the office late mornings and be back by dinner. We'll work on everything here the rest of the time—repairs, training, you name it." Right in front of her, green eyes gleamed above a smile she doubted many people ever turned down. "C'mon. You gotta admit killing two birds with one stone isn't the worst idea."

That was still debatable.

Ainsley cut a glance away from him and slid the baby feet charm on her necklace back and forth. As much as she wanted to, she really couldn't argue with needing his help on both accounts before Mama got there.

The Haygoods' criticism of the barn steered her focus to the kitchen window overlooking the property her father had poured his heart into. Seeing Kate round the corner with Josiah in tow didn't help. Between honoring Daddy and praying her choices hadn't been in vain, the growing list of motivators slashed through the remainder of Ainsley's reservations.

She lowered her voice. "Fine. But you're staying in the barn. And there will be rules." *Lots* of rules.

Connor ran a knuckle along the corner of his mouth. "I never doubted there would be."

"Including chores," she plowed on. "This isn't a condo where maintenance staff come do the work for you. You're going to have to get your hands dirty around here."

Lips slanting, he tipped his head in agreement. "I told you I'd pitch in."

"Good," she said, still flustered over this whole idea. "Then you can start with cleaning out the chicken coop."

When he didn't move, Ainsley motioned behind her to the door.

"Now?"

A quick appraisal of his dress shoes almost overrode her nerves. "Every minute counts."

Connor looked at her like he was waiting for the punch line. Not getting one, he buttoned the top of his jacket. "Okay, then."

Matty followed him out, probably for moral support. Heaven knew the guy was going to need it.

Kate flitted across the room. Knowing her sister, it likely hadn't taken much overhearing for her to fill in the blanks. "You didn't tell him we let the chickens roam this time of day, did you?"

"Nope." Ainsley grinned.

"Oh, you're mean, girl."

Maybe a little. But there was only one way to find out if he could truly hack it here.

Kate scarcely had a minute to toss Ainsley a look of reprimand before a blur of feathers and Nordstrom clothes passed the kitchen window. Both girls huddled in front of the sink with Josiah between them. Her son flapped at the window like it was a TV screen. It might as well have been. Because nowhere else would they see a usually dignified man flailing to get one of the hens off his shoulder without tripping over the others chasing him across their farm.

Ainsley couldn't decide whether Connor looked more like he was trying to dodge the flying monkeys from *The Wizard of Oz,* or if he was stealing one of Jane Fonda's signature workout moves. If he'd had sweatbands on, the latter would've won by a landslide.

Meanwhile, poor Matty helplessly tried to restore order to chaos, Josiah squealed his amusement, and Ainsley had to pinch her lips together to keep from losing it. Oh, what she'd do to be videoing this right now.

Kate leaned her free hip against the counter. "You do realize how much work you have cut out for you, right?"

"*So* much work." Ainsley laughed through tears on the verge of confirming she was as insane as this entire fiasco-of-a-plan sounded. "I'm going to regret this, aren't I?"

"That depends. How many miracles do you currently have at your disposal?"

"Not enough, girl." And only four weeks to pray for a new one.

Chapter Five

A blaring alarm Connor hadn't set jarred him awake. He bolted forward on his bed and almost fumbled around for a gun he didn't own. It took a dozen blinks for the rustic loft to settle into view. Once he'd gained his bearings, he flopped backward onto the stiff mattress. Until the noise that had awoken him pierced through the walls again.

Not an alarm. A rooster.

He flung the blanket off, reached for his cell, and squinted at the time. *You can't be serious.*

A bark outside answered his unspoken question. Ainsley wasn't joking about not wasting any time.

Cold wooden beams greeted Connor's bare feet in the third unpleasant welcome of the morning. A poorly insulated room with minimum essentials was a far cry from his city high-rise apartment, but he had a feeling she intended it that way. A test he wasn't about to fail.

He scrubbed his hands down his face to shake off the sleepiness. Nothing a few cups of coffee couldn't cure.

He threw on a pair of jeans and a Henley over his white undershirt. By the time he staggered down the narrow steps and made it outside, he didn't spot Ainsley anywhere on the grounds. Good thing. Because if she'd asked him to jump on a project before stealing the chance for a quick shower and some breakfast, he wouldn't have said no.

It was less about the need to prove himself, and more about the way she compelled him to want to be there. He didn't fully understand it, and it might possibly be the death of him, but it didn't really matter. He'd made an agreement and planned to uphold it.

After coffee.

Dew dampened his sneakers as he crossed the grass. When something slimy smooshed under his soles, the reminder of yesterday's chicken-shoulder-riding adventure jerked him to a stop. Thankfully, a merciful peek to the left confirmed the chickens were asleep in their coop.

The entire situation gave him a good laugh. When he'd set out to hit the road, a dirt one leading to the middle of nowhere wasn't what he'd envisioned. He couldn't deny the place held a peace about it though. A feeling of coming home.

He shook his head at the irony. He shouldn't have felt more lost in New York's nonstop whirl of activity than he did on a random North Carolina farm.

The endless grass stretching toward the blue-haze-covered mountains had something to do with it, he was sure. Even the old farmhouse with its stone chimney, wrap-around porch, and attached carport added to the charm. It all looked like something out of a storybook or maybe a movie. But mostly, the place looked as he'd imagined a real home should. One built on meddling families and antiquated values, as Ainsley had put it yesterday.

He glanced under the carport at the teal door bookended by two potted mums. The bright colored paint clashed with and complimented the house at the same time—something he had a feeling the unique girl who lived there had a way of doing herself. A girl who was eagerly waiting with a list of chores to hand off, no doubt.

Connor smiled to himself until a godawful smell nearly choked him out of nowhere. He turned toward the sound of something moving toward him. Make that *somethings*. Two horns to be exact. He squinted through the morning fog. His spiked adrenaline gradually subsided as a black and white goat came clearer into view.

The little guy was actually kind of cute. Happy, even. Until he noticed Connor, anyway. Once he did, the scared thing skidded to a halt like he was about to fall off a cliff.

A small pig trailing too close behind rammed into his hind legs, but the goat didn't so much as flinch. He stayed in place, battling Connor in history's most awkward staring contest. Were those horizontal eyes even looking directly at him?

A creepy shriek bellowing from somewhere behind them cut off his chance of finding out.

The frightened goat took off in a hurry only to collapse after two frantic strides. The pig took one look at his sidekick's legs sticking up in the air like a dead possum's and took great effort to tip over to the ground beside him.

Connor looked around, sure there had to be cameras hiding somewhere. Finding none, he let out a small exhale when both animals appeared to resurrect themselves a few seconds later. The goat stumbled around like he wasn't sure which direction to run next. But when another curdling yell grew closer, the little guy froze and fainted again.

Connor ran his hand over his chin. What was he supposed to do? Give the goat CPR? Given how strong that stench was growing, he'd be lucky if he could keep breathing at all.

He snuck in an inhale, gagged, and tried again. Giving up, he covered his nose and mouth with the front of his shirt—both to block the heinous smell and to shield himself from whatever lethal gas had to be floating through the air to keep knocking the animals out.

He glanced between the barn and the house, both a frustratingly equal distance away. Before he could decide which way to hightail it, the source of the weird yelling galloped to a stop a few feet in front of him.

Unlike the almost cute black and white goat who'd finally gained enough sense to stay down on the grass this time, the one looming in front of them looked more like a deranged mammoth with its crazy eyes fastened dead on Connor.

Something between sheer curiosity and bewilderment kept Connor in place. That, and the now-unbearable stench all but paralyzing him. No wonder the other goat kept passing out. Whatever that smell was had to be on some kind of toxic level.

Connor couldn't take it. He folded his shirt up an extra layer over his nose.

Wrong move. As soon as he broke the standstill, the bearded goat made a senseless blubbering noise. With his tongue waving all around, he pawed one leg on the ground, then took off after him like Connor was a female goat in heat.

Wait. He didn't really think—?

The goat had rounded Connor's legs and mounted the back of him before he had the chance to finish a thought no human should have to entertain.

That mystical sense of peace he'd felt a few minutes ago? Gone. Evaporated in a cloud of abominable stench and thrust to oblivion by the force of a one-track mind.

This couldn't truly be happening. Connor pushed to get away but almost tripped over the little pig who'd decided to join the mammoth in humping his shin. Meanwhile, the passed-out goat he'd previously felt pity for now stood perfectly stable on all four legs, watching like a spectator about to tip him for the entertainment.

Okay, that was enough. Connor broke free of his violators and made a run for the house. He didn't waste time knocking. He barreled right in, shut the freaky *Animal Planet* episode on the other side of the door, and backed against it.

The horrid smell followed him inside. Or was that actually *on* him? *Don't tell me.* He didn't make it an inch closer to his jeans before the odor flung him back against the door. "Aw, man, no. That's straight-up… foul." Those clothes were going in the trash, and he was going in the shower. Pronto.

"Ainsley?"

"She's not here," someone called from the kitchen.

Connor crossed the open space between the living room and kitchen and stopped just shy of bumping into a short-haired blonde. "Oh, sorry."

An awkward two-step continued until he finally slid to one side and gestured for her to pass. Without replying, she opened the fridge and pulled out a container of milk.

If she didn't think it was odd for a stranger to come waltzing into Ainsley's house without making introductions, he supposed he shouldn't think it unusual for a random girl to be making herself cozy in Ainsley's kitchen either.

Still not even asking so much as his name, she proceeded to fix her coffee, appearing perfectly comfortable in the silence.

At least one of them was.

"So," she finally said. "You must be the guy."

And she must've been the girl… who'd murder him if he was there with ulterior motives, or praise him if he was there to help out her roommate, best friend—whatever she was to Ainsley? Based on her apparent scrutiny, it was definitely a toss-up.

"Connor Allen," he said. "You live here too?"

"Most days."

Um, okay. He took another stab at it. "You're a friend of Ainsley's?"

"When she needs me to be."

He waited for more. Got nothing.

Well, that was clear as mud.

After another minute-long stare off, she looked to her left and right, scrunched her face, then lifted the jug of milk to her nose.

Connor glared at his jeans. "Yeah, sorry. That's probably me you're smelling."

The side of her mouth tipped as she looked him over again. "Interesting choice of cologne."

Funny. "So, do you know where Ainsley is exactly?" He jutted a thumb at the door. "'Cause we've got a serious problem to deal with out there." *Aside* from his offensive odor at the moment.

"What kind of problem?"

"You've got animals passing out, for one."

Her face muscles relaxed. "Mr. Tumnus got loose again, huh?"

"I'm sorry, who?"

"One of my mom's goats."

Connor blinked at her. "How'd you know…?"

"They're myotonic goats," she said like that clarified the situation whatsoever.

His obvious lack of goat knowledge must've ruled that out because her slow turn to the fridge didn't remotely hide her eye roll. She returned the milk jug and closed the door. "Most people call them fainting goats, but they're not really passing out. Their muscles seize when they're startled. It doesn't usually take more than a few seconds for them to shake it off though. They'll be fine."

"What about the pig?"

She lowered her mug. "Billy? Ignore him. He was raised by goats and thinks he's one of them, but he's really just a big ol' copycat." She finished the sip he'd interrupted.

Connor scratched the side of his nose, still stuck on the pig's name, never mind the rest of it. "Billy as in Billy goat?" Clever. Almost as funny as naming a goat Mr. Tumnus.

Based on the girl's deadpan stare, he was the only one who thought so.

He curbed his grin. Fainting goats from Narnia and identity crisis pigs. Totally normal. Okay, then.

She set her spoon in the sink. "I'll talk to my mom about keeping tighter reins on Mr. Tumnus when she gets back from her road trip in a couple of weeks. In the meantime, try not to scare him anymore."

"Me?"

"He doesn't freeze up for no reason."

"Uh, yeah, try the mammoth goat beast who sprang at me a second ago. I almost fainted too."

She peeked out the window above the sink and eased back down on the balls of her socked feet. "So *that's* the smell." An overzealous smirk wheeled her around. "Spock tagged you, didn't he?"

"Did you just call him Spock?"

"Hey, I didn't name them. When you meet my mom, you'll understand."

Not likely. Connor nodded anyway like it were possible for *anyone* to provide clarity to this bizarre scenario.

"He doesn't take to just anyone." An overly impish grin tipped above the rim of her mug. "You should be flattered."

"That he confused me for a female goat?" He angled a backward glance at his forever-tainted pant legs. "My ego's never been more stroked."

She full-on laughed then. "Don't worry, Doctor Love. The does will be all over you once they get a whiff of Spock's calling card. A buck's urine is irresistible."

Connor choked on nothing. "Are you saying he peed on me?"

"Technically, he peed on himself and happened to rub it on you." She laughed again when his face dropped. "Welcome to rut season."

"Do I want to ask what that is? Second thought, don't answer that." The image of the goat's stained fur was enough to cap an end to any more details on the topic. He didn't want to know how in the world an animal could cast enough trajectory necessary to reach all the way up to his beard. The only thing he wanted to know anything about right then was coffee. *All* the coffee. In fact, he was tempted to snort the stuff just so his scorched nostrils would be free of that pungent—now even more disturbing—odor.

He scoured the kitchen for a mug. His shower could wait five more minutes.

Maybe.

Hopefully.

By the time he'd hastily checked a few cabinets, Ainsley's nameless friend materialized next to him. "Mugs are beside the fridge."

"Thanks."

"No problem." She backed against the sink and proceeded to examine Connor's every move.

He stopped and started walking half a dozen times, wondering if her analysis ran all the way down to his stride. After filling up the largest mug he could find, he opened another couple of cabinets and shifted some canisters around on the counter.

"She doesn't keep any in the house."

He looked up. "Doesn't keep what?"

"Sugar. I assume that's what you're looking for. I'd offer you some from my own stash, but I used the last of it in an apple fritter earlier. So, sorry. You're on your own."

"But I watched her put some in her coffee at Common Grounds yesterday."

"She'd probably been talking to her mom. That's the only time she ever splurges."

She had to be joking. "You're serious?"

The girl shrugged like he was slow on the uptake, pulled a covered plate out of the oven, and handed it to him. "Biscuits and eggs. No bacon either, so don't bother asking. Ainsley's a vegetarian."

No meat. No sugar. Where in the world *was* he?

He hesitantly took the plate. "Thank you."

"I didn't make it. That was all Ains." She slid into a kitchen chair without pulling it away from the table and threaded her fingers through her mug handle. "And you can thank her by not ending up being a jerk. She doesn't need any more drama in her life. There's Irish cream in the fridge, by the way, if you're not strong enough to stomach your coffee black."

She casually crisscrossed her legs in the chair like she hadn't managed to threaten and insult him in the same tone she'd use for commenting on the weather.

Connor scoured yet again for hidden cameras, then cut a glance to the fridge and resigned to accept the cream evidently waiting to undermine his manhood.

A reusable egg carton marked with the hand stenciled words *Laid in the USA* sat directly underneath what appeared to be fresh milk from a dairy cow on the shelf above it. He smiled. Farm life perks. At least there was that.

He pulled out the chair opposite the second girl in this town who clearly didn't trust him.

Seated in front of a homemade breakfast, Connor noted the rooster patterned dishes and checkered tablecloth. He lifted a bite of eggs to his mouth, fully intending to keep his laugh blocked inside.

"Something funny?"

He lowered his fork to the plate. "A sugar-free vegetarian raised on a southern farm? You gotta admit, it *is* a bit ironic."

"Cliché busters usually are."

Wow. In less than twenty minutes, he'd managed to pin himself as a clueless, stereotype-casting Yankee skilled at winning over no one but hot and heavy goats. *Great start, Allen.*

He slanted a glance toward the window and his thoughts back to the much smarter fainting goat who'd learned when to stay down and keep his mouth shut.

Thankfully, Ainsley's friend must've been done saying her piece because the next few minutes passed silently in sips of coffee and a breakfast good enough not to need meat at all. He dragged his last piece of biscuit across the sturdy plate that looked like it'd been passed down through generations. Same way much of the house did.

A twinge of envy churned in his full stomach. For what exactly, he wasn't sure. But as he scanned the family pictures in the living room and the massive library filling a bookshelf beside the fireplace, Connor couldn't shake the feeling that Ainsley's story held something his didn't.

The sound of the front door opening followed a cry from one of the back rooms in perfect tandem. Ainsley heeled off her boots in the entryway while hanging a puffer vest on the wooden coatrack. "Sorry, Daphne," she said to the girl now standing up from her chair. "I meant to be back sooner."

"Why? You're supposed to be working." She cut off Ainsley's path down the hall. "I'll get him. That's part of our deal, remember?"

"I know, but—"

"Grab a refill on your way *back* to work." Daphne waved her toward the kitchen. "Josiah and I will be fine. Now, let me go get him before he wakes up Kate."

Connor wouldn't have been surprised if Ainsley saluted her. He almost did himself.

"Oh." Daphne called on her way down the hall. "And keep an eye on Doc, here, when you head back out, will ya? Spock has a crush on him."

Nice.

Rather than jump on the bandwagon left wide open for her, Ainsley crossed the kitchen floor as if she hadn't heard Daphne. "I didn't expect you to be up."

These girls really knew how to hide their honest opinions of him.

"Hard to sleep through the rooster wake-up call."

She retrieved a mug from the cabinet. "Sorry. I should've warned you about Herald."

He ran a knuckle under his bottom lip. "You named your rooster Harold?" The names around here were cracking him up.

"Well, he heralds in the morning, so…"

Naturally.

Connor brought his mug to his mouth to squelch another offensive laugh and pointed to the coffee maker. "Want me to make you a fresh pot?" Considering she'd made him breakfast, it was the least he could do in return.

"This is fine." She drained the last of the current one, topped it off with Irish cream, and shuffled in the middle of the floor as though searching for the least awkward place to stand.

Did he make her that uncomfortable? He was about to ask when a giggle from down the hall seemed to steady her.

She warmed to the sweet sound, her face aglow with the kind of love that made everything else fade into the background. But once seated in the chair Daphne had previously occupied, she breathed in the steam from her coffee like the fragrance alone could give her a needed boost. "You didn't hear him crying last night, did you?"

"From the barn?"

"I wouldn't be surprised." A heavy exhale lowered shoulders that looked six months past needing a good massage. Given the work and stress her life involved, no wonder her spine was out of alignment. "I'm sorry if he keeps you up at all. I think he's teething."

He'd sensed her apprehension about mentioning her son around him numerous times now. Yet as curious as Connor was to know the missing pieces of their story, seeing that apprehension extend to self-consciousness made him want to set her mind at ease even more.

"Nothing to apologize for. Parenting is hard enough. When they're this young and can't tell you what's wrong, well, my hat's off to all mothers doing the best they can."

Glistening eyes met his for the briefest moment before diverting to her mug again.

The sunbeams streaming through the kitchen window could've been a dozen spotlights, all gravitating to a natural beauty he hadn't encountered before then. It might've been the stain of hard work smeared across her cheek or maybe the gentle way she kept one ear tuned toward her son's bedroom. Whatever it was, Connor couldn't look away.

Ainsley turned clear eyes to him this time. "Thank you for that." Not a minute later, a gleam of sass sparkled in those clear baby blues. "Ready to get to work?"

An hour ago, he wouldn't have hesitated to answer. Now? He cast a glance at his jeans. "Mind if I shower first?"

"Up to you." She finished off her coffee and pressed on the table to stand. "But by the time we're done, you're gonna need a second one."

He raised a brow. "What exactly do you have planned?"

She turned without answering. But if that gloating look he caught meant anything, she was going to enjoy every second of whatever was about to go down.

Chapter Six

Out on the carport, Ainsley looked her new recruit over. Not half bad with the Stetson and boots she'd lent him, but looking the part was only half the battle.

Or maybe *less* than half. Connor strode forward with his thumbs in his belt loops, and Ainsley almost cracked up. Josiah would look more natural walking in boots than he did.

He adjusted his hat. "How much do I owe you for these?"

"Consider them on loan. You clean 'em up real good when we're done with this whole masquerade, and we'll call it even." She stopped mid-turn and faced him again. "And try to keep them away from the goats, will ya?"

Nearly blushing, he rubbed his jaw. "You smell that, huh?"

"Kinda hard to miss."

"Hey, you're the one who shot down my shower suggestion."

"And you're the one who shot down my warning that you didn't know what you were in for." Ainsley slid her straw hat on. "So, pony up, cowboy. You haven't begun to know what smells lie ahead."

A grin climbed his cheek. "Yes, ma'am."

She dropped her focus from his eyes to his arms. His very defined arms. Okay, maybe not her brightest idea. She stared at the ground instead, cleared her throat, and strained to regain her wits. *Terms, Ainsley.* "You were right about one thing yesterday. I need help fixing up the property before my mom gets here. So, here's how this is gonna work. When you're not at the office, we're gonna haul tail making repairs I haven't been able to get to. At the same time, you're gonna get a crash course on learning your way around a farm."

"Fair enough." He angled to meet the gaze she was purposely casting away from him. "Anything else?"

"The breakup plan," she spat out faster than intended.

"The breakup plan?"

"Well, yeah. We'll have to come up with a believable scene to act out when my whole family's here. Something that'll keep them from hoping the relationship can be saved, because trust me. They won't stop meddling otherwise."

When Connor kept staring at her instead of replying, Ainsley toyed with the zipper on her vest. "Don't worry. You'll be on your way to your next job before things get too crazy. You basically said so yourself. No complications or attachments, remember?" *Please remember.*

He dipped his hat in concession. "I did say that."

"Okay. So, I'm thinking the easiest way to handle this is to stick somewhat close to the truth. Your job requires you to travel. Coming to Whispering Pines was a trial to see if you could handle settling down instead. Obviously, you can't, but we're wise enough to recognize the alternative isn't going to work. We're simply not meant for each other. So, clean break. We go our separate ways. End of story."

Connor's intuitive green eyes zeroed in on her like they had a direct path to everything carefully hidden between her rushed words.

"What? That doesn't sound believable?"

"Only if you want your family to think I'm a self-absorbed jerk."

It wouldn't be their first encounter with one.

"I said we *both* realized it wouldn't work. No hard feelings."

"Uh-huh." He looked across the grass starting to dry in the sun. A minute later, he lifted his hat to rustle his hair, and Ainsley almost broke her zipper in half ogling at the unreasonably attractive motion.

Stupid, unruly eyes. She forced her attention to the barn. A lot of good it did. She looked back at him a second later. "Will you say it already?" she blurted out.

"Say what?"

"Whatever you're obviously dying to say."

"Nothing." He fit his hat back on. "Just debating whether I should be impressed with how easily you come up with these stories or insulted by how easily you expect the worst of me."

This time, she couldn't avoid gaping. Not at his arms or eyes or hair. At the unnerving way he could read her and wasn't afraid to call her out on it. He'd just met her, for goodness sake.

She fretted with her sleeve. "I'm not criticizing you. I'm being realistic."

"You mean cynical?"

"Sensible," she countered. "People looking to soar on open highways aren't satisfied getting stuck on country back roads. It's the way it is. Besides, all fiction has a thread of real life woven into it. It's unavoidable."

Leaving it at that, she straightened. "So, I sure hope there's some validity to your skill with tools. 'Cause I can only script so much fluff before no one buys it. And frankly, I'm depending on it." Man, it killed a part of her to admit that. Out loud. In front of him.

A slow grin mounted. "You might be surprised."

Doubtful. Still, a morsel of hope flickered deep inside. "We'll see."

His cell rang before he could plead his case. It didn't matter. One glance at the screen, and the eyes set on proving her wrong were already unknowingly proving her right. He lifted a finger. "Excuse me for a minute." Bringing the phone to his ear, he strode a few paces away. "Yeah, hey, Flynn. Tell me you have good news."

From the look on his face, that would be a no.

"Are you kidding me?" Connor rubbed his hand down his chin. "This is the second time things have fallen through. I don't understand what's going on. I thought you had everything squared away... I know, but—"

He tugged his hat off, wiped his forehead across his sleeve, and craned his neck to the sky. "You're right. I'm sorry. It's not your fault, but we're not exactly running on free time here. This job ends in less than four weeks. If I don't have something lined up soon..."

Releasing a hard breath, he closed his eyes under the sun. "Yeah, yeah. Okay. No, it's fine. We'll figure it out..." He tapped his Stetson against his leg and stared at the thing like he wondered how long he'd be stuck wearing it.

Something in Ainsley's heart winced. A memory. A scar.

She turned away from the one-sided conversation and headed to the barn. She shouldn't have been listening in anyway. They had work to do.

"San Francisco? That's perfect, bro. Call me as soon as you get it nailed down... All right, man. Later."

Ainsley kept walking.

"Sorry about that," Connor called on his way to catch up to her. "That was my buddy Flynn. He's sort of managing this impromptu consulting enterprise of mine."

Ainsley crossed her arms as if she could bar herself from the way his soft laugh warmed her. "It's not working out?"

"You know what they say about never mixing friends and business? They're not wrong." He chuckled again. "Flynn's a smart guy though. I'm sure we'll sort it out."

"I'm sure you will." She stopped halfway through the barn doors, more than ready to step away from things she couldn't change and throw all her energy into the ones she could. "Ever muck a stall?" Heaven knew an hour digging through manure would do the guy some good, and she could use the time to finish assessing the work the barn needed.

"I haven't quite made it to that item on my bucket list," he teased.

"Well, today's your lucky day." Ainsley led him to a wheelbarrow and handed him a pitchfork. "You can start with Shiloh's stall and work your way down to Buster's. There are fresh bales of hay in the open side of the loft when you're done, and each water bucket needs to be replenished."

Connor leaned against the pitchfork's handle, boots crossed, cheeks lifted.

"Do I need to write this down for you?"

Laughing, he scratched his smooth cheek. "I think I got it, boss. Unless you wanna show me how it's done, seeing as you probably have a set method I'm bound to get all wrong."

Ainsley stifled the grin he shouldn't have been able to coax out of her so easily. It was bad enough he could read her like an open book. She raised a noncommittal shoulder. "Surprise me, and I won't have to."

He belly-laughed this time. "Anyone ever tell you you're quick on your feet, Ainsley Grace?"

"You just try making it through the day staying on your own feet, cowboy."

He brought his fingers to the tip of his hat. "Yes, ma'am."

She forced her eyes to cut ties with the ones etching away at her opinion of him. At least he had his southern manners down. Pretend or not, even Mama would be impressed.

While Connor got to work in the first stall, Ainsley grabbed a flashlight and a clipboard from the small tack room in the back and began her inspection. Despite how much seeing damage to her dad's barn pained her, she relished the time to herself.

"You rent out all these stalls?" Connor called over the gate.

There went her sacred solitude.

"Most of them."

"And that's your main source of income?"

She clicked off the flashlight, wishing conversations were as easy to shut down. Though, she supposed she did have to give him at least a couple of bonus points for waiting this long to bring up business stuff. He'd probably been dying to cast his advice since he first stepped foot on the farm.

"It's one of the streams." She finished jotting down the last needed repair she'd come across. "We sell eggs and milk. My aunt pays to host her exercise classes on the property, and—"

"Wait. Your aunt…" he said randomly. "So, Daphne's your cousin then?"

"Yeah. She and Kate moved in after… several months back now. They both pitch in in more ways than I can count. Kate's a nurse, and Daphne farms part of the land for goods she sells at the farmers market." Ainsley braced her clipboard against her thigh. "We're doing fine as we are." Maybe not as comfortable as she'd like, but they got by.

"Didn't say you weren't."

He didn't have to. She knew his type. Could see his entrepreneurial wheels turning like she was one of his clients in dire need of consultation.

"Just because we live in the country doesn't mean we lack business smarts. We're not a bunch of stereotypical hillbillies getting our kicks drinking beer and going cow tipping."

Connor's brows pinched together but then shot clear up to his hat as he pointed behind her. "I don't suppose you've trained the cows to second that motion, have you?"

Of all moments, Mr. Finnigan's heifer waltzed into the barn with a giant bell around her neck like a scene straight out of a movie.

"Daisy." Shaking her head, Ainsley stroked the cow's side. "How'd you get out again?"

"This happens often?"

She avoided the sideways grin she knew he was flaunting. "Maybe."

If that weren't contradicting her previous comments enough, her out-of-breath neighbor hobbled in wearing coveralls, complete with boots up to his knees and a red handkerchief tied around his neck.

Ainsley cringed but only for a second. She refused to be embarrassed by her sweet neighbor, even if he shared an uncanny resemblance with Old MacDonald.

"Sorry, Miss Ainsley. I've never owned a heifer with such a mind of her own."

"You gotta watch those strong-willed types," Connor said from the stall.

Ainsley glared at him. He was lucky that gate stood as a barrier between them.

"Oh." Mr. Finnigan untied his handkerchief and wiped his face. "Didn't know you'd hired a ranch hand. Pardon my manners. Thomas Finnigan here."

"Connor Allen." He risked leaving the stall to shake his hand.

Brave man.

Ainsley's glare didn't yield until Daisy nudged her cud-slobbered mouth against Connor's already defiled jeans. She twisted to the side and tried to disguise her laugh as a cough. "Sorry. Allergies."

Connor's playful eyes looked full-on ready to meet her challenge.

"Well, knock me down, and steal my teeth." Mr. Finnigan patted Daisy. "Would you look at that, girl. Miss Ainsley found herself a beau."

She nearly choked on her fake cough. "No, he's not… we're not… I mean…"

"She means, I'm not her ranch hand." Connor cozied up beside her. "I'm her boyfriend. Just visiting for a few weeks. Getting a feel for Whispering Pines."

Her jaw dropped, but what could she say? He was following the script she'd laid out for him, effortlessly she might add. Somehow, that shouldn't have surprised her. She, on the other hand, obviously needed some practice.

"Just visiting," Mr. Finnigan said, as though trying to make the phrase connect with the first part.

Ainsley finally found her voice. "His job keeps him on the road a lot."

"A passerby, huh?" If he stared at Connor any harder, he'd brand him with the dozens of questions he wasn't saying aloud. "Well, ain't that a wonder."

And so it began.

Connor shifted under the silent scrutiny. "I wouldn't *exactly* call me a passerby."

"If you ask me, a job that takes you away from what matters most in life ain't worth a hill of beans."

Ainsley felt Connor's blank stare all the way down to her core. She twisted her hands together, half tempted to grab his for support.

"No, I suppose not, sir."

"Yer darn right I'm right." His weathered face softened as he tied his handkerchief. "But don't you worry, son. You'll come around. Even a blind squirrel finds a nut every once in a while."

The southernisms knew no end.

Ainsley pinched the bridge of her nose, but Connor only smiled. He was a good sport, if nothing else.

A breeze from outside whisked in. Mr. Finnigan leaned over Daisy and whiffed, then angled his nose in the air like a dog sniffing out which trail to follow. It stopped on Connor, and whatever lack of trust had been percolating in Mr. Finnigan's gut rolled into a smile. "Well now, son, I don't know nothin' about traveling. Nor dating, for that matter. But I know enough to tell ya smelling like you're bedding with the farm animals ain't gonna win you a prize girl like Miss Ainsley."

She bit her knuckle to block a laugh, unlike Connor who'd evidently reached his limit bearing the humiliation of wearing Spock's urine.

"Okay, that's it. I'm going to change." He strode for the stairs. "You guys got an incinerator somewhere around here?"

"I'd hold off on that if I were you," Daphne said from behind them.

They all turned toward her standing in the open doorway with Josiah on her hip. Ainsley's heart warmed at the sense of wonder lighting up her son's face.

"Everything's fine," Daphne assured her before Ainsley could ask. "We saw Daisy from the window, and Josiah insisted we come pet her." She walked him close enough to touch the cow's spotted back. Josiah squealed with delight at the soft feel of Daisy's hair, and everything preceding the interruption vanished at the sweet sound.

Ainsley caught a glimpse of Connor smiling at her, full of his own kind of enamor. She quickly willed away her blush and reached for Josiah to make sure he kept his focus on the animal instead of her fake boyfriend. "What does the cow say, sweet boy? Does she say, moo?"

Josiah waved his arms as he cooed.

"That's right. Mooo…"

Daisy whipped her tail at a fly and shuffled in a restless motion.

"Easy, girl." Mr. Finnigan's face scrunched in apology when Ainsley backed up. "She's always been so docile. I don't know what's gotten into her lately."

Daphne leaned against the nearest stall gate. "I'm sure Doctor Connor can shed some light on that for you."

Mr. Finnigan and Ainsley darted a glance from Daphne's loaded comment to Connor's now-white face.

"Doctor?"

"He's a vet." Daphne sauntered over and gave him a playful slap to the shoulder. "You probably run into behaviors like this all the time, don't ya? I'm sure Mr. Finnigan would be much obliged if you'd take a look at Daisy to rule out any medical problems."

Oh, she was so going to die. Ainsley shot her cousin an are-you-crazy glare, to which Daphne doled out a highly entertained grin.

"What do you think, Doc? Hormone related maybe? I bet we have a glove in the tack room. Why don't you grab one of those stools over there so you can get a good feel inside to see what's going on?"

"I'm sure Mr. Finnigan would feel more comfortable with his own vet's opinion," Ainsley piped in. "Besides, Connor's off duty."

Her neighbor cast Connor an apprehensive look. "When it comes to taking care of yer animals, a man's never off duty."

And... here we go again.

A silent minute lapsed until Mr. Finnigan finally stroked Daisy's smooth side. "But I guess I don't reckon it'll hurt nothin' for you to take a quick gander."

Connor's focus sailed around their four-person circle and landed on Ainsley's cousin. "I'd be happy to, sir," he said. "As long as Daphne assists."

Ainsley coughed down another laugh. Not that much could throw Daphne.

"Sure," she answered without pause. "But unfortunately, we only have one glove. Let me go get that for ya, Doc."

Connor didn't show any hint of intimidation until Daphne strutted back in dangling an arm-length glove. He took off his Stetson like he hoped the motion would shrink his horseshoe-size eyes back to normal, then turned toward Ainsley and whispered, "Now would be the time to intervene."

"I'm thinking." She looked around the barn. For what was anyone's guess.

Mr. Finnigan set a wooden stool behind Daisy and gave his cow a pat on the rear. "She's ready when you are, son."

"Right." Connor ran his shaky hands down his jeans as he walked around the heifer like she were a car on a sales lot in need of inspection. After a few more answerless glances at Ainsley, he stopped beside Daisy and began feeling her spine.

Lord, have mercy. What was he going to do? Give the animal an adjustment? Ainsley pinched her lips together, partly to tamp down another laugh, partly to keep from belting out some kind of signal for Daisy to make a run for it while she could.

She moseyed close enough to whisper to him and pretended to fiddle with an earring she wasn't wearing. "Sit on the stool."

Connor looked from her to the appraising stares zeroing in on them from opposite sides of Daisy. Mr. Finnigan splayed an arm out, and Connor nodded a dozen times before the movement freed his feet.

"I'll just..." He motioned to the small stool. "Right. Okay, then." With no other option, he took his designated seat and ran his hands over his thighs one more time. He slowly reached toward the top of the cow's hind legs but couldn't quite figure out where to place his hands. He cocked his head to the left, then to the right. If he was hoping to find a time portal to climb through in there, he was in for a rude awakening.

Daisy swatted at a pesky fly. Her tail whipped back and forth across Connor's face, smearing marks from a dingleberry stuck in the end of her hair from one cheek to the other.

Connor jerked back, not even attempting to downplay his reaction. He spat and flapped at his lips that were now more defiled than his jeans.

The poor guy looked like a frenzied animal trying to shake off a long hair stuck between his teeth. If Ainsley didn't have to keep Josiah from getting in the middle of it, she would've been rolling on the floor for sure.

Mr. Finnigan wheezed a hearty laugh on her behalf. "I thought smelling bad enough to gag a maggot set you apart, son." He wheezed again. "But this beats all."

Daphne's laughter bellowed into his.

Ainsley looked between the pair. If she didn't know any better, she'd have thought the two were in cahoots.

Connor jumped up from the stool, still wiping at his mouth, and made a beeline to the stairs without excusing himself.

Ainsley couldn't blame him. She faced her two conspirators once they were alone.

All smiles and innocence, Mr. Finnigan shook his head at her. "You done did it now, kiddo. Got yourself in a peck of trouble with that one, from the looks of it."

Daphne lolled an arm across her shoulders. "Ah, the price of love."

"Real funny." As much as she wanted to kick the living daylights out of her cousin right then, she had bigger problems to worry about.

If she and Connor couldn't even get Mr. Finnigan to buy their act, how in creation were they going to convince her mom?

Chapter Seven

Connor sprang forward on his bed at ninety degrees. Again. He was going to have words with that stinking rooster before his stint at Jamison Farms was up.

He flopped backward with the pillow over his face instead of chucking it at the window this time. A heavy exhale sank into the pillowcase. Splitting his time between the farm and the office these past two weeks was starting to take a toll on him. He didn't mind the hard work. In fact, the change was refreshing. Seeing things come along on the property had even incited an unexpected sense of satisfaction. Some days, though, he wouldn't have minded stuffing a pair of socks in Herald the Rooster's beak.

Connor slowly lowered the pillow at the sound of something clattering around the floor.

Not something. Someone. Right in front of his face.

The crazy horizontal eyes and stained beard didn't give him a chance to think. He straight-up jumped smack against the wall behind him with his flimsy pillow as a worthless barrier clasped to his stomach.

Spock tilted his head at him like *Connor* was the one out of place.

"Dude, ever hear of personal boundaries? And what'd you do? Beam yourself up here?"

At the sound of his voice, the goat stared at him a moment longer, then nudged his nose along the edge of the mattress.

"No, not the bed, man. Not the bed!" He waved the stink machine away with his pillow, but the stubborn goat barely budged.

Connor scanned the floor for any sign of Spock's sidekick. Despite how short Billy the Pig's legs were, he wouldn't put it past the pudgy thing to have found a way to follow his mentor up the tall staircase. But from the looks of it, they were alone. Fabulous.

A standoff ensued.

With the pair of too-far-apart eyes zeroed in on his every move, Connor was tempted to spread his fingers apart in the classic "Live long and prosper" salute—half out of curiosity if the animal would live up to his name, half out of desperation.

Spock hung his tongue out and blubbered at him before he could lift his hand.

Whatever language that was, he knew profanity when he heard it.

Connor grasped onto the sound of someone stirring downstairs. "Ainsley?" he called without moving from the corner of the bed.

"Everything all right?"

"That depends," he hollered back, "on whether you'd hate me forever if we have goat for dinner tonight."

Boot steps rushed up the stairs. Ainsley peeked around the doorway, assessed the goat-man stare off, and flung both hands over her mouth.

"Glad you're amused." Connor flicked his chin at the mammoth. "You want to help me out here?"

For a second, she looked dead set on letting him fly solo, but then she walked over to lead Spock to the doorway. "You wait until Aunt Penny finds out you escaped again, mister."

Her baby-talk threat might've held more water if she weren't rubbing the goat's heinously stained chest with all the affection in the world. Connor had always had a bit of trouble conceptualizing love, but that image right there had to say it all.

She prodded the stink bomb down the stairs. It was only after she turned back around that she seemed to take stock of the fact that Connor was standing on the mattress in nothing but his pajama pants.

Either she'd instantly developed a deep fascination with the cobwebs decorating the ceiling's four corners, or his bare chest flustered her enough to avoid eye contact.

He tried not to show how cute he thought that made her. "Something wrong?"

"Nope. I was just... You should..." Rocking on her heels, she cleared her throat. "We should get a jump on the day. I'm gonna go turn out the horses while you..." She waved in his general direction without looking at him. "Find a shirt. One that covers..." She kept waving. "All... that."

If she only knew the effort it took to keep a straight face. "I'll see what I can find."

"Good. So, I'll be downstairs. Well, outside. By the house probably. Waiting." She rolled her eyes. Following a silent about face, she hesitated in the doorway like she wanted to say more, then rounded the threshold with determination this time.

Once he was alone, Connor chuckled. He'd learned how to do a lot working with her these past two weeks. Managing how easily she got the best of him, however, definitely hadn't made the list.

Dressed and freshened up, he headed toward the carport, stopping once to laugh at good ol' Billy perched on an oversized rock like his buddies usually did. As long as the pig kept his underside to himself, Connor was happy to let him play goat all he wanted.

Herald strutted along his own perch on top of the doghouse, and Connor swore the bird was gloating over waking him. One of these days, he'd beat him to it. Getting up before Ainsley... now that would be the real challenge.

She was waiting by the house as promised. Despite the brisk morning air, the slightest sheen of sweat already glistened on her forehead. Fretting with her broken-in boots, she looked every bit the hardworking farm girl he'd grown to admire.

He stopped at the edge of the carport and lifted the sides of his not-so-broken-in flannel. "Better?"

She fanned a nonchalant glance at his shirt. "As long as you don't mind getting it dirty."

"Wouldn't plan on anything less, boss."

"Great." She pushed off the side of the house. "We should get moving then."

All work, no play. He should be used to her lead by now.

"Would you mind if I sneak inside real fast to—?"

"Already got it." She handed him a travel mug.

Connor raised an impressed brow, took a sip of the unexpected coffee, and smiled. "Have I earned bonus points or something?"

"Chalk it up to southern hospitality." She dished his impish grin back at him. "And to me being too tired this morning to pay attention to how many cups I made."

He laughed. "Now there's the honest country girl I know."

Blue eyes fluttered as she turned.

He almost bumped into her when she crouched toward the cement out of nowhere. An earthworm, from the looks of it, wiggled beside her boot. She picked the thing up, escorted it to the edge of the slab, and gently set it in the grass like she was sending a rescue animal back into its natural habitat and kept right on walking.

Connor scratched his jaw. "Um, what was that?"

"What was what?"

He hustled up beside her. "It looked like you just released a worm into the wild."

She stopped and stared at him like it was stranger for him to ask than for her to care about fish bait. "The rain floods them out of the soil, but if they don't get back in it, the sun will dry them up for sure."

Connor tried so hard to match her honest to goodness straight face. Couldn't. "I would've said being a mom and farmer bumped you up to superhero status, but a worm saver... That has to top the noble charts."

"Better to be compassionate than indifferent," she replied without missing a beat.

He surveyed the headstrong, compassionate woman in front of him, taken aback yet again by how intriguing she was. "Hard to argue with that."

"Good." She tossed him a pair of pliers. "'Cause a hard day's work doesn't leave any time to argue." Ainsley stopped beside the wire on the coop that had gotten the better of his fingertips his first day there.

And just like that, her grin ended his miraculous two-week streak of avoiding his feathery attackers. He shifted uncomfortably at the mere sight of the little leg peckers. But to his great surprise, Ainsley didn't bring up his last run-in with them.

Work-focused, she demonstrated an issue with one of the two main doors instead. "We need to readjust the hinges. Make sure there are no gaps for any critters to get through. Same with the walls—checking for any holes, warped siding, loose nails." She pointed to a corner in the fencing. "I'm worried a snake might be getting in through this spot here."

He nodded like her casual mention of a chicken-eating snake wasn't the least bit alarming and followed her inside the coop. A few steps in, a brown chicken flapped toward him. She landed on his shoulder and settled into her apparent new favorite nesting place.

Connor froze. *Not again.*

"Don't worry," Ainsley said. "She won't get *that* much poop on your shirt."

"You think this is hilarious, don't you?"

She gave a noncommittal shrug. "I might be enjoying it *a little.*"

"Uh-huh." In an awkward one-handed grasp, he lowered the hen to the ground and did a double take at her sad eyes. The thing actually looked hurt by his rejection. What was with these animals?

Ainsley didn't slow down to show she noticed. She motioned to another section of the coop and continued on with her list of tasks. "The nesting box needs to be cleaned and bedded with fresh straw. Trust me, if you think Spock smells bad, wait 'til you get a whiff of the ammonia that can build up in here. Oh, and be sure to mind any eggs while you're working. We collect them each morning but, seriously, you do *not* want to have to deal with cleaning up broken eggs in here if we miss any."

When she finally paused, Connor rubbed his chin. "Anything else?" he said playfully.

"Oh, we're just getting started."

Of course they were. "You sure you wouldn't rather start with mending the goats' pen instead? 'Cause those things are a menace to society when they escape."

The faint freckles dotting Ainsley's cheeks glistened above a quirky grin. "You should try yoga with them. You might find they're not so bad. Even relaxing."

Relaxing. Sure. She apparently thought he had a death wish. Either that, or he wasn't the only one who'd found buttons to push... and was enjoying every second of it.

He took her in under the morning sun—auburn locks hidden under a straw hat, fitted flannel topped with a rust colored vest, worn jeans bearing the marks of rough work and even more heart. The thought of women back home having to buy pre-worn jeans to get the same look gave him a laugh.

A set of barks tore his gaze away from her. From across the property, her Blue Heeler charged straight for them. The friendly dog, who'd warmed up to him the last couple of weeks, now looked like he could put Connor in the hospital if he made the wrong move. Despite being protected inside the coop, Connor raised his palms in a reflex.

"It's just us, Matty." Ainsley slipped out to rub his head. "Good boy, watching out for the chickens." Matty landed his muddy paws on her waist and returned every bit of praise with a slobbery kiss. "You're the best guard dog around, aren't you? Yes, you are."

Connor captured a mental picture of the cute dance. Though New York offered a plethora of interesting people, he had a feeling Ainsley Grace might rival them all.

He joined them on the opposite side of the coop. "Where'd you come up with Matty?" At this point, he would've expected something more tongue-in-cheek.

"The name?" She lowered his paws to the ground. "It's short for Matthew. Well, Matthew Cuthbert, to be exact."

"Who?"

Her silent dismay left a sharper bite than any snake could've.

He rubbed his neck, but even Matty looked flabbergasted. "I assume I should know who that is?"

"Marilla and Matthew Cuthbert... *Anne of Green Gables*." She returned his blank stare. "Do you have zero taste in literature?"

He smiled at the horror claiming the innocent shine in her eyes. "I take it you read a lot?"

In all their time together, she hadn't openly revealed a lot about herself. Ainsley, the farm owner, yes. But Ainsley, the girl, she kept mostly hidden.

Connor tipped his hat toward the house when she raised a brow. "That floor-to-ceiling bookcase you've got in there might've given off a subtle hint."

She seemed to grant him that. "I used to. All the time. But ever since I..."

"Had a baby? That's what you kept cutting yourself off from telling me that day at the office, isn't it?"

"I get enough judgment for being a single mom without broadcasting it. And when it comes to men, I prefer to keep Josiah out of the picture." She rubbed her arm as she swayed in place like she did when holding her son. "It's not that I'm ashamed. I'm trying to—"

"Protect him. I get that." With him not planning to stick around, he couldn't fault her for wanting to keep his interactions with Josiah at a minimum.

"Anyway," she said to avoid the silence. "Running this place is pretty much full-time. I couldn't keep up with it during the last half of my pregnancy. And those first few months postpartum..." Her bewildered face said enough.

She looked toward the house, and her gentle laugh lulled into a pensive smile anyone could see belonged only to her son. "Being a mom's the best part of my life though. I wouldn't change that for anything."

"I can see why."

A twinge of uncertainty—either about him in general or simply on how to respond—flitted past her eyes. She peered around her. With fingers adorably entwined and fidgeting together, she scanned the property he didn't blame her for admiring. "But so is this farm. The best part of me, I mean. I know it probably doesn't look like it after having to take a back seat for a while, but I'm working on changing that. Little by little." A confident inhale brought her face forward again. "We'll get there."

As the sunshine met the hope in her eyes, Connor couldn't help believing her. "I'm sure we will."

"Oh." Her sun-kissed cheeks turned a deeper pink. "I didn't mean *we* we." She waved between them, stopped mid-swing, and stuffed her hands in her pockets like it struck her she was only making it worse. "I meant..."

"I know what you meant, but I'm here to help too, remember? I know I'm not fully trained on farm life yet.

Okay," he admitted in response to her snicker. "I'm *barely* trained. Doesn't mean I'm a slow learner. I might surprise you."

Another uncertain look battled a soft smile. "So you keep telling me."

"Some things are worth reiterating."

"Presumptuous and persistent."

"A good ol' cowboy in the making."

Her laughter clearly disagreed. "You learn to walk in those boots without looking like a cat in socks, *then* we'll talk about if you'll surprise me." She winked. "*Cowboy.*"

He'd do whatever she asked if she kept looking at him like that.

"Challenge accepted."

She shifted under his transparent gaze and lifted a hand to her neck behind her ear. If she was trying to look less attractive, she was failing. Miserably.

"You know, it wouldn't hurt to toss in some personal lessons with all this farm training. You're a reader. What else should I know about you?" He scratched his cheek. "I mean, I *am* kind of your boyfriend, so I should probably know more than the basics."

Rolling her eyes, Ainsley maneuvered past him to shut the coop doors and bent down to a toolbox. "I don't like to waste time."

Connor tossed his head back. "That's hardly a secret."

"I know how to use every tool a guy can." She stood and thrust a hammer and wrench into his chest. "And can probably do the work faster."

Fighting a smile, he clasped the tools. "If I didn't know any better, I'd say you like a little competition."

"If *I* didn't know any better, I'd say a girl who isn't afraid of manual labor intimidates you."

Face to face, mere inches apart, he'd be lying if he didn't admit that nearly everything about her intimidated and intrigued him at the same time.

He searched her eyes. "I guess some secrets aren't very hard to hide."

She didn't look away, but the flutter on her neck revealed more than her eyes were letting on. "I... made flash cards for you," she stammered. "So, you can learn all you want. *After* you work."

Of course she did. More surprising was how cute he found that. So much so, it drew him another step closer.

The pulse on her neck ticked faster. "No secrets," she said through an airy breath. "Just facts."

"Facts." Did that include the reason she was straining not to break eye contact with him?

"Ainsley?" someone behind them called.

It was a good thing they weren't still in the coop, or Ainsley would've hit the ceiling from flinching so hard. They both turned toward a woman in her forties and a guy about Connor's age, from the looks of it, heading toward them.

The woman darted a glance from Connor to Ainsley and smiled wide enough to split her tight yoga pants in two. "Why, Ainsley Grace, why didn't you tell me you were dating someone?"

Either the woman was mighty presumptuous herself, or Connor hadn't imagined the way Ainsley had been gazing at him. No time to analyze, he caught his pretend girlfriend's wary glance, winked, and slipped his arm around her shoulders. Ready or not, it was go time.

Chapter Eight

When Yoga Pants Lady's expectant eyes kept fishing for an answer, Connor reached for Ainsley's reluctant hand. "We wanted to keep things private for a while."

He counted the seconds it took for the look ping-ponging between them to give way to an accepting smile. If it'd taken any longer, his hand might've turned purple from Ainsley's death grip.

"With Josiah involved, I don't blame you, honey." She set a large thatched bag in the grass, laced her fingers together, and stretched them overhead from one side to the other. "That poor boy's already been through enough with Jonathan—"

"You know what, Aunt Penny?" Ainsley jumped in.

So, *this* was her elusive aunt who'd been road tripping the last two weeks. So many things clicked into place then.

"I checked it out earlier," Ainsley went on, "and I think the east pasture is a bit too muddy for your class today. You might want to scope out some other options before everyone gets here. Oh, and Spock escaped his pen again."

Without giving Penny a chance to respond, Ainsley turned to the guy clearly avoiding getting in the middle of it. "You didn't bring my grandparents with you, did you?"

His confused-yet-guilty expression landed him a swat to the arm.

"Easton."

"What?" He rocked forward on his boots to catch his balance. "How was I supposed to know you had some clandestine soap opera thing going on?" He adjusted his cowboy hat. "Not like you have a fighting chance keeping anything from your grandpa anyway."

Another swat.

"Hey, even if you'd warned me—which you didn't, by the way—you know how your nanna is when she has a hankering to come see Josiah."

The slightest reprieve loosened Ainsley's tight lips. "Where are they?"

Easton pointed behind them to a pickup on a lift kit parked in the driveway.

Connor barely got a good view of the redneck vehicle before Ainsley jerked him in the opposite direction.

"Tell them we had to go out to the north border to rig up a fence," she called over her shoulder to Easton. "We'll be back later, but they probably don't want to wait for us."

"But—"

"They'll understand."

She kept hauling Connor across the yard toward a smaller, detached carport.

"Whoa." He tugged her to a stop. "Easy, Whiplash. I gather that was your aunt, but who's the guy? And you wanna tell me what this high-speed escape is all about?"

"Easton's a childhood friend we grew up with. Basically a brother," she rattled off. "And I'm sorry, but I don't want my grandparents to meet you."

Well, that was blunt.

"Thanks."

She tipped her head at him. "I didn't mean it like that. I'm just not ready to do the fake relationship thing around them yet. Look, we'll talk about it later. Right now, we gotta move." She tossed him a set of keys.

Connor glanced from the single key ring to the outdated Ford work truck they'd stopped in front of. The thing looked like it had seen better days. As in, back in the sixties. "We're taking this?" And how big could her property possibly be that they needed to drive to get to a fence?

"It's either her or Oprah, and as much as I love my Odyssey, she's not built for these dirt roads."

"Did you just call your minivan Oprah?"

"That van's had to listen to her share of sob stories through the years." She shrugged. "Seemed fitting."

When a glare topped her crisscrossed arms, Connor reined in the laugh he hadn't meant to let loose. "Sorry. I'm sure she's been a trusty advice giver in return."

There went another attempt at keeping a poker face intact.

Thankfully, hers cracked too. "Better than some." Her wry once-over launched an arrow of insinuation his way, to which he laughed all over again. If it meant drawing out that playful grin, he'd gladly be a target all day.

"You have nicknames for everything, don't you?"

"Mostly." Smiling, Ainsley whirled toward the pickup. "Including people."

The glint in her eyes warned him not to ask what name she had for him, and yet…

"What's mine?"

"I'm still deciding."

So was he—about a lot of things. Not the least of which was what to make of the tool-wielding, earthworm-rescuing girl who kept him on his toes.

She pulled herself up into the passenger's side and caught his gaze over the hood of the truck. "Ready?"

As he'd ever be.

The rust-paneled door squeaked shut as he settled into the driver's seat. He cranked the engine, shifted into drive, and eased the wheels out of the half-dried mud. The old pickup sputtered at first but quickly fell into a bumpy pace along the red dirt's tire-ridden tracks.

Not all rocky starts were lost causes. You just had to find the right rhythm.

Connor cut a glance at Ainsley and smiled to himself. Once on the road, away from potential run-ins with her grandparents, she seemed to relax. It looked good on her. With her boots propped up on the dash, she turned on the radio and sang along to the country lyrics. Sort of. Almost. Okay, more like she was botching up every few lines with made-up versions of her own. The best part was, she had no clue how impossibly adorable that made her.

Another stolen glance across the seats left him baffled over what kind of fool let a girl like her go. It had taken less than ten minutes with her that first day for him to see it. Heck, any guy with half a brain could tell she was a girl worth hanging on to. A little broken. *A lot* quirky. And stubborn as all get out. But for all that and more, she was the kind of girl you could see yourself coming home to every day.

Her aunt's mention of Josiah's father soared to mind, and Connor had to rub his jaw to stop himself from prying for details. It wasn't his place to ask. He certainly had no qualifications to offer advice, anyway. Fun and diversion were safer bets—even if they involved twangy banjos. Casting his taste in music aside, he turned up the radio and joined Ainsley in singing along to words he didn't know.

As the world's most fudged duet to ever disgrace the music industry carried on, grassy fields spanned across miles on either side of them. Even wider, the open sky stretched forever. It was one of the enigmas of being tucked in the valley. At times, there was no mistaking he was in the mountains. At others, the land could almost convince him they were out on the plains.

After several more minutes down the seemingly endless road, Connor shifted in his seat.

"Getting restless?"

He ran his thumb down the corner of his mouth. "Considering the yards back home are all of fifty feet, having to drive to get to a fence might be a little unusual."

"Welcome to the country." With her straw hat shadowing a contagious grin, Ainsley soaked in the sky's reflection pouring through the window.

The image could've been on a postcard—the perfect depiction of everything his life wasn't. Connor snapped another picture in his mind. One of the many he doubted he'd forget after he left.

The unwelcome reminder of needing to secure his next client weighed on his chest. The unknown usually didn't get to him. Winging this trip was kind of the whole point. No restrictions. No unwavering demands or boxed-in expectations placed on him. Without that, he would never figure out what life apart from Pop's shadow looked like. Maybe the answers weren't here, but—

"Connor?"

His foot slipped off the clutch, and the truck stalled out.

"You okay?"

"Yeah, sorry." He turned the music down. "Did you say something?"

Ainsley motioned to a fence up ahead. "Welcome to your awaited destination."

Though clearly teasing, her words staggered over him.

"You sure you're good?"

He would've answered in a heartbeat if the tender way her hand reached for his arm hadn't thrown his normal tempo off kilter. He averted his attention to the steering wheel. *Pull it together, bro.* Now wasn't the time or place.

He grabbed the keys from the ignition, opened the door, and lifted a steady smile toward a girl capable of shaking it. "Absolutely. You good?" He notched up his hat along with his faux southern accent. "'Cause time's a-wastin'. And ain't nobody got time to waste when a full day's work is calling."

Her fully expected eye roll led her out of the truck. Ainsley hefted a toolbox out of the back, met him around the front bumper, and handed him the box. "Then you best get *a-movin'*."

He didn't know the first thing about mending a barbed wire fence, but something told him he was already being schooled in more than he'd planned.

With one hand securing the toolbox and the other tipping the front of his hat, Connor winked. "Yes, ma'am."

He watched, waited.

There it was. The coveted smile.

"Okay, country boy." She nudged him toward the fence. "Time to focus on the real work."

Oh, but he was.

"And Connor?" she added after he'd already turned. "Don't nobody say a-anything around here."

He laughed at the way she mocked his evidently offensive stab at mimicking the local dialect. "Duly noted."

Something rubbed against his shin and continued weaving to the next leg. He looked down at the random cat now meowing up at him with two different colored eyes.

"Hey, Sox." As soon as Ainsley said the gray tabby's name, Connor noticed its four solid white paws.

The cat's ears perked toward her voice. Instant purring followed as the tabby trotted toward the familiar sound.

"This is one of yours?"

"Daphne's, actually. She got her from a litter at the farmers market probably… six years ago now. She's blind in one eye."

He scanned the vast openness surrounding them. "Isn't it a little odd for her to be this far away from the house?" Not to mention dangerous.

Ainsley lifted a shoulder. "She's a bit of a roamer. Always has been."

A cat he could relate to. Now there was something he'd never expected to find no matter how far he traveled.

"Daphne doesn't strike me as a cat person."

"You gotta watch out for those assumptions," she said in a singsong voice.

He laughed. "Speaking of… Penny seems kind of young to be your aunt."

"She is. Nanna calls her their happy accident. She was over forty when they found out she was pregnant. She wouldn't trade her for anything though."

"I'm sure she wouldn't." Their family might have some interesting characters, but no one could deny the fierce love between them. "So, I guess Penny decided to make sure she had her own daughter young?"

"Like, nineteen kind of young. *Also* not planned."

"I take it Daphne's dad didn't stick around?"

When sorrow clouded Ainsley's eyes, Connor regretted bringing it up. Once again, it wasn't his business.

"Sorry. I shouldn't be prying."

"It's nothing she wouldn't openly tell you herself."

"Still. I should give her that chance and not put you on the spot."

Ainsley stared at him with surprise or maybe curiosity. If they ever reached a point where she let go of some of her skepticism about him, he'd be surprised himself.

Sox rubbed her cheek against the post between them and meowed like she knew they needed the interruption.

"You think she's telling us to get to work?"

The tops of Ainsley's cheeks lifted. "She *is* a smart cat." She tapped the post. "Ever rig a fence?"

"Not so far this month."

"Then I guess you're lucky November's not over yet." She waved a pair of pliers at him. "'Cause if we're gonna sell my family on you being my type, you darn good and well better know how to mend a fence."

"Fence mender. Got it." Connor adjusted his Stetson, losing count of how many proverbial hats he was going to have to wear to pull off this charade. Better a ranch hand than a vet, he supposed. Easier, anyway. He hoped.

"See that?" Ainsley motioned to a busted spot in the wire. "That right there's an open invitation."

"To who?"

"Anyone who's not welcome."

If he read the look on her face right, Connor was glad not to be lumped into that group.

She gestured to the back of the pickup. "We're probably gonna need the fence stretcher. Maybe a splicer. There's some extra wire in the toolbox as well."

So much for Connor's working knowledge of tools. He squatted beside the fence to get a closer look at the damage.

"Uh-uh." Ainsley swatted his hand away from the barbs, then pulled a pair of soiled work gloves out of her back pocket. "Lesson number one: never touch wire without gloves." She tugged out a pair of her own and squinted at the grin he'd meant to lose before she looked up again. "What?"

"You seem prepared for everything is all."

"As any respectable southern woman always should be." Her exaggerated southern drawl cost him another battle against a laugh there was no point in stifling around her.

That is, unless it meant getting drenched in the rain. He nodded to what looked like storm clouds swelling in from behind her. "Did you prepare for *that*?"

She turned for a split second, flung right back around, and got to work like someone had set fire to her backside.

There went their training. No instruction. No play-by-play. Nothing was diverting her single-focus mission.

After several minutes, Ainsley tossed her hat on the ground and shoved her bangs back with her forearm. "Stinkin' wire," she mumbled. Just when he was convinced the girl couldn't get any cuter, she gave the fence the stink eye. "Don't think you're getting the better of me 'cause I'm rushing."

"You sure there's nothing I can do to help?"

"Another time."

If those fast approaching clouds had anything to say about it, time didn't appear to be on their side. He'd never seen the sky darken so quickly, nor heavy wind pick up faster.

Thunder rippled across the pastures, and Sox took off like a banshee. Clearly, *one* of them had enough sense to get the heck out of there while they still could.

"Um, Ainsley? I'm thinking we should hit the pause button for now and come back after this blows past us." Based on what he'd seen of the area so far, the weather didn't tend to hold back in these parts.

"I'm not leaving the fence this vulnerable. I need another five minutes." She twisted the pliers. "I've almost got it."

Lightning streaked the sky.

"We don't have five minutes." A closer roar of thunder backed up his claim. The first raindrop splattered onto the brim of his hat. The second. Third. Wind howled. "Ainsley?"

"Almost there—"

"We're out of time." He grabbed her hand and pulled her to her feet.

Beads of unforgiving raindrops pelted them from every angle. In a matter of seconds, the earth turned to sludge under their boots as fallen leaves whirled past them on the tail of another clap of thunder.

Ainsley pulled in the opposite direction. "The tools…"

"Will be here later." He admired her determination, envied her loyalty to the farm. But right now, protecting her was more important.

He whipped open the truck's passenger door and closed it behind her. He slid around the front of the pickup, grabbed the hood to keep from falling, and blinked through the rain soaking his hat. Even with the wipers going at full speed, it'd be pure insanity to try to drive in this.

Flashes of lightning jolted him away from the bumper.

They had no choice. They needed to get to shelter.

His boots slogged through the red mud as fast as he could make them. Finally inside, he yanked the door against the wind and fished the keys out of his sodden jeans' pocket.

"You should've let me finish. Storms like this blow through here all the time," she said, as if they weren't sitting ducks in the middle of one right now.

"All the same, I'd rather not watch one while standing next to a wire fence or from inside this rusted lightning rod." The heap of metal might as well have had a flashing beacon on the hood, drawing bolts straight to the only viable target within miles of nothingness.

He turned the key. The engine sputtered, then stalled.

"Come on." He tapped the wheel. "You can do this." If Ainsley could talk to inanimate objects, he could too.

He cranked the ignition again. Churning, it turned over a dozen times before the motor's glorious roar rumbled against the thunder.

"Yes." He strapped on his seat belt. "Thata girl."

A glance out the back window snagged on the cute way Ainsley was pinching her lips together. "What?"

"Nothing," she said the way he usually did. At least she was smiling again.

Another lightning bolt sparked across the sky. Connor thrust the gearshift into reverse. The wheels spun but only sank deeper into the mud. He cast Ainsley a wary glance, then pressed the gas again. Same.

"You've got to be kidding me." He shifted into drive instead. Nothing.

The passenger door clanked open. "Come on."

"Wait, what?" Connor grabbed the keys and hustled out after her. "Ainsley, hang on. What are you doing?"

"There's a barn an eighth of a mile that way." She pointed behind her. "We can make a run for it."

Crazy hadn't made it to the list of words he'd use to describe her until right then.

"You have a better option?" she added when he didn't move.

He looked around, shook his head, and finally relented. They might as well be crazy together.

By the time they reached the wooden structure, Connor had mentally revised all his usual workout routines to include running in the mud from now on. If nothing else, the burn helped counter the chill from the rain.

He slid the doors shut, backed against them, and stopped himself short of shaking out his clothes like a wet dog. He hung his soaked hat on a nail and settled for shaking out his hair instead. "Well, that was fun."

The witty remark he'd expected in return didn't come. Instead, Ainsley's eyes scanned the old barn like it held more to her than overworked farm equipment. She grazed her fingers along a dusty workbench but still said nothing.

"You come out here often?"

"To check the fences, yeah. Perimeter checks are pretty routine. Another lesson to remember," she said with less inflection than her usual instructions.

"But you don't come in here," he said like Captain Obvious yet again.

"Not in a while."

From the looks of it, no one had. The damp smell put off notes of old hay and stale oil. No telling when any of the tractors had last been used. At the same time, the tools scattered beside a coffee mug on the workbench would've made him guess someone came out here to work regularly. Or used to, anyway. It looked as if they'd left mid-project with every intention of returning to finish it.

Ainsley dusted off some kind of manual she'd picked up from the bench. The dark clouds dimming what little light the barn offered couldn't hide the torn look misting her eyes.

"It doesn't seem right to give up something you miss so much." He nodded at the book. "Reading, I mean."

She quickly masked her surprise at the random comment. "Who said I miss it?"

"It's just the sense I get."

"You mean an assumption you're making."

He'd give her that. "Doesn't mean it's wrong."

With her eyes fixed on the book in her hands, she opened the hardback cover. "I already told you. No time."

"Not even for *Anne of Green Gables?* It's your favorite series."

"Another assumption."

"You named your dog after one of the characters." He cocked a brow at her even though she wasn't looking at him. "Are you really gonna deny that one? Even if you try, the worn spines on those books don't lie. You have to have read them a thousand times minimum."

"Maybe a few hundred." The slightest quirk nibbling at her lips slowly waned. "That's what happens when you fall in love with love when you're eight."

Connor crossed the hay-strewn floor to the bench and picked up an old handheld radio. "Seems like a little heavy reading for grade school."

"No one said I read them alone."

"Your dad read to you?" It wasn't an assumption this time. More of a gut feeling based on the esteem her eyes held any time something seemed to trigger a memory of him—this old barn and the book in her hands included.

Her fingers glided over the faded print on the opening page. "My mom, actually."

So much for his gut. Surprised, he angled toward her. "You two are close?" That definitely wasn't what he would've banked on given what he'd picked up on so far.

"We used to be." Ainsley closed the cover, set the book back on the dusty bench, and strode over to the window. She leaned against the trim and stared outside like she could drive the storm away with sheer willpower. If anyone could, he didn't doubt she'd be the one.

"What is it about books you love so much?"

Seemingly struck again by his random questions, she turned. "Everything," she said as if that were the only—and glaringly obvious—answer.

"Can you be a little more vague?"

The ghost of a smile surfaced. "Sorry. It's not something a *non-reader* would understand."

He laughed. "You know, for someone who's always calling me out on being presumptuous, you have a hefty streak of your own."

"Fair enough. What's the last book you read?"

"Stop avoiding my question."

"Look who's talking." Rather than run with their banter, she let his evasion slide as she peered outside again. After a few minutes, she lifted a hand to the trim and seemed to sink deeper into the place where her love of fiction flourished. "There are a ton of reasons, really. Getting to escape to another world, another life. The power words have to speak to your heart and awaken emotions you didn't know you had. There's something magical about it, something... powerful."

A shade of sadness gradually shrouded her unmistakable reverence for art. "Maybe more than anything, I love the peace of knowing you can trust the ending that's coming. Through all the turmoil they have to go through, the characters inevitably get their happily ever after." The hint of another slow grin snuck up her cheek. "I still cheat and read the end first most times."

"*You* cheat?"

She turned and waved off the appalled expression he'd feigned at her. "I can't help it. I *have* to know. It's the only thing that gets me through all the doubts and obstacles."

Despite the tease in her voice, she probably wished she could skip ahead to read the end of her own story. Connor could hardly blame her. It was too easy to lose faith during the middle. If he could, he'd hold the pages open for her himself. Read them to her and assure her of the happily ever after she deserved in real life.

She faced the window again. Light from outside sprawled over her hair, and Connor stumbled over reactions spurring out of nowhere.

Open the pages for her? Okay, all this old hay had to be getting to him. He needed something practical to focus on. He tinkered with the near antique in his hands until a staticky station filtered through. "Ha." He lifted it up like a trophy. "Still works."

"I'm not surprised."

That made one of them.

Ainsley's eyes didn't stray from the rain-coated windowpanes. "My dad loved that thing. He insisted it worked better than any modern invention." She half snickered. "Same way he felt about most things."

It didn't take a genius to piece together the fact that her father had passed. How and when, Connor didn't feel comfortable asking. From what little he'd observed of her so far, he gathered she preferred to keep most of her life private.

He got that. Appreciated it more than she probably suspected. Nonetheless, seeing a bird with broken wings never sat well with him. She'd thrived once. He saw it in glimpses, heard it in snippets when she dared to let her guard down. His stay in Whispering Pines might be short-lived, but he couldn't think of a better way to spend that time than to show her flying again was worth the risk.

The commercial on the radio ended, and a good old country ballad filled the barn. Connor set it on the bench and met Ainsley at the window. "May I have this dance?"

"Come again?"

"Dance with me."

The look she gave him had her name written all over it. "Are you kidding?"

"Not kidding." He directed her eyes to his outstretched—still empty—hand. "But maybe a little deflated if you keep standing there turning me down."

Her arms a shield, she stayed in place. "We're soaking wet, stranded in a musty barn in the middle of a storm."

"All the more reason to make the most of our time." He clasped her hand. "There's no work for you to do right now, so c'mon. Have some fun."

She reluctantly let him draw her into his arms. "Is that what you call this?"

He returned the smile she was fighting. "Is there any other name for swaying to staticky oldies?" He twirled her around, drew her back in, and rested his chin near her temple. "See? A little Patsy Cline goes a long way."

Ainsley laughed against his shoulder. "That's definitely not Patsy Cline."

"Dolly Parton?"

"You better quit while you're ahead."

The playful warning struck deeper than intended. No doubt, a girl as closed off as she was had a valid reason to be. He didn't have to be a therapist to know how easily he could add to those reasons if he wasn't careful.

He loosened his hold at the thought. But when a mix of unvoiced questions looked up at him, he couldn't silence his own.

"So, this whole fake boyfriend thing…" he said slowly. "I don't get it. You're clearly more than capable of standing on your own. Why pretend to need a relationship?"

The brief look of surprise at his blunt question gave way to resignation. She backed out of his arms. "You don't know my mom. If I'm not already in a relationship when she gets here, she won't rest until she gets me in one."

"Can't you tell her to butt out?"

"You've obviously never met a southern mama. I swear," she went on. "The woman's worse than Mrs. Bennet."

Connor chuckled on the inside. He had a feeling that was another Austen reference, but he wasn't about to add to his literary naiveté at the moment.

"What about Easton then?"

She stared at him. "What about him?"

"You two seem close." He shrugged. "Wouldn't it be easier to pull off a pretend relationship with someone who knows you well?"

She snorted. "Not if we actually wanted anyone to believe us."

"Best friends can fall in love. It happens in books all the time, right?"

Ainsley lifted her hand to her neck and a grin he wanted to hang on to with all he had, but her countenance dropped a second later. "If real life followed books, we'd all get happy endings."

"I thought all fiction has a thread of real life woven into it." Connor rubbed his jawline. "I believe unavoidable was the exact word you used."

She looked up from the floor, and another dance with amusement brushed her cheeks. "I need to be careful what I say around you, don't I?"

"Maybe."

She shook her head. "Unfortunately for Easton, the thread he wants from Kate is still wrapped around her ex-boyfriend."

"Wait, wait." He rewound her words. "Easton likes Kate?"

"The guy's been in love with her since we were, like, twelve."

"Unreciprocated," he gathered.

"Unacknowledged altogether. But Easton has no room to talk. He's just as clueless about how long Daphne's liked him."

Connor raised a finger. "Okay, hold on a second. So, Daphne wants to be with Easton. Easton's pining for Kate. And Kate's still hung up on an ex."

"Pretty much." A weak laugh followed the admission. "I guess it sounds a little soap opera-ish when you say it out loud like that."

Or a lot. But something warned him neither to confirm nor deny how much.

A sheen of sympathy touched Ainsley's eyes. "Like I said, most of us don't get the happy endings we read about."

He could concede to not involving Easton and the complicated family-best-friend saga he brought with him into Ainsley's relationship predicament, but Connor didn't believe for a minute she'd go forever without a happy ending.

"Okay, forget fiction for now. Look at your grandparents." He inclined his head at her, knowing she couldn't deny that one. "If they found lifelong mates, why doubt you can too?"

Ainsley stepped farther back as if distance would improve how absurd his questions were growing by the second.

"Let me guess," he said when she didn't respond. "Too busy."

"As a matter of fact, yes." She lifted her necklace to her chin and twisted the tiny charm on it back and forth. "It wouldn't matter if I wasn't. I'd have better luck chasing after dandelion seeds in this storm than chasing after real love."

In all honesty, he resonated with the tired struggle more than he wanted to admit. Maybe not a chase for love but for something missing.

He released a hard exhale. "Guess we're all chasing something."

She looked back at him, brow raised. "And what is Connor Allen chasing?"

It took him a minute to look away from the blue eyes searching his. Peering off to the window, he squeezed his shoulder. "I'm still trying to figure that out."

"It's hard to know you've found something if you don't know what you're looking for."

Rather than reply, Connor simply stared. At her insight, her brokenness, the frail armor not so unlike his own. She might've been right, but the opposite unnerved him more. What if you don't realize what you've always been looking for until you've finally found it?

Though his feet retreated, his gaze hung on. He swallowed. "You should start reading again," he prattled off again. "It'll be good for you."

"There you go with those presumptions again."

Better than other things he could let his mind run away with.

He strode for the radio, turned it down, and faced another window.

"The storm's fairing off," she said from right beside him now. "Told ya. They blow out of here as quickly as they blow in."

Like him?

He'd intentionally arranged for it to be that way before ever stepping on the first tarmac. Each stop a momentary pass-through.

"Too bad you don't have running shoes on."

Connor whipped his head up, certain she'd heard what he hadn't spoken aloud. "Sorry?"

She motioned to his mud-caked boots. "Those may keep your feet dry. But when we get back to the house, you might be wishing for something with even more tread."

"Why?"

"'Cause if you think that storm was something to run from…" She walked backward to the door with a look on her face that made him want to backpedal in the opposite direction. "Wait 'til you meet my grandpa."

Chapter Nine

Their long trek back to the house passed in less comfortable silence than they'd shared on the way out. At least, for Connor. He could get away with attributing it to nerves about meeting Ainsley's grandpa as long as he didn't have to convince himself that was all it was.

They'd parked the mud-covered truck under the carport and headed to the nearest pasture when Ainsley's phone rang. "Sorry," she said as if receiving a phone call was somehow rude. "I've been waiting for this call. Would you mind giving me a minute?"

"Of course not." He gave her some space.

She turned toward the fence and propped her boot on the bottom rail. "Hey, Donna. Did you hear back from the Fenways?" She picked at the splintered wood. "Uh-huh... I understand... It's fine. I'll keep looking. I need to get myself together and post an ad online anyway. I shouldn't have put that off... No, no. I'm good. Really. I appreciate you asking around for me."

One of the horses approached the fence and nuzzled his nose to Ainsley's neck. Smiling warmly, she rubbed his forehead. Connor had never seen anything like the way she connected with the animals here. No words required, trust and acceptance easily transferred between them in simple acts of love.

"He's doing great, Donna. Teething up a storm but good. Thank you for asking," she continued. "Yep, my mom will be here the day before Thanksgiving... Mm-hmm. I will. You take care too. Bye now." Ainsley looked at her phone long enough to push the end button, stuffed it in her pocket, and drenched the horse in front of her with all her attention. "We'll be all right, boy," she whispered.

Connor doubted she'd meant for him to hear her, same way he doubted she would tell him what that phone call was about. If he had to guess, she'd lost a prospect on filling the empty stall she was trying to rent.

He peered at the rest of the horses grazing in the muddy pasture. Such strong creatures. Such beauty and fortitude. Just like their caregiver. He expected her to be too proud to ask for financial help, but that didn't stop him from wanting to offer it.

"Ainsley, if there's anything I can—"

"Oh, no."

He turned from her panicked face to the source behind him.

Matty proudly followed a classic southern couple looking like they'd stepped off the pages of a timeless magazine. A sturdy arm led a silver-haired woman who clearly held her husband's heart.

"If it isn't the prettiest gal this side of Georgia."

"Hi, Grandpa." With the kind of expression accustomed to humoring his compliments, Ainsley squinted into the sun, which had finally decided to return. "Y'all didn't have to wait."

"Of course we did, sweetie." He removed his black Stetson and kissed her cheek. "Now, there's that smile I've been missing."

"You just saw me at church on Sunday."

He tipped her chin. "With a smile that lovely, I miss it before you ever leave." He positioned his hat back on, circled his wife's arm through his again, and patted her aged hand. "A trait you inherited from the loveliest gal in the country."

"Oh, stop now, Henry. You're gonna embarrass her." Instead of pulling away, his wife nestled closer to him, and a hint of admiration deepened on Ainsley's face.

Connor couldn't fault her for turning starry-eyed. He was almost tempted to do the same.

Daphne headed over with Josiah strapped to her back, while Easton and Penny brought up the rear.

Wow, a whole family gathering. That wasn't intimidating in the least.

Daphne stopped by Ainsley to let her kiss Josiah's cheek. "Did you pick up that order of feed yesterday?"

"Yeah, but don't worry about it." Ainsley rubbed her son's hair. "I'll take care of it in a few."

"Are you kidding? No chance, girl. Josiah *loves* feeding the horses." She hopped to bounce him. "Isn't that right, Smalls? Besides," she added. "It'll give us something to do. If I have to listen to one more nursery rhyme, I'm going to end up in a padded room. And seriously," she said so her grandparents couldn't hear. "That toy your mom got him needs to die."

Ainsley cracked up. "I keep trying to think of a way to ditch the creepy thing without her knowing."

"I'm sure I can come up with something."

"I'm sure you could. You better wait 'til after Thanksgiving though."

"No promises," Daphne called on her way to the paddock.

Ainsley shook her head but kept smiling as her cousin and son led the first horse through the gate. When Josiah practically leaned out of his carrier to reach for the horse's mane, Connor couldn't help smiling too. The kid was lucky to get to grow up here.

An ache pressed in out of nowhere. Before he had time to dissect it, Matty surprisingly trotted to his side. He nudged his wet nose against the fingers Connor still had wrapped around the truck's keys. He would've dropped them to pet the dog if he didn't think it would draw attention to himself. Then again, Matty must've already had that covered, because a semicircle of faces now stared at the pair of them.

Not knowing what else to do, he extended his free hand to Ainsley's grandpa. "Connor Allen. Nice to meet you, sir."

"Henry Jamison." The firm handshake alluded to hard work, weathered years, and maybe a bit more warning than anything else. He set his hand on his wife's back. "And my beautiful bride, Ellie."

Connor tipped his hat in what he hoped would pass for a genuine cowboy-ish gesture. "Howdy, ma'am."

Easton laughed until Ainsley side-eyed him.

She angled in front of Connor and whispered in his ear, "You're in North Carolina, not the Wild West. No one actually says howdy."

Right. Compensating, Connor nodded at her grandma and tried again. "Pleasure to meet you, Mrs. Jamison."

She returned his nod with an unreadable glint in her eye. "Pleasure's mine, dear. But if you want to keep an old woman from feeling her age, please, call me Ellie."

"Yes, ma'am."

Henry sized Connor up and down. "Easton, here, tells us you're helping out around the farm."

"That's one way of putting it," Easton mumbled.

The guy was either foolishly brave or an outright fool, because the look Ainsley speared through him sure as heck made Connor want to clear the yard faster than a jet clearing a runway.

"Speaking of help." She prodded a shovel into Easton's sternum. "Brie's stall hasn't been mucked yet this morning. You should be right at home digging yourself out of piles of cow manure."

The corner of his mouth tipped in acceptance of being outplayed. "I'll get right on that... *after* I get some more coffee." He propped the shovel against the fence and cast an almost casual glance to the house. "Is Kate home? I'm surprised she's not up yet."

Ainsley and her nanna shared a knowing look. "The hospital extended her shift later than usual last night, so I wouldn't hold your breath on her getting up anytime soon. But… I'm sure Daphne would have another cup with you." Her lips twitched. "Either her or Brie."

Easton turned without biting. He made it up to the carport before Ainsley tacked on, "Don't think you're getting out of spending the morning with Brie, buddy."

"Wouldn't dream of it." He spun around, brought his hand to the brim of his hat, and walked backward the last few steps before trailing out of view.

Connor wouldn't have minded following him when another lick from Matty brought his attention back to the group huddle. Downsizing their semicircle by one did nothing to diminish the volume of silent conversations crisscrossing between everyone. He would've wagered a month's salary on guessing Henry's thoughts. Unlike Penny's. He didn't have enough in the bank to bet on what that look in her eyes meant.

She bit her lip the way Ainsley often did and bounced on the balls of her feet like an antsy girl waiting to go to a slumber party. "When are you going to tell us how you managed to keep such a prize from us all this time, love?"

Ainsley's stammer lasted two point five seconds before her grandpa's eyes narrowed. "You're seeing my granddaughter?"

There had to be more than a hundred acres of mostly open space around them, and Connor would've sworn he was standing in the close quarters of a principal's office. He cleared his throat. "Yes, sir." He glanced overhead. No lightning bolts. That was a good sign. Then again, Henry's eyes could quite possibly cause more lasting damage.

"I thought you were helping out around the farm."

"He's pitching in while he's here," Ainsley quickly added.

"Here? As in *living* here?"

Oh, boy.

"In the barn... sir."

Ainsley motioned behind them. "We were actually just getting ready to jump on some work in there."

They were?

"So we should probably... you know... go *that* way," she mumbled mostly into her sleeve.

"Sweet pea," Henry said to Ainsley with his eyes still fastened on Connor. "Why don't you take your nanna in to warm up with some of the coffee Easton's making and let her visit with that sweet great grandbaby of ours for a while? Mr. Allen and I'll take a gander over the barn he's staying in." He landed a solid grasp on Connor's shoulder. "If that's all right with you, son."

That depended on whether the pitch forks inside were in reachable distance.

Connor hesitated. But when Ainsley gave him a look of reliance, he didn't want to disappoint her. He rolled his shoulders back. "Of course, sir. After you."

Ainsley caught his hand as he turned. She didn't say anything. She simply held on and nodded, to which Connor offered an assuring smile. Easton might not be the only one digging himself out of manure this morning. But for her, he'd dive in with both hands.

He dried his palms on his jeans as he and Henry entered the barn. Painted in golden rays of sunshine now, the rustic structure stole his focus. No one could challenge its need of some repairs, but they'd be hard pressed to deny the quintessential country icon its character. No doubt, the same caliber of charm was what had drawn his brother to break away from the family business for a job as a Texas vet.

With his boots crunching over loose pieces of hay tracked out from the stalls, Connor couldn't avoid the irony of ending up in a role far better played by Reed. Not that he should have been surprised the man best suited to fit in with a family like the Jamisons would match his brother to a T. Still, he'd never felt the strain of differences between them more than right then.

"You handy with tools, son?"

Connor looked up from the ground to a stall gate Henry was inspecting. "Yes, sir." Common tools, anyway. It wasn't his everyday type of work, but he'd picked up a number of skills along the way. No thanks to his father. Or his absentee grandfathers, for that matter. He'd taught himself out of necessity or mere interest in varying circumstances.

"That's a good trait to have in these parts." Henry hung his Stetson on a nail, positioned himself to get a solid hold of the stall gate, and heaved it back into the right angle it'd fallen loose from. "Come make use of that screwdriver over there, will ya?"

Connor did as instructed. After double-checking the hinge was secure, he tapped the top of the gate. "That oughta do it."

Henry released the wood and flexed his fingers. "She's a beauty, isn't she?"

At Connor's raised brow, Henry nodded inside the stall to the same black horse Ainsley had shared a moment with earlier by the fence. "Shiloh."

The horse stuck his head over the gate in response to hearing his name, and Henry rubbed his nose. "Ainsley's had him since he was a yearling. A special bond these two have. Built on years of investment, trust."

He didn't need to slant a glance his way for Connor to sense the shift this conversation was taking. He also didn't need to know Ainsley very long to already appreciate how much she loved everything life on this farm encompassed.

"Your granddaughter has a very compassionate heart."

"A very fragile heart," he qualified.

Connor challenged the old man's blue eyes without thinking better of it. "I have a feeling she's stronger than some give her credit for."

The horse shrank back into the stall as if he had the sense to take cover. Unlike Connor, apparently. He crossed his arms instead, in case Henry happened to be skilled at knife throwing and decided to grab that screwdriver in a pinch.

To his surprise, a whiskery smile released a slow chuckle. "That she is. You can thank her daddy for that. Walker worked his fingers to the bone running this place."

"He passed it on to her?" He couldn't stop his inflection from revealing the curiosity he'd been reserving.

"And I to him." Henry unhooked his hat and peered around the barn that must've been in their family for generations. "Ainsley wasn't ready to see that legacy end."

"I don't blame her. The land holds a lot of charm."

"It holds much more than that, son." He gestured for Connor to walk with him. "You should've seen it in its day. A working cattle ranch did mighty fine for itself back then."

"Cattle?" Stopped by the doors, Connor scanned the property, wondering if he'd managed to overlook a herd of livestock somewhere.

"You can look 'til the cows come home," he said with a self-humored laugh. "You won't find 'em on this land no more. Unless you count Brie."

Connor watched Matty run in the distance where he envisioned a magnificent business once flourishing. Ideas churned in the wind whirling the cool morning into the barn. Maybe he could help Ainsley turn this place around more than he'd originally expected. He'd make a few calls, lay out some plans. This property could really thrive again.

Henry fit his hat on. "If my nose ain't lying, I believe there's a pot of coffee waiting inside for us."

They were done out here already? That went more smoothly than expected. "Perfect. I could use another—"

A firm grasp to Connor's shoulder brought his rambling—and his relief—up short. Henry's grip equaled the intensity of his no-nonsense stare. "Just 'cause my granddaughter's learned to be strong doesn't mean she's beyond breaking. You play a part in that, young man, and you'll find out good and well where she inherited her strength from. You follow me?"

Willing himself to maintain eye contact, Connor nodded. "Loud and clear, sir."

"Good." He followed the word with a swift pat to Connor's back. "Then what do you say we go wet our whistles."

"You got it," he managed.

Once Henry strode ahead of him, Connor checked his phone. Only an hour left before he had to be at the office— an hour that was about to confirm he'd already unknowingly lied to Ainsley. Keeping things simple and unattached wasn't going to be as easy as he'd told her it would be.

Proving him right, the beautifully intriguing girl he'd first laid eyes on at Common Grounds two weeks ago slipped out of the house to meet her grandfather with a steaming mug of joe. Her hair glistened above eyes anxiously searching past Henry to Connor. She must've sensed his hesitation. She whispered something to her grandpa, latched onto Connor's gaze, and headed farther into the sunlight showering over a day that just turned a heck of a lot more complicated.

Chapter Ten

Ainsley slipped her hands in her back pockets when Connor met her halfway across the lawn. "You good?"

No telling what Grandpa had asked while he had him to himself in the barn. More fretful, one slipup from Connor could've ruined everything. He wasn't prepared to be thrown into the lion's den.

"All good." Though his confident voice backed up the affirmation, his eyes told a different story. He diverted them to his phone. "I was just wondering what the game plan is for telling your family why I have to leave in an hour. If any of them sees me in town, it might be a tad difficult to explain why a vet's working in a chiropractor's office."

Ugh. Ainsley wasn't expecting to have to deal with that part yet. She faced the sky on the off chance an answer was waiting to smack her in the head.

A minute later, she looked from the answerless sky to eyes starting to hold more doubts than hers. "You're right." She sighed. "I'll have to tell them I made the vet part up."

"Because?"

"Because... I wasn't sure they'd accept a chiropractor. I already told you. You're not exactly my type." That was legitimate enough.

The annoyingly cute hitch of his lips returned. "You're pretty quick on your feet, Ainsley Grace. They got lying rodeos around here?"

"Hush up." She shoved him in the arm. "I already feel like I'm going to hell in a handbasket for all this." She knew keeping up the act would be hard, but not being forthcoming with her grandparents had drilled guilt past what she was prepared for.

If she read the way Connor searched her eyes right, he sensed it too.

He edged close enough for his aftershave to make her feel heady. "Are you sure this is what you want?"

Was he expecting her to make an audible response when he looked at her like that? Heart racing, she reached for the back of her hair like it could save her from sinking any further into those green eyes.

"I…" She forced her attention behind him to her family's barn, and her thoughts to the precious baby boy inside the house she'd grown up in. She knew what she wanted as well as she knew it was worth any cost. "I thought you were supposed to be the sure one. *You* convinced *me* we could do this, remember?" She couldn't afford him to be second-guessing now too.

His focus strayed to the grass. Despite logic telling her it couldn't have been more than a thirty-second pause, Ainsley would've sworn ten minutes lapsed before a heavy inhale brought his eyes back to hers.

"You're right. I did, and I'll see it through. But if we're going to do this, we're going to have to really sell it." The assurance that embodied Connor Allen inched yet another step closer. "And we should probably work out those rules you mentioned soon." His all too familiar dimples sank in as he reached for the hair her fingers had fallen from seconds ago. "Because with your family glued to the kitchen window right now, I might have to kiss you to stay in character."

When the tips of his fingers grazed her neck, Ainsley was positive she would drown right then and there in her own mud puddle. Until the first part of his comment registered. She whipped toward the house and the four faces vying for the best view from the window. Unbelievable. Did they think she was sixteen still?

"I'm so sorry." Her face burned against the cool air. "I honestly don't even have an excuse for them."

Connor's laugh slowly drew one out of her.

She lifted both shoulders to her ears. "All I can say is welcome to Whispering Pines, country cliché at its finest."

His laughter tapered as his hand found its way back to her neck. He leaned in. "I'm starting to like it here more than you think." The lightest touch of his lips to her cheek sent his whisper all the way down her body.

Rules. They definitely needed rules. Without them, a boarder for the empty barn stall would be the least of things she needed to worry about losing.

She jutted a thumb over her shoulder like her elbow was some kind of slingshot. "We should probably go inside."

Still smiling, Connor offered a tip of his hat while motioning her ahead of him.

Surely her legs could handle walking. She tested one out, then the other. Once her back was toward him, and the kitchen window out of view, her eyes reached for the sky again. *If you're not gonna give me answers, you could at least loan me some dignity. Levelheadedness. Non-noodled legs. Something!*

Apparently, that was too much to ask for.

Inside, everyone beamed at them coming through the door like they were homecoming king and queen. She might've been able to give them a reason not to if the feel of Connor's warm hand on her lower back weren't coursing straight to her cheeks.

"Eee!" Josiah stretched his arms toward her, and, just like that, the world diminished to the one smile that always realigned her life.

"Hey, sweet boy." Ainsley lifted him off Nanna's lap and ate up his chubby cheek. "You ready for a diaper change?" She felt his puffy diaper. Oh, yeah. Definitely past ready.

"Here, let me," Connor volunteered.

Okay, the guy's confidence got him a little ahead of himself sometimes.

When Ainsley didn't hand Josiah over, Connor silently pleaded for her not to leave him hanging in front of everyone. In all fairness, she understood that he was trying to make their relationship believable, but his involvement in Josiah's life was still one part she wasn't comfortable with. Fine, one of the *many* parts.

He reached for Josiah. "We've got this. Right, big guy?"

Ainsley reluctantly handed him over along with a look of caution. His tender nod of acknowledgement eased her shoulders a bit until Josiah stared at him like he was a complete stranger. She bit her lip, waiting for the inevitable cry. When it didn't come, she tried to ascertain whether to blame the unexpected reaction on fascination or fear.

Josiah ran a curious—and slobbery—hand over Connor's jaw, popped him a good one, and squealed through a smile.

Connor wiped his wet cheek. "Thanks, buddy." He laid Josiah on a changing mat on the living room floor. "You ready for diaper time?" He made a plane motion with the fresh diaper, and Josiah wasn't the only one fascinated.

Maybe because he was from a big city. Maybe because he was a single guy focused on his career. Whatever the reason, Ainsley never would've pegged him for being good with kids.

The image distracted and warmed her. Almost as much as the sudden stream of pee soaking into his shirt was probably warming Connor.

"Cover it. Quick!" Ainsley rushed over.

Connor scrambled to block the projectile torrent with both hands but only ended up looking like a dog trying to paw at a popup fountain.

Ainsley landed on her knees beside him, clamped a dry diaper over the fountain, and turned the best straight face she could pull off toward the frozen one drenched in urine and shock.

Fighting a grin, she handed Connor a clean burp cloth. "At least you waited to shower."

A slow blink broke the barely contained silence in the room. Full-on laughter at Connor's expense outshot Josiah's impressive trajectory and brimmed all the way to the ceiling.

"Not quite like using a wrench, is it, son?" Grandpa rasped.

Nanna popped her husband in the arm while stifling a chuckle of her own. "Leave the poor guy be, Henry. He's obviously still learning."

Josiah flailed his legs with uncontrollable energy. Ainsley grabbed a new diaper before the little wiggle artist ended up scooting around on his bare backside.

Connor helped keep Josiah in place with one hand and dried his face with the cloth in the other. When Ainsley motioned to trade places with him, he stretched forward and whispered, "Just so you know, I blame your lack of sugar as the culprit here."

She smiled behind her shield of hair. "You do, huh?"

"Without sugar in my coffee, my whole game's thrown off."

"Ah." She leaned in close enough for her lips to hover near his ear the way he'd done to her outside. "Welcome to what happens when you level the playing field." Letting her satisfaction linger, Ainsley sat back on her heels.

If she was smart, she'd soak up her momentary victory instead of relinquishing it to the green eyes she knew would be waiting to regain the upper hand.

One look. One blasted look. He didn't even have to say a word, and her composure slipped away from her faster than a greased piglet in a pig scramble.

Smart obviously wasn't in her wheelhouse today. Or any day, for that matter. This entire predicament vouched for that.

"Guess I should take that shower now."

If he didn't hurry it up already, she'd need a second one herself. What was with this guy's ability to fluster her so easily?

She glanced at the thermostat, knowing full well the heat wasn't on. Not that her increasingly damp shirt cared at all about silly things like logic. She fanned it away from her body, probably looking as casual as she sounded. "Sure. I need to feed Josiah anyway." Which happened to come with a glorious twenty-minute free pass to hide out in his nursery.

"And you, big guy…" Connor arched above Josiah. "We should talk about those mad skills of yours before—"

Josiah landed a flailing karate chop dead to Connor's windpipe.

Coughing, he reached for his neck, and Ainsley couldn't help joining the rest of the room cracking up. She would've felt sorry for him if he weren't laughing himself. Leave it to Mr. Smooth to not let embarrassment get to him.

"I think it's past time for that shower." He pointed to the hallway and excused himself, leaving the aftermath of another easy smile in his wake.

Better than the one Daphne was not so subtly aiming in her direction.

"What?"

Daphne circled her hands around her mug. "Josiah's not the only one with skills."

Of all the things Daphne was trying to imply, Ainsley was sure her cue to leave the room lay somewhere near top of the list. She finished getting Josiah changed and avoided the other loaded looks she wasn't about to respond to.

Her shoulders relaxed once she was finally alone with Josiah to nurse. But as always, the sweet snuggle time passed too quickly. She smoothed his hair off his forehead and kissed her little bundle of energy. "Love you to Neverland and back, sweet boy," she whispered.

Using her thighs as a springboard, he bounced up and down.

"I'll take that as an, 'I love you too.'" She laughed. "But if you really want to show me some love, save some of that spit-up for Daphne." She carried him back down the hall to her cousin, who obviously needed longer than twenty minutes to lose her telling grin.

Ainsley dodged it, along with any accompanying conversation, and headed straight to the coatrack for her puffer vest.

Grandpa stood by the stone fireplace that he and Daddy had built together before she was born. Nanna sat at the end of the couch with a mug in hand and a distant gaze out the window. While part of Ainsley wondered what had each of her grandparents lost in thought, another part warned her now wasn't the time. She turned to Daphne instead. "Did Connor already leave?"

Her cousin switched Josiah to her opposite hip. "Were you waiting for a kiss goodbye?"

"No," she answered too quickly. Though, if she wanted to get technical, shouldn't even fake couples at least say a regular goodbye to each other?

The mere thought warranted a full-on beating of common sense. She mentally slapped herself upside the head in lieu of the slap Daphne probably would've eagerly given her.

"Uh-huh," she said with a look ruling out any doubt.

On that note, Ainsley turned. "I need to milk Brie before she explodes." She didn't wait for a retort. She tugged the door behind her and started for the barn. She had work to do. Nothing complicated about that.

Unless that work took a detour straight into a certain non-cowboy's chest.

"Oh, sorry." Inside the barn doorway, Connor caught Ainsley by the elbows.

In a sleek button-down with the sleeves halfway rolled up, dress pants, and stylish shoes, he looked anything but the part he was supposed to play, and everything like the businessman it made no sense to be attracted to.

Reason obviously bypassed her eyes, or she would've looked away by now. Or at least stepped out of his arms, for heaven's sake.

Smiling too wide, he nodded toward the driveway. "I was on my way—"

"Sorry, I thought you already—"

As if their simultaneous babbling weren't awkward enough, now they were having a two-person shuffle, trying to get around each other. Classic.

Connor finally stepped far to the left and motioned her inside. "You first."

"Thanks." Ainsley strode ahead but stopped a few feet in and turned. "I wasn't looking for you or anything."

He ran the back of his finger under his bottom lip. "Good to know."

"I was on my way to milk Brie. Believe me, you don't want to see a dairy cow with engorged udders. It's not a pretty sight," she rambled relentlessly. "You're lucky you're a guy." *Have mercy.* What in Sam Hill was wrong with her? Cringing at his grin, Ainsley angled a thumb behind her. "So, yeah, I'm gonna go… rescue her." And herself. She headed down the barn again.

"Ainsley?"

Steeling herself, she stopped and turned reluctantly once more.

She should've kept going. Under the trusses' shadows, those doggone green eyes could've passed for headlights beaming at her. "I was thinking…"

This couldn't be good.

"I should probably grab those flash cards before I go."

She caved to a smile. "You think so, huh?"

His laugh filtered through the rafters. "Maybe."

No maybes about it. She draped a pair of work gloves over the nearest stall gate. "Give me a sec, and I'll go get them."

"One other thing," Connor said before she could slip past him.

His expression rooted her in place. "Yes?" she managed to eke out when he stalled.

He leaned a hand on the gate, lowered his eyes for half a moment, then found hers again. "What would you say to going out to dinner with me? Tonight."

Of all the responses competing for the quickest route from her brain to her mouth, not a single utter made it past the mere thought of going on a date with Connor Allen.

Chapter Eleven

Ainsley was plumb off her rocker. There simply wasn't another explanation. Pretending to be a couple probably warranted a few in-public appearances, true. She could see that. But a *real* date? Did she even own anything suitable to wear to dinner with a guy like Connor?

Brie mooed when Ainsley's grip around her teats accidentally tensed.

"Sorry, girl." She leaned back to stretch out her muscles, adjusted the bucket, and repositioned herself on the stool to finish the job. If she didn't stop thinking about this whole ordeal, she'd never get her work done.

Brie mooed again.

"I feel your pain, love." Ainsley patted the cow's side. "Believe me." Though milking was different from nursing, becoming a human pacifier was much the same.

"Ainsley, dear? You still in here?" Nanna said from the front of the barn.

"In Brie's stall," she called without standing, lest she spook the cow.

Nanna curled her aged hands around the top of the wooden gate and a warm smile around Ainsley's heart. "A farmer's work is never done."

"Don't I know it."

Unlike Mama, Nanna never chided her for taking up Daddy's mantle. She'd always loved farm life. Loved the work, the fruit of the labor—passions she'd passed on to Ainsley through the years. It was one of the many reasons she admired her grandma and the life she was able to provide for her family. The same kind of life Ainsley longed to give Josiah. Even without needing to hear the words, Ainsley somehow knew Nanna understood that.

"Are all the chickens back in their coop? I thought I saw some feathers in Connor's hair before he left."

Ainsley laughed. "I think one of the hens has a crush on him. But yes, they should all be back in now. Matty's standing guard."

"I'm sure he is, and loving every minute of it, no doubt. Males need tasks to keep them busy." Nanna winked. "Makes them feel useful."

"Is that what it is? I thought it was pride."

Nanna swayed her head. "That too." Letting an indulgent grin pass between them, she scratched Brie's head from over the gate. "But I suppose we all have our vices. Especially when it comes to love."

Not her too.

Ainsley rubbed post-milking disinfectant on Brie's udders and carefully balanced the bucket as she stood. "No one's talking about love here, Nanna."

"No?" The loaded question dangled between them. "You could've fooled me back at the house. I may be old, dear, but I haven't fully lost my sight. You and that Connor boy make a mighty fine couple."

Mighty fine at pretending to be something they weren't, maybe. Her gut clenched at the genuine belief Nanna's eyes held.

"Where'd he run off to anyway? Your grandpa didn't embarrass him too much, did he?"

Ainsley locked Brie's gate behind her. "I think his ego can take it."

"What about yours?"

"Nanna."

"Now, you know I love you enough to speak my mind when it calls for it. So, I'll say this and then let it be. No one expects you to pretend Jonathan didn't leave scars behind. Grief's a lifelong road, honey. I'm not sure it's something that ever fully leaves us."

She curved a flyaway strand of hair around Ainsley's ear. "But that voice telling you you'll never love again? That's just a tired lie running out of breath. Don't you give it permission to take up residence in your heart." She ran a hand down Ainsley's arm and squeezed her fingers. "That precious space is meant for greater things than doubt, honey. Not the least of which is someone with whom you can share all that love you have to give."

It's hard to share love from a sieve.

Ainsley offered Nanna an assuring smile nonetheless but couldn't hold it in place for long. She faced the gate as if she hadn't already latched it. And there, hidden, her thoughts swam through wave after wave of conflicted feelings Connor had stirred these last couple of weeks. She hadn't let herself dive into them until he'd asked her to dance in Daddy's old work barn. Even now, the comfort of being in a man's arms again waged war with the reservations hedged around the places she kept buried inside. Broken places.

No, it was a good thing Connor's stay was only temporary. She couldn't deny being attracted to him—to his humor, his confidence, even his larger-than-life vision if she was being painfully honest. But that meant little to a damaged heart. Even less to one that was here but always somewhere else. Ever the wanderer. She saw it each time he was drawn to his phone and to the whispers of a borderless life. She knew that same drive by heart. It was, after all, what had drilled holes through hers to begin with.

Nanna gently touched her back, transferring hope Ainsley wished more than anything she could still believe in.

She turned, but any response zipped out of mind at the sight of Daphne strolling in alone.

"Where's Josiah?" She checked her phone. It was too early for another nap.

"Kate stole him from me." Daphne stopped beside Nanna. "As much time as I spend with him, you'd think I'd be his favorite."

"You start giving him cookies, and I bet you will be," Easton said on his way in after her. He leaned a bulky shoulder against one of the beams they'd carved their initials in when they were kids. He took another bite from a cookie he must've snagged from Ainsley's stash in the kitchen and nodded at her. "If you ever decide you want to change professions and bake instead, I'd buy a batch of these from you every week."

"You would, huh?"

He exaggerated an over-agreeing bite. "Any day."

Daphne locked eyes with Ainsley but amazingly contained her laughter long enough to give Easton a swift pat to the chest. "I don't think your pecs need any more."

"Any more what?"

"Lactation cookies."

Easton froze with the last of the oatmeal cookie in his mouth. "Lactation?" he mumbled.

"To help keep Ainsley's milk supply up for Josiah."

She had no idea how Daphne managed to say that with a straight face. Especially in light of Easton's rather green one.

Gagging over the realization of what was in his mouth, he spewed out what he hadn't swallowed faster than a hot knife cutting through butter.

That did it. Even Nanna let a laugh slip through.

Daphne squeezed his pec this time. "Yep. Definitely working."

Easton eyed her with a look Ainsley would've been running from if she were her. "You think that's funny, do you?"

"Hilarious, actually."

"Oh yeah?"

Daphne skirted his attempt to lasso an arm around her waist and sprinted to the front of the barn.

"You're in for it now, Daphne Duck," he called on his way after her.

"Only if you can catch me."

Ainsley shook her head as the teasing duo disappeared into the sunlight cresting the door. "You think he'll ever figure out she's the one he should be chasing for real?"

"Not until he opens his eyes to what's right in front of him."

Ainsley left Nanna's pointed insinuation unacknowledged. Her intuition might be spot on most of the time, but being able to see into Ainsley's heart wasn't the same as being able to protect it. That was up to her alone. Smart decisions, right priorities—that was all she needed to focus on chasing right now.

She motioned to the house. "I need to go place an ad online before the rest of the morning gets away from me. Do you want some more coffee?" Or anything that passed as an excuse to end this conversation?

Nanna dipped a patient smile at her, then cast a nostalgic look around the barn she'd spent more time in than Ainsley had been alive. "You go on in, dear. I'll be along after a while."

Ainsley understood the need to soak in the peace nowhere but home had ever been able to provide her. She left Nanna to it and strode for the house.

Halfway across the yard, a soaring rocket of fur sprinted for her and landed two paws onto her thighs.

"Hey, boy." She rubbed Matty's cheeks. "We have a good thing going here, don't we?"

A single bark defended her plea.

"You always get me, you know that?" She gave his head a vigorous scratch and lowered his paws back to the grass. "How 'bout you help me go nail this ad?"

Matty nestled up to her leg. And with her best companion this time, Ainsley headed inside.

At her desk, she opened her laptop but somehow ended up digging out the copy of *Anne of Green Gables* she'd left tucked in a drawer these last several years. She brushed her thumb along a binding as cracked as she felt on the inside. Burying the reaction, Ainsley let go of the book and straightened in her seat. She was in a different season of life now. One where certain drawers were meant to stay shut.

Matty let out a whine from by her feet.

"It's okay, boy." She stroked his ears. "It's all okay." If she could convince her dog to believe it, maybe she stood a chance herself.

She redirected her attention to her laptop but had to blink against the glare streaming in through the window. She twisted around. Sunlight trickled across her nightstand, streamed over the flash cards she never did give to Connor, and landed smack on the clock counting down the hours until their date.

Her stomach dropped. She glanced at her phone, tempted to call him and cancel, but something drew her to the full-length mirror across the room instead. A reflection of a country working mom looked back at her—hair always up, no makeup on, a figure now shaped by the toll of childbearing. She clamped both hands over her love handles, as if that would do a blessed thing to change the song blaring through her head.

Do you know the muffin man, the muffin man, the muffin man?

She pulled the elastic band free from her hair and shook out her wavy locks. Too bad they weren't long enough to cover that muffin top. She probably couldn't pull off Rapunzel's charisma anyway. Connor, on the other hand... Now there was a rival for Flynn Rider if she ever saw one, all the way down to his impossible-to-deny charm. If there was a boat ride and lanterns involved tonight, she'd—

Cries erupting from her son's room jolted her from all Disney fantasies. Part laughing, part rolling her eyes at herself, Ainsley swept her hair back into a ponytail where it belonged. She clearly had nothing to worry about tonight.

She hoped.

Chapter Twelve

Eight hours later, Ainsley's reflection hadn't changed in the slightest. Different clothes now, different hairstyle, same girl. She ran her fingers down the tip of her loose side braid, feeling half naked without her boots on. The heels Kate insisted she wear were a death trap. The dress, at least, had a more slimming effect than she expected… as long as she didn't breathe. Or eat. The perfect choice for a dinner date.

Ainsley dropped her head into her hand. What was she doing?

"You're a single woman who deserves to go on a date and have some fun for a change," Kate said from the doorway.

Ainsley stared at the old wooden trim surrounding her sister like some kind of telepathic communication enhancer.

Kate pushed off the frame. "I know you, and I know what you're thinking." Behind her now, Kate slipped a strand of hair free from Ainsley's braid so it dangled alongside her earring. "And I can tell you exactly what Connor's going to think when he sees you tonight. Because you, girl, look straight-up hot."

A snort laugh bellowed deep from Ainsley's chest.

Kate popped her in the arm. "I'm serious." She slid around her. "Every guy in that restaurant is going to be checking you out."

"Until they see past the makeup and realize it's me."

When her sister's eyes reached for the ceiling, Ainsley perched a hand on her hip. "You do remember where we live, right? Everyone knows everybody *and* their business." A jilted ex-wife and single mom wasn't exactly a tempting calling card.

Kate waved off her argument. "First of all, half the guys in this town are clueless. Second of all, you're missing my point."

"That playing dress-up is as ridiculous as going on a fake date with your pretend boyfriend?"

Kate returned her mock smile. "Can't be more ridiculous than a girl trying to convince herself she's not interested in said pretend boyfriend."

This time, Ainsley blew *her* off. She turned for her dresser and the bobby pins she'd left there. "Thanks, *Mama*. I was starting to go through a whole day of matchmaking withdrawal."

"Don't try to tell me you're not attracted to him. I've seen you two together. You're totally into each other."

"We're not *into* each other. He's not even my type."

"What type is he?"

She fluttered a hand in hopes the motion would fan up believable adjectives. "The clean-shaven… well-dressed… successful business type."

"Yeah, I totally see that. Who would possibly be attracted to a clean-cut, good-looking man with a solid head on his shoulders?" She scrunched her nose. "Gross."

Ainsley made a face at her. "Okay, fine. So, he's attractive, but it doesn't matter. We've set terms." She kept meaning to anyway. They did have their breakup plan in place at least.

"Of course you did."

"Something wrong with that?"

"Only if you never want to fall in love again."

Ainsley stopped short of snorting. "Maybe I don't."

"Yeah, you know the really annoying thing about love? It has this nagging way of changing your mind. Trust me. Nothing pursues your heart like love."

Except for loss.

"Attraction isn't love. And you know as well as I do attraction isn't enough to make a relationship work." The hasty words hung heavy on lips already wishing they could retract them. She turned, shoulders slumped. "I'm sorry. I shouldn't have said that." Just because Kate had experienced a failed relationship, too, didn't give Ainsley a free pass to rub it in her face.

As usual, her sister willed away the crease of pain lining her forehead as fast as she dismissed the reference to her ex-boyfriend. "I'm not you, and I'm not Mama." She reached for Ainsley's hand. "But I *am* a bossy sister who's telling you to stop denying yourself possibilities." Kate turned her around and fixed the bobby pin Ainsley hadn't finished securing properly. "You look great, Ains. Seriously. Even if nothing comes of all this, it's good for you to get out there again. It's time."

Was it? Her focus strayed toward the closed bedroom door across the hall where her seven-month-old lay asleep in his crib—protected, unaware of where his mama was going or who she'd be with. He was too young to know whether she dated or not, but she didn't want to be *that* mom. The one who gambled more than her own heart.

The look on Kate's face matched the empathetic sigh tilting her head at Ainsley. Great. Even outside of the magical doorframe, the girl's telepathic wonders were in overdrive. Either that, or Ainsley's inability to keep her emotions off her sleeve promised to make tonight even more of a debacle than she'd anticipated.

Kate turned her to the mirror again. "Listen, I'm not saying you have to be reckless or impulsive. I get you have Josiah to think about. I do." She clasped Ainsley's thin silver necklace beneath her hair. "But you can't go through life expecting every guy to hurt you the way Jonathan did either. That's not fair to anyone. Including Josiah."

Ainsley lifted her fingers to her necklace and wrapped them around the tiny baby feet charm she'd worn every day since having Josiah. But even as tightly as she squeezed, she couldn't stave off the question thoughts of Jonathan always spurred. "How am I supposed to tell him, Kate? How do you tell your boy his father loved his career more than his own son?" And his wife.

"I honestly don't know. And I absolutely hate that he left you with the predicament of needing to have that conversation at all." She breathed in, rested her chin on Ainsley's shoulder from behind, and locked eyes with her in the mirror. "But I know beyond any doubt that the love you pour into Josiah's life every day will be what gets you both through it."

Blasted tears.

Ainsley dabbed under her eyelashes. "I hate you."

"Love you too." Kate kissed her cheek and spun her around. "And after tonight, so will Connor. 'Cause, girl, you're gonna crush this date."

She laughed. The only thing she wanted to crush right then was an entire bag of Dove dark chocolates.

Kate rubbed Ainsley's arms. "When he brings you up to the door to say good night, you're not going to be fretting about any of this. Promise. It's going to be great. Now, c'mon, repeat after me. Thank you for a perfect date."

Facing the mirror, Ainsley batted away the last of her tears and offered a half-hearted, "Thank you for a perfect date." Her shoulders caved a second later. "You sure you don't want to go for me?"

"And let Mr. New York City sweep me off my feet? Don't tempt me." Kate squeezed Ainsley's hand one last time and headed for the hall. She stopped over the threshold with her lips cocked to the side. "But you better come back with details."

Ainsley saluted.

"And hey. If it doesn't work out, don't worry. You can always fall back on Hank."

The girl was lucky Ainsley didn't have anything to throw at her. "Funny."

"Aw, c'mon, he's had a crush on you since we were, what? Like, seven? You gotta give him props for longevity."

"I'll give him props when he stops spouting off the most random comments known to man."

Kate laughed. "You sure that's the only turnoff? 'Cause I was thinking it might've had something to do with…" She waved her hand all around the top of her head.

Ainsley cracked a grin. The poor guy's toupee could've passed for one of the hundred guinea pigs he kept at his house to train for racing. Yes, *racing*. Ainsley still had no idea how that was actually a real thing.

If Hairpiece Hank or Set-up Steve were her only options for a relationship, her love life wasn't only in dire straits. It was quite possibly up for the award for the most pathetic of the decade.

"I've heard the guinea pig race club is the happening place to meet your spouse."

This time, Ainsley did find something to chuck at her sister—a wadded-up pair of the oversized underwear Mama had sent her.

A trail of laughter flitted around the doorway and beckoned another round out of Ainsley too. *Crazy girl.*

Once alone, she toyed with her necklace again. All jokes aside, Kate had a point. It was one date. One night. It wasn't going to kill her to go.

Ainsley almost made it out of the room before remembering the flash cards. Smiling to herself, she grabbed them from her nightstand but stopped at a glimpse of a family picture frame hidden inside the half-opened drawer. She pulled it out, sank onto the mattress edge, and stared at the empty frame she'd bought when she'd first found out she was pregnant.

Memories poured in as she picked at the price tag of stolen dreams until a noise from the hallway threatened another pep talk from Kate.

Enough with the past. Ainsley returned the pictureless frame to the drawer as she'd done with her book and headed to the door without looking back.

In Josiah's dark room, she kissed two fingers and pressed them lightly to her sleeping son's cheek. "Love you to Neverland and back, sweet boy," she whispered as always.

She released the crib rail and clutched the flash cards with both hands. This whole thing might be silly. Maybe it'd end up going absolutely nowhere. But maybe—just maybe—hoping in possibilities again would be worth the risk.

She cast one more glance at Josiah's silhouette outlined in traces of moonlight. She'd do anything to give him the world he deserved.

A shaky confidence led her to the van. With one hand on the door handle, she paused under the kind of night sky she used to turn to when looking for answers she couldn't find anywhere else. It'd been a while. A *long* while. Yet despite losing track of how many times she had searched the stars for any sense of her father still being with her, Ainsley lifted her eyes to the heavens yet again.

Silence didn't waver. Answers didn't come. But sometimes assurance, even borrowed, was all faith offered. If she wanted to move forward, she had to believe it would be enough.

As usual, her mom's uncanny ability to know when Ainsley was at her most vulnerable prompted an untimely call before she'd made it even halfway into town. She wouldn't have answered if the late call weren't a little unusual.

"Hi, Mama. You okay?"

"A woman passes sixty-five, and the whole world thinks she's got one foot in the grave and the other on a banana peel. Heck, they're ready to *kick* you into the hole themselves. You know how many funeral package solicitations I get in the mail each week?"

Almost as many headaches as this phone call was bound to give Ainsley?

"I'm fine, sugar bunches. As fit as an ox. It's you I'm worried about."

"I'm good, Mama. I had my last check-up a month ago, remember? I told you, Doctor Miller said—"

"Oh, Doctor Miller doesn't know his tail from a hole in the ground when it comes to diagnosing a broken heart."

Ainsley almost swerved off the two-lane road. She steadied the van and her tone. "Can I give you a call in the morning? I'm driving right now and should really be—"

"How many times have I told you to let the dishes air dry? It's more sanitary."

"Dishes?" It took a second for her brain to connect the scattered dots. "No, Mama. I'm *driving*. Not drying."

"Diving into what? It's November, for gracious sake. Are you trying to catch your death?" She gasped. "See, I told you Doctor Miller doesn't know what he's talking about. If he did, he'd see the signs of depression a female doctor wouldn't have missed."

Jesus, take the wheel.

"If I were depressed, I wouldn't be on my way to a date right now," she blurted out.

"A date? Well…"

Ainsley could practically see her mom sitting up straighter.

"So, things are really moving along with the veterinarian? What was his name again?"

A stiff competition between guilt and pressure crept up Ainsley's chest, closely tailed by the fear of what a genuine answer to the second part might mean. She swallowed. "His name's Connor. And yes," she reluctantly admitted. "There might be real possibilities here."

Some of the details of this convoluted situation might've been made up. But if they led to something real, the route to get there didn't really matter, did it?

Ainsley glanced in the rearview mirror to eyes wanting to convince herself more than her mom. She fastened her attention back on the road, flipped on her blinker, and slowed in front of the turnoff to the restaurant's parking lot. "I'm pulling up now, Mama. Can we—?"

"Are you wearing earrings?"

"What?" Ainsley circled the wheel, the question throwing her for a loop.

"Earrings, punkin'. To show off your neck. Men need a little something that draws the eye. A girl should never leave the house without them. Same as lipstick. And panty-hose," she quickly amended. "Ainsley, baby, tell me you at least put hose on before you left."

Oh my stars. She revved the engine. "Sorry, Mama, it's loud here... I... really... go... breaking... bye." She didn't doubt her mom knew when she was pretending to break up a call, but Ainsley would rather face that particular backlash later than listen to What Men Want 101 right then. Though, she supposed she should be grateful Mama hadn't asked her if she was wearing the granny panties she'd mailed. At least there was that.

She tucked her phone away, along with all unsolicited dating advice, and opened the door, but she only got one leg out before halting in place. An exasperated sigh craned her neck back. "Blast it." A second later, she rifled through the bottom of her purse for any sign of the tube of lipstick she'd probably last used in high school. She twisted it up, stared at the matte color, and shook her head as she stretched to face the mirror. Oh, the things her mom's voice was capable of making her do.

Lipstick approved, Ainsley headed inside the restaurant where a guy in his early twenties, from the looks of it, greeted her from behind a podium.

"Table for one?"

Maybe she should've worn those hose after all.

She almost feathered her hair back, as if displaying her dangling earrings would answer his question. She gripped her purse strap instead, unsure which was worse—the fact that Mama was stuck in the fifties, or that Ainsley was actually listening to her.

"I'm meeting someone."

Before she could stammer her way through further explanation, she caught sight of Connor's easy smile from the far back corner of the restaurant. It didn't matter that he wasn't looking at her. Something about seeing him caused her shoulders to settle and her pulse to escalate at the same time. Nerves locked horns with anticipation as she motioned past the host. "May I?"

"Of course." He nodded. "Enjoy your evening."

"Thank you." Ainsley offered him a final smile on her way onto the bustling floor.

She bumped into someone only a few feet in.

"Ainsley? I thought that was you."

No, this wasn't happening. Hairpiece Hank was not standing in front of her right now. If Kate had anything to do with this, so help her...

Whatever he'd said next got lost in the sound of the air-conditioning kicking on and in the sight of the front of his toupee flickering under the vent. She strained so hard not to stare. Oh, how she tried. But when a waiter walked by with a flaming skillet, all she could envision was a burning guinea pig coming to life on his head.

He leaned every which way to follow her eyes no matter where she averted them. "Are you okay?"

"Yeah, sorry. You surprised me is all. I didn't see you hair—*there*." She cleared her throat. "It's real nice of you to comb-over. *Come*... It's nice of you to *come* over!" she practically shouted to overcompensate. "To come say hi... is what I meant... to say." Like a blithering moron. "How are you doing tonight, Hank?"

"I'm finer than a frog's hair split three ways now that I've run into you." Chin down, he scuffed his boot along the floor. "You're so pretty, you could make a hound dog smile."

"Oh, um, thanks. That's very kind." In a very redneckish kind of way. "Listen, I was just on my way—"

"If you gotta hit the bushes, remember studies have confirmed the middle stall is the dirtiest."

"Wow, that's, um..." Incredibly random. "Thanks for the tip."

"You know I'll always look out for you."

Okay, Kate was right. The guy was sort of sweet in his own weird way.

"I have some hand sanitizer if you need it."

"Come again?"

He whipped out a miniature bottle from his pocket. "For the ladies' room."

Ainsley looked behind her to the escape route he'd perfectly set up for her. "That's very thoughtful of you, Hank, but I think I'll be good." When no response came, she angled a thumb to the restroom. "I should probably get going then. I hope you have a nice night," she added while turning.

"The *middle* stall," he called after her. "Don't forget!"

No chance of that happening, despite there being, oh, so many things about that interaction she would've liked to forget completely.

After a quick peek behind her showed Hank returning to his table, Ainsley grabbed a menu to hide her face, made a U-turn, and hustled down the opposite side of the restaurant.

Conversations overlapping background music brimmed from tables scattered throughout the room. Though she preferred the gentle lull of the farm, something about the energy reminded her of parts of her life she'd long ago resigned. Another wave of anticipation trilled through her.

Until she caught sight of someone sitting opposite of Connor—a man, probably fifteen to twenty years their elder. An aura of business defied his casual clothes as much as Connor's jeans did.

Ainsley cast a glance down her ridiculously overdressed self and slipped behind a tall partition. Engrossed in conversation, neither man had noticed her yet. Thankfully. She eyed the exit. With all the noise, she could easily hightail it out of there without anyone noticing. She'd make an excuse for why she hadn't shown. It'd be fine. She'd just—

"Ainsley?"

Crud.

She dropped the menu, caught a welcoming look from Connor, and instinctively ducked below the partition. Her purse clattered to the floor, followed by her knees a second later. The booth in front of her squeaked, probably from the person in it turning to find out what class act was making such a ruckus.

Way to draw more attention to herself.

Ainsley unclasped her earrings in a hot hurry and raced to wipe her lipstick off with the back of her hand.

A shadow stretched above her. "Lose something?"

Her sanity. Clearly.

On her hands and knees, it took her a minute to lift an open palm toward Connor without looking up. "An earring." She fudged her way through standing gracefully in a dress and heels and scooped up her purse. "Found it."

"Uh-huh." Connor motioned back to her hiding spot. "You sure you didn't lose your flash cards too?"

Gah. Why'd she bring those blasted things? Ainsley bent to snag them from the floor, but he beat her to it.

"The well-kept secrets of Ainsley Jamison." He fanned through the stack. "I'm honored to be privy to them."

She fidgeted like a schoolgirl. "I wouldn't call them *secrets*. More like—"

"You have a thing for hot chiropractors?" He looked up from the top card with a glowing mix of charm and feigned scandal. "I knew you were a forward girl, but wow…"

"What?" Horrified, she reached to snatch the cards from him. "I did *not* write that. I…"

He backed up with the cards behind his back and his maddening dimples egging her on.

She glared at him. "Real funny."

"You looked like you could use a laugh."

Or a shot of whisky.

When Ainsley let out a slow breath, he dipped his head under hers. "Seriously, are you sure everything's all right?"

"Fine," she spouted off too quickly. A peek behind him to the man at their table knocked her voice off kilter even more. "I just thought…" What? That her pretend boyfriend had wanted to take her on a non-pretend date? *Stupid.* She made herself face him. "I didn't realize this was a group dinner party. A heads-up would've been nice. That's all."

By the time he'd finished studying her, the crease of confusion tightening his brow had worsened to a look of keen understanding. "You're right. I'm sorry. I wanted it to be a surprise, but I should've considered you might've thought—"

"It's fine." Or it would be as long as he didn't finish that statement. Ever. Ainsley stared at her heels with a fool's hope that pure determination could magically turn them into running shoes. But when Connor bent to intersect her line of sight again, there was nothing to do but steer their conversation away from the direction it was heading… and fast.

"Have you ordered yet? I'm starving."

He graciously let the forced transition go and gestured to the seat waiting for her. "There's an appetizer on the table."

"Tell me it involves bread." Carbohydrate therapy had never been more urgent.

The side of his mouth pulled to the left. "I'm afraid not, but I'm sure we can arrange that." He stopped a waiter passing them, leaned close enough to say something above the clamor, and nodded while stepping back.

As the waiter continued on to the kitchen, Connor set a hand on Ainsley's back. "Shall we?"

Though her feet moved, her thoughts remained tangled around the smoothness he exuded in every situation. To be honest, she admired that about him. Maybe even envied it some. But under the dim light at their three-person table, that same confidence set her heart aflutter again.

Ainsley folded the hem of the tablecloth like an accordion fan she wouldn't have minded using right about then. Heck, she'd even consider rushing back to stare at Hank's toupee again if it meant getting to stand under the blessed air-conditioning. She searched the ceiling for a vent. Finding none, she shifted as casually as her glued-together thighs would let her and rubbed her foot against her calf.

A sandpaper feel drew all her fidgeting to an abrupt halt a hot second later. *What in tarnation?*

Somehow, she'd missed shaving an entire stretch of her leg. She couldn't even blame it on a huge pregnant belly anymore. Seriously, how'd she miss that? And for crying out loud, if her mom's advice to wear stockings sprang to mind one more time, she'd—

"Ainsley?"

Her whole body jerked, including her fingers—the ones still wrapped around the tablecloth. All of their place settings shifted before she had time to open her mouth. She let go, but a stream of water and ice cubes was already racing over the edge for the guy adjacent to her.

He shoved his chair back. Too late.

"I'm so sorry." She jumped to her feet with a cloth napkin in hand. "Here, let me—"

"I've got it." He grabbed his own napkin and wiped the now-wet seat of his pants while excusing himself to the restroom.

Ainsley cringed. The only thing that would've been more embarrassing than trying to dab at the most inappropriate part of the man's jeans was if she'd stood up with the tablecloth tucked into her dress. It was like a prom date straight out of some terribly written and equally adored eighties rom-com. All she had to do was come back from the ladies' room with a strand of toilet paper stuck to her shoe, and she'd sell the clichéd scene for sure.

She scoured the room for an excuse to leave, an apparition of Molly Ringwald—something. Empty-handed on all accounts, Ainsley set her balled-up napkin down and hooked a thumb behind her without a word.

Apparently, Connor took her silence as a challenge and, of course, one-upped her non-verbal cues. He didn't have to make a single peep, and Ainsley found herself seated in her chair again, entranced by everything he managed to say through his ridiculously unfair green eyes.

Lordy mercy, she should've stayed home and eaten that bag of chocolates. Where was that forsaken bread already?

On cue, the waiter placed a basket of pumpernickel rolls in front of her as if he'd heard her inner meltdown. Or maybe the bread was simply drawn to her. She wouldn't have been surprised. The steam, the scent, the comfort. It was like it knew her deepest yearnings.

She didn't wait, didn't even grab the butter. She stole a roll, tore into its steamy goodness, and took a self-indulgent bite.

Amusement trailed from one dimple to the other as Connor openly watched her love fest with a piece of bread.

Ainsley set the half-devoured roll onto her plate and crossed her legs. She accidentally bumped Connor's knee and yanked her leg back like she'd touched a fired-up hibachi grill. Cringing again, she slid her ankles under her chair.

There was no way Connor could've felt her Harry Henderson leg through his jeans. Still, Ainsley focused on smoothing out her wrinkled napkin instead of making eye contact.

After a minute that felt more like ten, she released the world's longest exhale. With any luck, it'd ward off whatever fire her disaster dating skills were bound to cook up next.

She risked peeking up. Wrong move. Connor's eyes gave the bread's magnetism a run for its money. Once locked in, she got the feeling he was waiting for her to respond to a question she must've missed.

She cleared her throat. "Sorry, did you say something?"

He motioned to his guest across the table who'd, at some point, returned to his seat probably as reluctantly as Ainsley had abandoned her roll. "Before the, um, water incident," Connor said through a smile she wanted to douse off his face, "I was getting ready to introduce you to a business acquaintance of mine, George Landy."

Ainsley froze with her fingertips a centimeter from the butter dish.

A business acquaintance. She glanced from Connor to their third wheel and back. She'd called it all right. He'd arranged a business meeting under the guise of a dinner date, and she'd been a fool for expecting the latter.

George moved his empty water glass beside his fork and nodded. "Pleasure."

"Likewise." Returning pleasantries on autopilot did little to relieve how tense Ainsley's forced smile must've looked.

It obviously didn't deter him. "I hear you have quite the piece of land you're operating on," he continued. "Ever considered investing in livestock? We could settle on a cost per head that would be well worth your money."

Logically, a blink had to have passed in the length of time Ainsley sat there staring at the businessman, but her dried-out eyes refuted rationale as much as her heart had by letting her come here tonight.

Stupid. Utterly stupid. She pushed up from the table and walked away from a mistake there was no point in prolonging.

She made a hard turn to the right at the sight of Hank starting to stand from his chair. Great, and now she proba-

158 | CRYSTAL WALTON

bly looked like a guinea pig maneuvering through a maze of tables in a race to get out of there.

Thankfully, he must've decided to sit back down. Either that, or she simply couldn't hear anything above the frustration still blaring in her head. Livestock? Unbelievable. The farther she strode away from the table, the faster the whole idea of Connor pushing his business agenda on her made her madder than a wet hen. If he only knew what that—

"Ainsley, wait up." Connor slid in front of her. "Are you okay?"

"I have to go."

"No, you don't."

"No, really, I do. I never should have come." She sidestepped the nearest table, but his persistence drove him in front of her again.

"Hey." He caught her hand, and it took all her strength to ignore how much his touch mirrored the concern in his voice. "If you want me to ask George to leave, I can."

"This isn't about George, Connor. It's about you." Despite his distinct features arguing otherwise, Ainsley could've been looking at her ex-husband. She tugged her hand free. "My property isn't some business venture to be exploited."

"That's not what I was trying to do."

"But that's just it. I don't need you to *do* anything." Fuming, she clutched her purse. "Look, this was obviously a mistake. All of it. Don't worry about Thanksgiving. I'll figure something out." She started for the door.

"Ainsley…"

The timbre in his voice drew her to a stop. Hurt sliced through his usual confidence as he searched her face for answers she didn't expect a guy like him to understand. But when mixed emotions clouded his eyes, she had a hard time containing her own. And for a minute, her irritation melted.

"I'm sorry." She nearly said more but didn't. Couldn't. She turned instead. Only a step away, her feet gripped her in place again. Four breaths passed before she could convince her legs to move. She had to keep going. Away from a man she could never be with. Back to a home he'd never belong in.

The glass exit door blurred through tears proving Mama wrong. Not even lipstick and earrings could rewrite an ending she needed to stop trying to change.

Once hidden in the shadows of the van, Ainsley lifted a broken smile to the rearview mirror and sighed. "Thank you for a perfect date."

Chapter Thirteen

Connor's eyes flung open. He glared at his traitorous cell that was supposed to get him up before Herald could. He swiped his phone, scrolled past a missed call from Flynn, and opened the alarm app. He'd set it for p.m. instead of a.m. Figured. His head hadn't been the sharpest when he'd gone to bed. Even after a full night's sleep, questions were still suffocating him.

The flash cards on the nightstand hadn't offered much insight. They held trivial facts about Ainsley's family rather than herself. Yet again, he wasn't surprised.

He slid his feet into a pair of slippers he'd learned to keep in front of the bed and stretched his neck from side to side. Only a glimpse of sunlight snuck through the window, but it was enough to prod him toward the beginning of a new day and a chance to figure out where things had gone terribly wrong at dinner.

Then again, knowing Ainsley, whatever chores she had planned for him today wouldn't require nearly as much work as pulling answers out of her. Assuming she'd even let him stay this morning. Had she officially kicked him out last night?

Only one way to find out. He got dressed and hustled to the main house. Across the lawn, Connor pointed at Herald standing tall and proud on the doghouse. "Tomorrow, buddy. Tomorrow."

Country breakfast scents welcomed him inside. As usual, Ainsley had already cooked, eaten, and had probably made her way to the pastures by now. If the girl ever got more than five hours of sleep a night, he'd be shocked. Honestly, he'd never met someone quite like her. Driven business associates, sure. They were a dime a dozen in his circles. But Ainsley's commitment to her work held its own pulse. Almost as if her heart beat in tandem with the daily ebb and flow of a farm that defied business sense.

He didn't fully understand it, didn't know how to articulate it, but one thing was clear. Something tied Ainsley to a life unlike any he'd ever known. And if he didn't figure it out soon, he was positive he'd lose his chance to.

His talk with her grandpa stirred to mind as it had done numerous times since listening to the old man share stories of generational legacies. The kind Connor hadn't realized how much he wished his own family held.

Without overthinking it, he strode toward the kitchen window with his phone to his ear. This was probably a bad idea. What would he even say? He picked at the edge of the sink like he could unearth some sense underneath the stainless steel.

Too late. The line picked up. "Hello?"

"Ma?" Connor glanced at the screen to make sure he'd dialed the right number. Pop never left his phone unattended. "Everything okay?"

"Oh, Connor, it's you. Yes, sweetie, everything's… just fine."

"Then why are you answering Pop's phone?"

Though it would've helped to see her face, her pause gave off enough reluctance for him to know something wasn't right.

"Ma, what's going on?"

"Nothing, honey. You know how your father is. Always caught up in something." Her strained laugh didn't convince him. "He must've run off to the office and left his phone by mistake. He'll be sorry he missed your call. We've been worried about you. Are you getting enough to eat? Rose made your favorite last night. Her Beef Wellington truly is worth every penny we pay her. Your father thinks she robs us blind, but after a meal like that, I don't know how he can compl—"

A man coughed in the background—the *only* man who'd be in the house with her.

Connor's jaw constricted. "Pop's at the office, huh?" More like he was avoiding taking his call. "Glad to see he's worried enough to talk to me."

"Connor…"

"Don't bother." She'd made up enough excuses for him to last a lifetime.

"You don't understand."

"Believe me. I do." More than he ever wanted to. "Listen, I gotta go. I'll call again when I get to my next client."

"Honey?" she rushed in before he could hang up.

Connor breathed out. "Yeah?"

"Your father loves you," she said gently. "We both do."

A second exhale came harder this time. "Love you too, Ma." He couldn't say more. There was no point anyway.

He slid his cell into his pocket, gripped the counter with both hands, and hung his head. Overlapping frustration twined up his muscles. He shouldn't have expected anything different. Disappointment was, after all, the only legacy passed down from father to son in his family. He'd do good to remember that.

A soft cadence drifted from down the hall. Connor released the counter and thoughts that would lead him nowhere. Drawn to the sound, he quietly eased down the hallway so as not to interrupt and stopped in front of Josiah's cracked-open door. Wrapped up in visible love for her son, Ainsley held him in the rocking chair, singing softly against his fine hair.

The scene chafed against the aftermath of his phone call home. Such tenderness. Such connection. The profound beauty of their bond rooted so deeply into Connor's chest, it anchored his feet in place and his heart in a moment he had no right to be eavesdropping on. He would've moved if he could have. Would've tiptoed away and preserved the moment for the two of them alone. He stood there instead, enraptured by an ache he couldn't describe.

"It's sweet, isn't it?" someone whispered.

Connor's shoes broke free from their cement hold. He backed away from the bedroom door to find Kate standing in front of her own with a knowing look on her face.

"I was…" What could he say that wouldn't make him sound like the peeping Tom he probably already looked like? He pointed over his shoulder. "I was on my way to the bathroom. Morning breath and all that."

Morning breath? Really? He clearly needed something a heck of a lot stronger than Listerine right now.

Connor turned and hightailed it to the bathroom, away from the hole he was continuing to dig himself into.

He leaned on the corners of the sink and hung his chin again. What was it about this place? This family? It was one thing to be thrown off his game. He could admit when something surprised him. But this was different, deeper.

Another breath brought his head up and shoulders down. He needed to get a grip on something besides the sink.

He grabbed his razor and ran the backs of his fingers along his stubbly cheek. The unshaven look was actually starting to grow on him. He tossed the razor back into his toiletry bag and shook his head. Whispering Pines really was something else. Only here would he feel more at home looking like his brother.

After brushing his teeth, he headed to the kitchen and found Kate seated at the table topped with two place settings and breakfast keeping warm under a large lid. He leaned into the corner of the wall. "You didn't have to wait for me to eat."

Her sassy smiles could compete with Ainsley's. "I didn't. I'm waiting for Easton."

"Oh." *And the embarrassment continues.* "Right. Makes sense." Nodding longer than the statement warranted, Connor eyed the food left on the stove. "I should probably take mine to go anyway. I need to get a head start out there." With any luck, working with his hands would keep his mouth shut for a while.

Farther into the kitchen, he did a double take at a giant bag of 100% raw turbinado sugar sitting beside the coffee maker on the counter. He looked around, sure he was missing something.

"She got it for you." Kate casually picked at a piece of toast she'd snuck off the plate.

"Ainsley got this?" Yeah, he had definitely missed something. The image of her eyes before she'd walked out of the restaurant ransacked his smile. "She must've gotten it *before* I ruined everything last night."

"*Everything* is probably a bit of an overstatement."

"She told you what happened?"

"Not in detail, but I got the gist."

He strode to the table and to the hope of figuring some things out. He slid into the chair meant for Easton. "Then you know why she was so upset."

"It's understandable."

Maybe to her. "It's hard to understand if she won't talk to me. I get that this place is important to her, but—"

"It's more than that."

"It's a part of her. I know." Connor rocked his empty mug on its bottom edge as he peered around the kitchen. The single room held more roots than his entire life did. The thought pulled at a string he didn't want to search for the beginning to. Not here, now.

He let go of his mug and sat forward. "But if you're that tied to something, seems like you'd be willing to do anything to keep it. Or at least *consider* a potential solution to make things easier." She hadn't even heard George out last night.

"Maybe she already has." Kate nibbled on another pinched-off piece of toast as if totally unaware of how much he was hanging on to each of her cryptic responses.

When she noticed his prodding stare, she sent a sympathetic smile across the table. "You're a good guy, Connor. Anyone can see you have the best of intentions wanting to help my sister out, and that means a lot. Really. But a word of advice?" She covered his hand with hers. "A girl doesn't need a man to fix her problems. She needs a man who'll stand beside her even when he can't." Her pensive stare wandered off to the window. "Sometimes, simply choosing to stay is all it would take to change everything."

Connor breathed in—at the weight of her words, yes, but more so, at the sorrow in her eyes. Even without looking directly into them, he saw enough to feel the emotion as if it were his own.

A quick knock, followed by the door opening, brought Easton inside. He zeroed in on Kate's hand over Connor's and stopped midstride. "I'm not interrupting, am I?"

If Connor read the guy's face right, any answer but no would likely end in a punch to the jaw.

Kate, however, didn't seem to notice at all. She slipped her hand free as she swiveled in her chair to face him. "If you count Connor keeping my mind off how starving I am, then yes." She crossed her arms and legs. "You best have a good reason for being late, buddy, and it sure as heck better not involve mud on those monstrous tires of yours."

Easton's tight mouth surrendered to the kind of smile a guy had little control over. As often as Connor had been donning the same one since meeting Ainsley, it was hard for him to miss.

He cast a sideways glance toward Kate's oblivious expression and chuckled. He didn't know Easton well, but he sure could empathize with the guy.

On that note, Connor left the chair out for him, thanked Kate for their talk, and returned his unused mug to the counter. He'd probably regret skipping his coffee, but something told him it was past time to take his leave.

"On your way out?" Easton asked while hanging up his hat.

Connor pretended not to hear the relief in his question. "Work's calling."

"Always is."

"You got that right." Connor stopped beside him in the entryway and held out a hand. "It's nice to see you again, man." He clapped him on the back and dropped his voice. "Be sure to give her all the toast. Trust me."

Midway through the door, he turned toward Kate. "When Ainsley comes out, can you tell her..." What exactly, he still wasn't sure. He only prayed he'd figure it out before she was standing in front of him again.

Kate's eyes warmed with understanding. "I'll let her know where to find you."

"Thanks." He nodded and closed the door on a conversation that still had his mind reeling.

Around the corner of the house, fresh air streamed through his shirt's cotton threads. It would've been nice if it penetrated his thick skull while it was at it. He could use some clarity.

When all else failed, there was always entertainment. Billy the Pig stood like a statue on a stump near the chicken coop. Connor shook his head. At least he wasn't the only clueless one around here. His laughter trailed a panoramic look across Jamison Farms. Despite its quirks, it wasn't hard to see how easily one could sink roots here. The place had a draw to it much like the girl tethered to it.

Matty torpedoed out of his doghouse as though his keen ears had heard Connor's inner thoughts about his owner. Four feet away, the dog still hadn't slowed. Two feet. One. At full speed, he lunged on his hind legs at the last moment.

Connor caught his front paws against his thighs and stumbled backward a good five steps. The dog had some force to him. No question about that. Connor would've been a little nervous if the attack hadn't ended in a slobber of licks to his hands and face. Strong yet tender—traits Matty, no doubt, had learned from Ainsley.

The thought swept him back to his conversation with her grandpa.

"Just 'cause my granddaughter's learned to be strong doesn't mean she's beyond breaking."

Breaking. The single word hadn't stopped needling at Connor since Henry had put the fear of God in him. He stared into the fog clouding his view of the barn until the rumble of an engine drew him out of questions he still didn't have answers for.

Matty's ears whipped toward the sound of tires rolling up the gravel driveway. Connor rubbed the dog's head while shielding the sun from his eyes. Though the glare kept the person approaching hidden, he caught a glimpse of Ainsley coming out of the house with Josiah on her hip. His stomach tightened—partly from the way she strode toward the front porch like a linebacker, partly because something about the situation didn't feel right.

Matty must've agreed. It took all of three seconds for him to abandon the backyard to be by Ainsley's side. Kate's advice to do the same prodded Connor toward the woman he wanted to protect and his prayers toward the hope she wouldn't view his presence as interference this time.

He slowed his stride once he reached the bend leading to the porch.

A baritone voice brought an older man in a tan cowboy hat into view. With one boot propped on the first step, he looked up at Ainsley with a smile that left a bad taste in Connor's mouth. He had no clue who the guy was or what his relationship with Ainsley was. But, honestly, he didn't have to. Without any specifics, Connor sensed the only thing he needed to know.

Trouble.

Chapter Fourteen

Connor waited around the corner of the house to give himself a chance to assess the situation.

"I already told you I'm not interested in selling the farm." Ainsley shifted Josiah to her opposite hip. "We're doing fine as is."

"Aw now, Miss Ainsley, I've known your family too long for you to be giving me the runaround." The man adjusted his hat. "I know a fib when I hear one. Just like I know a good investment when I see it." He held up a hand. "Before you go getting up in arms, be sure to think about what your daddy would want to become of his land."

"You don't know a *thing* about what my dad would want."

"I knew your daddy a long time, sweetheart, and I can assure you. Boarders taking up his barn, hippie exercise classes on pastures meant for cattle..." He shook his head. "Walker would be rolling in his grave if he saw what you've turned this place into."

"What I do with my property is my business." Her voice held authority. But even standing tall, her chest quivered. Matty barked from beside her and rubbed his head under her hand in a reminder she didn't stand alone. A deep inhale raised her eyes to the man's again. "For the final time, Mr.

Hudson, Jamison Farms is not for sale, so I suggest you take your solicitation elsewhere."

"It'd sure be in your best interest to reconsider."

"And it'd be in yours to leave." Connor edged forward then. "Now." He slid Ainsley an assuring glance. He'd apologize later if she felt he'd overstepped his bounds. He couldn't take watching her hurt, no matter how well she hid it.

Mr. Hudson turned a plastic smile to Connor. "With all due respect, young man, I don't believe I was talking to you."

"With all due respect, sir, I don't believe you misheard the lady." Connor stood firm beside her and rested a hand against Ainsley's lower back. "So again, we suggest you leave."

Ainsley surprisingly leaned into his side with what he sensed was relief. He would've gotten lost in the feel of her slender shoulder fitting under his if their unwanted guest wasn't digging his heels deeper into the dirt.

Connor motioned to the driveway with his eyes. "I'd be happy to have your truck towed if you can't figure out how to move it yourself."

Tag teaming, Matty pawed at the edge of the porch and added a snarl for good measure.

The tight lines around the guy's mouth were barely keeping him from spitting nails from the looks of it. His gray mustache twitched. Before his car salesman veneer could crack completely, he brought his hand to the tip of his hat and lifted a splintery look from the dog to Ainsley. "Ma'am."

Matty steered him to the driveway like a bouncer. Even in the cloud of dust from the tires peeling out, Matty continued to stand guard at the edge of the gravel and barked what were probably more than a few choice words Connor wouldn't have minded saying himself.

Ainsley didn't move until the extended cab had fully cleared her property. An exhale curled her shoulders forward and her eyelashes down. "I'm sorry."

He'd never known how much emotion a whisper could hold until right then. Though part of him wasn't ready to lose the feel of her in his arms, he angled away enough to dip his head under hers. "Sorry for what?"

She adjusted her hold around Josiah. "For letting him get to me. I should've been able to handle that on my own."

The fact that she truly believed that cut him to his core.

"You're one of the strongest women I've ever known, Ainsley Grace." He didn't doubt she could handle anything that came her way, probably with more finesse than most. Before he met her, he would've vouched he could do the same. Now, he couldn't even handle tearing himself away from her.

Bravery, passion, commitment. With a single look, she undid every certainty he'd held about the way life worked. What had once made perfect sense now made none at all. Because at the end of the day, mastering all the confidence in the world meant nothing when he realized he was just a boy captivated by a girl who made him want to be a better man.

With emotion pulsing all the way down to his hands, Connor risked lifting her chin and exposing what he doubted she'd miss in his eyes. "Just because you're capable of doing everything on your own doesn't mean you have to."

Tears she'd likely suppressed while Cowboy Jerk of the Year was there now stormed her lashes. She blinked them away while smoothing Josiah's hair to the side in spite of the breeze blowing it in the opposite direction. She wrapped her hand around one of his and brought it to her chest. "I should probably get him back inside. It's cooler out here than I thought it was."

Connor nodded without saying anything until she'd made it to the corner of the house. "Ainsley?"

When she turned, whatever he'd planned to say lodged in his throat.

"Yes?"

"Can we, um…? Can we talk?" He ran his palms down his jeans. "I mean, when you're free. If you have a few minutes."

Her hesitancy to answer settled any question of how lame he sounded.

"If not, it's cool. I'll just…" *Keep rambling like an idiot?*

The longest pause known to man stretched between them.

"Give me a minute?" she finally said.

"Of course. Take your time."

He swallowed at the way she hovered in place a moment longer. Even more so when her hand drifted down the edge of the house on her way around the corner and out of sight.

It might not have made sense for him to feel as if her fingers had grazed his heart instead of the house's siding. Yet he stood there, willing to wait as long as it took to feel that close to her again.

What was going on with him today?

Matty barked from the steps and met Connor at the top the second he sat down. He rested his chin over Connor's thigh, followed by an empathetic paw.

And now he had a therapy dog. Perfect.

"Do I look that bad?" Connor couldn't help laughing. "Yeah, well, I guess of anyone, you know what an amazing girl you have here, don't you?"

A soft bark of confirmation prompted Matty to paw at Connor's leg again.

"Don't worry, boy." Staring into the field across the street, he stroked Matty's back. "I won't do anything to hurt her."

The vow struck him more than any of his questions. Nothing inside him wanted to see any part of Ainsley hurting, but his intentions weren't what concerned him. Making promises he couldn't keep was.

"Better be careful," Ainsley said from behind him.

Connor choked through a cough. "Sorry?"

She joined them on the steps. "If you're not careful, you might end up becoming a certified country boy after all." She ruffled Matty's ears. "Never underestimate the power of an animal's big, sappy, brown eyes. Before you know it, the city's bright lights won't hold a candle next to these babies."

The dog scrambled across Connor's lap to get to Ainsley's.

She laughed at each slobbery lick to her cheek. "Now tell me how you could deny such priceless love?" Though her smile remained unshakable, something in her eyes wavered as Matty settled beside her. She leaned down to kiss his head in her lap. "It'll change your heart forever."

Lost in visible affection, she had no clue how capable she was of doing the same.

Connor rubbed his knees like they were crystal balls that could tell him how his time in Whispering Pines would end. Or at the very least, that they could tell him what in the world to say right then.

All the traces of lightheartedness in Ainsley's voice trailed off with a sigh. "Ever feel like you're getting everything wrong?"

If she only knew.

"It takes a lot of time and work to manage a place this size. Especially for a single woman, as my mom so *aptly* reminds me every chance she gets." She shook her head. "I don't know. Mr. Hudson's probably right."

Connor raised a brow, caught off guard more by how she could think that than the sudden change of topic. "About how you're running this place? 'Cause if that's the case, believe me, he couldn't be more wrong."

"But what if he isn't?" She pulled her feet up to the step beneath them and drew her legs close. "It's nothing like the way it was when my dad ran it."

"Your father ran this place the way he saw fit at the time, as I'm sure your grandpa did too. I get that those roots stretch deep in the soil here, and I admire you for wanting to honor them. But this isn't your dad's house anymore. It isn't his property or your grandpa's. It's yours. You don't have to keep second guessing your decisions." The advice ricocheted back to his gut. Head lowered, he picked at the edge of the stairs. "Different doesn't mean wrong."

"But it could mean disappointment."

Connor pivoted to face her. "I never knew your dad, Ainsley, but something tells me that's not possible." He scratched Matty's head, sure he agreed. "If anything, I'd be willing to bet he's awful proud of you."

With sunlight draped across her face, she released her legs and a breath laced with doubts Connor wanted more than anything to take away. He let his last comment hang in the brisk air instead and welcomed the distant murmur of a tractor filling the silence. Whether she opened up to him or not, it was her choice. His was simply to be there regard-less.

Ainsley rubbed her arms a few minutes later. "He died in a cattle accident," she said without looking at him. "My dad."

Slow and deliberate, the unexpected words settled into a place of understanding.

"Which is why you don't want anything to do with owning them again." No wonder she'd dismissed George's offer so quickly.

"They were everything to him. Took everything from him too. Blood, sweat. No one worked harder than he did. Even in his sixties, the man swore he could pull the same weight as a twenty-year-old. *Despite* what his doctor told him." A laugh tied to memories broke through. "Stubborn as a mule."

"Nothing like his daughter."

Mock offence met Connor's teasing grin, but it didn't take long for her smile to wane. "It probably sounds stupid to you, but I don't know. Every time I tried to bring myself out to the pasture they grazed in, I... couldn't." She closed her eyes. "I couldn't look at them, Connor. I couldn't care for them, couldn't forgive them. It's been years, and I still can't go out there without hearing the sound of the trailer gate knocking the wind from my dad's chest."

"He was...?" He couldn't get the word "trampled" out of this throat.

"He died from a heart attack." She twisted a thread hanging from a rip in her jeans. "The doctor said it was better that way. That recovery would've been too hard for a guy like him."

She wiped at her cheeks and kept her focus on the open field. As the overgrown grass swayed in the wind, Connor could almost see the haunting memories weave across her eyes.

"It wasn't the cows' fault. Daddy had just gotten them. There's no telling if they'd been rough handled before. And with being separated from their normal herd, it's no surprise they got spooked." Her fingers flexed around Matty's fur. "He never should've been out there loading them alone. And I…"

When she stalled, Connor got the impression a hundred "should haves" weighed down a sentence that likely looped endlessly through her head.

She curled an arm around her legs again. "I shouldn't have sold them. I know you're probably thinking they were just cows, but they were more than a business to my dad. The whole farm was."

"As it is to you." Connor reached for her. "I'm sorry for trying to get George involved. I never would've brought up the proposal if I had known."

"I know." She slipped her hand free and tucked both under her legs. "It wasn't fair for me to hold you responsible for something you had no way of knowing about. I appreciate you wanting to help. Honestly, it has more to do with how much you remind—"

Matty heard something around the corner of the house and soared off the porch like he had a bona fide cape on.

Ainsley laughed at the little torpedo. As much as Connor wanted to backtrack and beg her to finish her thought, the moment had passed as quickly as it had come.

"You know, if I didn't get to see his sweet side, I think that dog might scare me."

Ainsley raised both eyebrows. "Connor Allen, afraid?"

"It happens occasionally."

"Oh really?" She angled the full intensity of her gorgeous eyes at him. "This I might pay to see."

She didn't have to pay. All she had to do was look at him—right now, every moment he was with her. Even when he wasn't, he wanted to be. She had to see it.

He leaned his shoulder against the porch rail in a sad attempt at playing it cool. "You should've been there when I first met Daphne in your kitchen... *alone*."

Ainsley laughed at his look of horror. "That would do it. Sorry. She can be a little protective."

"As a good cousin should be." Connor toggled his head. "With anyone but me."

"Is that right?"

"Well, you *did* buy me a bag of sugar, so you can't think I'm *that* bad."

Her adorable and completely benign scowl nearly did him in.

She faced forward. "It isn't white sugar, so don't get too excited."

Too late for that.

Her lips tugged sideways, and he could barely control his own.

Another breeze swirled by as they both soaked in the sun glistening across the field. At home in the comfortable silence setting between them, Connor took her hand in his again. "I really am sorry, Ainsley."

"Me too." Her lashes feathered together.

Whatever she was thinking of saying next seemed to pull her in two directions. But when she didn't withdraw, Connor ran his thumb along her knuckles. "If you're okay with it," he said tentatively, "I'd still like to stay and be here for you through the holiday."

A piece of him had almost said he'd stay longer, but he couldn't offer that. As winsome as Jamison Farms was, not to mention the girl beside him, it was a temporary stop on a rootless path he needed to follow. He hadn't fully understood why until coming here and seeing how different life was for someone like her.

Ainsley's focus wandered to her lap. A deep breath raised her shoulders, then slowly released them.

If they were standing, Connor was sure she'd be swaying in place the way she did out of habit from soothing Josiah. It was a sweet tic. Something he'd learned to associate with her way of mulling something over. Not for the first time, he wished he knew what she was thinking. Even more so, he wished he knew how to dismantle her reservations.

He could reassure her he'd avoid complicating things between them, but that was another promise he couldn't keep. Of the few things he truly was afraid of, that scared him most.

A notification from his phone wormed into the standstill of their conversation. Connor ignored it despite Ainsley's sad smile confirming it was fine to take it.

"Business comes first." Audible hurt trembled in the short phrase. Keeping it buried, she pulled up on the rail.

"Speaking of, I need to get back to my own before Josiah's appointment with the pediatrician."

Connor closed out the reminder on his phone and shot off a quick text to Flynn before Ainsley had fully risen off the steps. "Hold that thought." He stuffed his cell into his back pocket and rose opposite her. "How about a helper?"

"Don't you have to get to the office?"

"It's my day off. And I just canceled a Skype meeting I was going to have with Flynn this morning, so I'm all yours." He shrugged when she squinted at him. "I figured I could stick around the farm today. Maybe finish turning Spock's pen into Alcatraz."

Ainsley's mouth pulled to the side. "I'm not sure even *you* have enough skills for that."

"You don't think so, huh?" He caught her fingers when she started to turn.

The playfulness in her eyes yielded to something he couldn't walk away from. Pulse drumming, he edged closer. She was right about his lack of skills. He'd need an entire army's worth to withstand the urge to kiss her right now.

He'd reminded himself again and again that he was only here until Thanksgiving. He'd even convinced himself he could last that long and be here for her without getting attached. But when the slowest movement brought her eyes to his again, he knew surviving two more weeks was nothing compared to the undeniable truth driving his feet another inch toward her: No military force in the world could save him from the next five minutes.

Chapter Fifteen

Ainsley took her time brushing down Shiloh. She never needed an excuse to prolong moments with her horse, nor to spend time in her favorite place. The barn had always been a source of comfort for her. If she was honest, it'd even been a hideout at times—tonight clearly being one of them.

She wasn't exactly avoiding Connor.

Shiloh nickered at her unvoiced thoughts.

"Okay, fine," she said out loud to the little mind reader. "Maybe I am avoiding him, but can you blame me?" This morning on the porch had been mortifying enough. They'd shared some close moments before—times when his suave confidence had drawn her in and made her wonder about possibilities, but this was different. His *eyes* were different. The way they'd held her, brought her close. She was positive he was about to kiss her. Worse, she'd stood there waiting for—visibly *wanting*—him to. The embarrassing moment hadn't stopped replaying through her head since it'd happened.

Thank heavens she'd left her lipstick stashed inside the house this time. Truly, when your lips are parted like some overeager pucker fish, you don't need bright pink lipstick drawing any more attention to those suckers. Then again, plain ol' *naturelle* style must've done a mighty fine job communicating her intent, or Connor wouldn't have backed away like he'd regretted the mistake before ever making it.

He couldn't possibly have missed her reaction—before or after he'd withdrawn. But he never showed it. Not once. No awkwardness or backtracking. Not a trace of being uncomfortable around her or distracted at all. Throughout the day, he'd been nothing but… thoughtful, hardworking, focused.

She glanced around the trusses and stall beams he'd spent a good part of the afternoon reinforcing. Despite the substantial progress they'd made today, they had work to do yet. No question. Nonetheless, the scent of new oak boards infused the barn with fresh life it'd been lacking for years.

Ainsley fluttered away tears rising from that beautifully devastating place inside her where hope and doubt intersected. The rust-free nails didn't only hold a relic of a building together. They undergirded a vision that Connor had embraced with such honest fervency, she could've believed they were in this together. Like it was his home too.

Instead of the pushy, business-driven man she'd pinned him to be, he'd undeniably, unsettlingly been a man Ainsley could too easily wish were a real part of her life. A part she wouldn't be losing at the end of the month.

Shiloh prodded his nose under her hand.

Smiling at her horse's uncanny intuition, Ainsley set the brush on top of the stall gate and stroked his neck. "See," she whispered. "You'd be hiding, too, if you were me."

"Hiding from what?"

Ainsley jumped at the sound of Connor's voice approaching. She quickly pulled herself together—mostly—before turning around. "Hey. I thought you were inside getting cleaned up."

He held his arms out with his shower-fresh look on display: damp hair with the slightest curl grazing his forehead, scruff trimmed to the perfect level of tantalizing, an untucked button-down hanging over relaxed jeans.

Good gravy, could her eyes take any longer trailing his profile? She fixed them back on Shiloh a good forty seconds too late to hope Connor hadn't noticed her ogling. She cast her horse a don't-you-dare-laugh glance of warning as she exited and locked up the stall. "I guess I've been out here longer than I thought."

"Out here *hiding*."

Why did he have to overhear that? And for the love of stable smells, why couldn't her brain work on the fly around him the way it did around anyone else.

"From the horseflies," she zipped off.

Connor's line of sight followed one buzzing into the stall no sooner than she'd said the word. "You're hiding from horseflies… in a barn."

Okay, not her most impressive excuse.

"Between them and the mosquitoes," she blathered on like an imbecile, "I feel like I'm trapped in a *Twilight* movie half the time."

"*Twilight*, huh?" His shoulders shook, and Ainsley could've died right there.

She spun toward the stall gate like she was getting ready to do-si-do with the thing, gripped the top to keep her grounded, and did her best to contain an exasperated sigh.

Shiloh nuzzled her neck over the gate—always there for her, always knowing.

Ainsley ran her fingers down his thick mane and smiled at the feel of his whiskers tickling away her embarrassment.

"You really love him."

She peeked over her shoulder at Connor's pensive expression. "Shiloh? He's been my best friend for as long as I can remember. Seen me through every season, even the hardest ones of my life." She rubbed her horse's forehead as memories surfaced. "It just about killed me when I had to leave him here alone."

"Leave him here? When?"

She knew they had to broach the subject at some point. Still, the words came hesitantly. "When I got married."

The vibration from a horsefly's wings had never echoed louder.

Ainsley didn't turn to read Connor's expression this time. His silence held her in place until Shiloh nudged his nose under her neck again. Leaning on his comfort, she went on. "We couldn't afford a property where we could board him, so my dad kept him and exercised him for me on days I couldn't get here."

Shiloh turned for his feed tub, and Ainsley folded her arms over the gate. "I know it was good for him to stay in a familiar place. And amazingly, he didn't seem to resent me for not being around as much, but saying goodbye each time never got easier."

The pain in those memories triggered deeper ones. "I'm honestly not sure which is harder: knowing a goodbye is coming or being completely blindsided by it."

Ainsley turned at the sound of a footstep behind her.

Connor stopped mid-step and gazed at her as though she were standing in front of a newly discovered Monet piece instead of a colorless old barn gate.

She looked away from admiration she didn't understand and toyed with the charm on her necklace. Why was she telling him all this? "Sorry. I didn't mean to ramble."

"You didn't."

Her eyes found his. "Then why are you looking at me like that?" She was almost afraid to know. Afraid it would make her heart beat faster than it already was.

Connor started forward again but stopped and dropped his chin to his chest. "I'm just sorry for how you had to say goodbye to your father."

A breath whooshed out of her, half from relief he hadn't asked how she'd said goodbye to Jonathan. "Me too." She turned back to the stall gate and waited for one steady inhale to lead to another.

Warm, invitingly strong hands rested over her shoulders from behind. She didn't startle or try to slip away, only grasped the wood tighter.

So much for staying grounded. Her body melted at the feel of Connor's deft fingers massaging away tension he probably had no idea he'd played a part in causing. Even now, her heart stayed caught up in a war her muscles had no chance of winning.

His fingertips grazed her necklace as he drew her loose ponytail over her shoulder.

Ainsley closed her eyes at the tender way he regarded her—the slowness, each pause. When he let a breath out behind her, she struggled to release her own.

Connor cleared his throat, then felt along the vertebrae on her neck. "You could use another adjustment."

That was one way of putting it.

She smiled in spite of herself until she turned around. This close to him, she had two choices. Pull him to her right then and there or spare herself unneeded pain and cling to lighthearted banter with all she had.

"Well," she said, choosing the latter. "I'd make an appointment, but those chiropractors can be pretty hard to get in to see."

"Is that right?"

"Mm. Taking days off whenever they want... They're actually kind of full of themselves now that I think about it."

"Oh really?"

"It must be that presumption they run with all the time."

"Ah." Connor's grin nearly tipped him over the gate. "You know, you might want to cut them some slack. At least the ones running dual jobs. It can make life feel a little..." A quick glance at the trusses beckoned a look that felt torn. "Complicated."

And there went her hope of keeping things playful.

Her back creased against the wooden board as she stared at the hay strewn across the ground like broken pieces of her life. "I guess no one ever promised us it wouldn't be." At some point, she'd learned to accept that. "We do the best we can."

"What if it's not enough?"

She knew that question by heart. For years it had woven a jumbled knot inside her that only got harder to swallow with time. "I guess we keep pretending it is until we learn to believe it."

The whisper hung between them. Raw, unsatisfied.

She let go of her necklace but couldn't release the yearning for a better answer. One that felt real and safe. The kind her dad had always been able to give her.

Traces of his memory surrounded them—in every beam, every hook and latch, nail and bolt. They should have soothed. Instead, the fingerprints he left behind hollowed his absence all the more. Same way most of the farm did.

"You're thinking of your dad again?" Connor asked without really needing to.

"Sometimes I feel like I'm still a little girl. Out here with the horses, waiting for him to come in from the pastures so we can go riding together." She smiled softly toward the door he'd never walk through again. "There's an alcove far on the east corner of the property. It was our favorite spot. I used to stay out there for hours under this giant Cypress tree, watching him caught up with his tools when he thought I wasn't looking."

The weight of losing that time with him pressed her deeper against the gate. "You would've liked him. No one could argue he was a man of few words. But, oh, he worked and loved fiercely. He had an amazing home to show for it too. I knew even then I wanted the same when I grew up. The family, the farm. I'd work every bit as hard if it meant being able to give my own kids the kind of childhood Kate and I had. Playing hide and seek in the fields, sneaking carrots to the horses." She laughed. "Coming home positively covered in mud, knowing Daddy and Grandpa would have to shove a wad of tobacco into their mouths to keep from laughing when Mama came out."

Connor shifted without interrupting.

"I was supposed to have that life. *Josiah* was supposed to have that life." Regret frayed her voice. "But then Jonathan…"

"Walked out on you." An ache of compassion pulsed in the way Connor looked at her. "Your ex-husband," he continued. "At first, I figured he must've died. I couldn't fathom anyone bailing on you and Josiah, but then I realized you still have your maiden name."

"Yeah… I might've been a *wee* bit upset with him when I changed it back."

"Who could blame you?"

"My mom, for one." She huffed. "Jonathan was a respectable man. Real business savvy. Going places. I should've followed and tried harder to be the wife he wanted," she said in her mom's notoriously southern belle tone. "And I did. I tried. Begged even. But he left long before he ever bought his plane ticket." She shook her head, more at herself for how naïve she'd been.

"Jonathan dreamed big from the time we were kids. I think I might've even loved that about him. The way he wasn't daunted by things out of reach. He worked his way up his company ladder, closer to a life that drew him away." Memories closed in. "It was subtle at first. Always on his phone. Attending more and more meetings. If anything, I thought finding out we were pregnant would be the one thing to draw him back." She rubbed the skin between her nose and eyes. "I was *so* sure."

Connor stood as straight as the stall beams. "Are you saying he left *while* you were pregnant?" If he could've crunched the rafters in half with his bare hands, Ainsley wouldn't have been surprised if he tried.

"Oh, but don't misunderstand. That was his mercy," she said with more sarcasm than she should've. "It would be easier on Josiah if he never met his dad to begin with."

Connor walked a few feet away with his fingers clenched through the base of his hair.

Though she didn't hear every word he muttered, Ainsley caught enough between "crock" and "coward" to fill in the blanks.

"We both made our share of mistakes. But at the end of the day, a simple farm girl content to stay in Nowhere, North Carolina forever can only overshadow a trapped man's wanderlust for so long."

Lines creased Connor's forehead when he turned. "Is that all you think you are?"

"It's fine, really. I'm good with who I am. I'm good with living right here. It's just that I had hoped for more for Josiah. He doesn't know the pain of his dad's leaving yet. But one day, when he's older…" Her heart pounded with words she'd never know how to say. "No son should be without a father. I can't fill that role for him. I know that. And I'm giving him the *best* of me here on this farm as *best* as I can. But there are moments—days—when I worry it's not enough."

"Ainsley…"

"I know. I promise, I know."

His shoulders rose and caved. He lifted his head. And with slow and deliberate effort, gentle strides brought him to her again. Though he could've said a dozen things, he didn't have to. The look on his face was enough to back her into the stall. He braced a palm against the gate and searched her eyes. "You deserve your happy ending, Ainsley."

The wordless battle she'd seen claim his eyes time and again seemed to withhold what he wanted to say. A tendon on his neck pulsed as he looked away. His hand skimmed down the wood. "Don't ever give up on it."

He stepped back, crestfallen in ways Ainsley would've done anything to understand.

"Connor." She reached for him without thinking.

He looked from her hand in his, back to her face. Silence hovered. Heartbeats stretched. Neither of them moved until gradual steps finally brought him close again. Even slower, Connor tilted her chin up toward eyes so full of compassion and torment, she didn't have the willpower to shield him from her own. He could see it. He had to have. The yearning, the doubt, the fear of opening up a door that would inevitably lead to another goodbye.

"Ainsley..." Connor's gaze drifted to the floor again. "I—"

"Ains!"

They both whipped toward Daphne barreling into the barn with Josiah in her arms.

"Something's wrong," she said on a rushed breath. "He's burning up."

Chapter Sixteen

Ainsley hit the speakerphone button and chucked her cell on the counter. "He spit up the Tylenol both times I tried to give it to him. I sent Daphne out to try to find some Ibuprofen, but I don't know what else to do."

"Relax," Kate said.

Easy for her to say. She wasn't standing in their kitchen with a screaming baby, unable to get his temperature down. He'd had fevers before but never anywhere close to this high.

"Start a lukewarm bath," she instructed in the serenest voice imaginable.

Ainsley appreciated her sister's soothing nature.

Usually.

Right now, she had to breathe through the urge to strangle that calm voice right out of her throat. Ainsley set Josiah on the edge of the counter in order to take his pajamas off. She flipped on the faucet, plugged the sink, and brushed the sweaty hair off his forehead. When his beet red skin burned against her fingers, she fought back tears for the second time since rushing inside from the barn. "Don't worry, baby. We're gonna get you cooled down." They had to. *Please.*

She balled up his clothes. Where was Daphne already?

She frantically swished her fingers in the sink water. "How cold is too cold? I don't want to shock his body." She'd read the books, heard the stories. If she changed his temperature too quickly one way or the other, he could end up seizing.

The possibility sent her own body shaking. She stuck her elbow in the water but couldn't trust her temperature to be a normal gauge right now. She yanked her arm out. "What does lukewarm even mean?" she practically yelled.

Startled, Josiah cried louder and almost squirmed off the counter.

Ainsley brought him close. "It's okay, sweet boy. I'm sorry. You're okay." She cupped the back of his head with her cool, wet hand and desperately strained to shield him from how helpless she felt. But when sturdier hands than hers rested against her tense shoulders, what was left of her frail composure threatened to crumble. She gripped the sink's edge.

Josiah climbed inconsolably up her stomach, crying in her ear. Connor reached for him, but Ainsley held on.

"I can only help if you let me." He transferred a supportive hand to Josiah's back, the other to her arm, and dipped his head. "Please."

With a release from some unknown place inside her, Ainsley slowly handed her overheated boy to him. She stood motionless for a minute. Watching, breathing. Though Josiah didn't fully calm down, something about Connor's presence soothed him. And her.

She clutched her elbows across her stomach as if they could shield her from the way seeing him hold her son nearly pulled her apart. She turned to the counter and stared at her phone. "Kate? You still there?"

"I'm here."

Ainsley drew her shoulders back. Josiah needed her to focus. She felt the water one more time, added some cooler water, and tossed in a washcloth. "Okay, lukewarm bath. Got it. What do I do after?"

"Keep him stripped to his diaper for a while. Try to get him to nurse. It might settle him some."

"Only a diaper. Nurse him. What else?"

Kate's pause snuck through Ainsley's plastered-together emotions.

Even miles away, Kate knew. She always knew. "Ains, listen. I know you're scared. Every mom is when their little ones are sick. But try to remember a fever is his body's natural way of fighting infection. It's a common reaction after immunizations."

Ainsley picked up her phone, wishing she could hold her sister right then instead. "Are you sure he's going to be okay?"

"Keep a cool washcloth on his head. After you nurse him, try a fever reducer again. Check his temperature periodically."

Ainsley half smiled. "Nice job skirting your way around my question."

"Occupational hazard," Kate teased. "Seriously, Ains, if you need me to come home, I will."

She turned and expelled a slow breath at the sight of Josiah calming down even further in Connor's arms. Truth was, Kate's patients needed her there at the hospital tonight. And despite not being entirely sure how she felt about seeing Josiah cradled snugly against Connor's shoulder, she couldn't deny what scared and comforted her more than anything else right then. She wasn't on her own.

A bonk to the corner of the couch brought Ainsley's head bobbing up and her eyes fluttering open. The quiet living room settled into view, followed quickly by a reminder of the hours that had led to her dozing off. She looked from Daphne passed out in the armchair to Connor sitting on the opposite end of the sofa.

With his head tilted to the side and arms keeping Josiah securely asleep on his chest, he had to be as exhausted as she felt. Yet she didn't doubt for a second that he'd stay there, holding her son until dawn if she'd let him.

Josiah wouldn't have argued. It didn't matter that she couldn't see his face nestled under Connor's neck. The slow rise and fall of his back spoke his contentment. The longer she watched, the more her own breathing evened. And for a moment too long, she wished he wasn't the only one in Connor's arms.

Apparently, Matty did too. He'd eagerly invited himself into his new buddy's lap for the night the moment they'd sat down. Given his protective instincts, he'd likely chosen a post near Josiah. But if she was a betting woman, Ainsley would wager her dog was getting used to having Connor around the farm as much as she was.

She slid her leg—and the thought—out from under her.

"You should keep resting," Connor said without opening his eyes.

"I didn't mean to fall asleep."

He looked at her then. "You took care of him most of the night. You deserve a break." He rested his cheek against Josiah's head, probably to check his temperature. Though his fever had finally broken much earlier, it'd taken him quite a while to settle enough to fall asleep. Ainsley, even longer. "I think he's going to be out 'til morning. Really, try to rest." He smiled tenderly at the boy cozied under his chin. "I've got him."

The weariness of being a single parent pressed in— maybe from the night's fatigue taking its toll, maybe from the fatigue of her hectic routine catching up to her. Her emotions didn't waste time sorting out the source. They brimmed without thought or resistance. "Thank you for helping tonight," she whispered. "I'm sorry I was such a mess. It's just that he's my whole world. If anything were to happen to him…"

Connor's eyes grabbed hold of hers. "You don't ever have to apologize for loving your son."

But was love enough? She begged her lips to smile without quivering. "It's the hardest thing I've ever faced in my entire life. Parenting, I mean." She looked at Josiah. "I've never experienced a deeper exhaustion or a more earnest love. But I honestly don't know what I'm doing half the time. Like I'm winging every choice, hoping beyond hope I'm not making the wrong ones."

"I think you just described how every parent on the planet feels."

"Not every parent is raising their child on their own." She stiffened, not meaning to have said that last part out loud.

Empathy filled Connor's eyes in place of the judgment she expected. "You're not alone."

"I know, but I made the decision to raise him here. It was my choice, and if it was the wrong one…" She grazed Josiah's hair with her fingertips. "I'm so scared of falling short for him." The deep-seated confession seeped from a mama's vulnerable heart.

"Falling short doesn't make you a failed mom, Ainsley." Connor stretched a hand to hers. "It makes you a real one."

The simple words struck against the courage she always tried so hard to maintain.

Josiah turned his head, and a glimpse of the peace on his sweet face fanned into the comfort Connor offered them both.

He shifted gingerly. "I can give him another adjustment when he wakes up if you want," he whispered. "I think it made a big difference."

Ainsley didn't doubt it had, but she knew something deeper than an alignment was at the root of her son's contentment.

"It helps that you're such a natural with him." More than she ever would have suspected. "You have kids of your own?"

The minute the skin around his eyes crumpled, she realized how that might've sounded. As if she pegged him for the kind of guy who had no problem leaving a family behind.

"I'm sorry. I didn't mean—"

"Don't worry about it, but no," he said while edging up the couch. "No kids. Nieces. Two of them." Sorrow trailed the warmth filling his voice. "They're pretty amazing girls. But they live out in Texas, so I don't get to see them much."

"I bet they miss their uncle."

"Nah. They have a one-of-a-kind dad who doesn't leave anything lacking. Trust me."

His broken smile drew Ainsley across the cushions. "Are you close with your brother?"

"In any way besides age?" A sad laugh answered the rest. "Reed's always known who he was and what he wanted."

"And you haven't?"

His shoulders rose and fell in the moment it took for him to respond. "I used to think I did. But either way, Reed wasn't afraid to risk everything for the life he chose— including standing up to our father." He traced figure eights along Josiah's back with his fingers. "It's probably part of what enabled him to become a great dad himself."

Which was something Connor didn't think he could live up to, from the sounds of it.

"What do you mean, standing up to your dad?"

"He turned down his designated spot in the family business. Didn't bat an eye leaving either." Something bordering admiration clung to his words. "Man, the look on Pop's face when Reed told him he was moving to cowboy territory to become a vet, of all things…"

"Of all things, huh?"

Connor let out a short laugh. "You don't know our dad." He pulled a throw pillow into his lap to support his arms. "Honestly, it wouldn't have mattered what profession Reed had chosen. If it's outside of Pop's empire, it's grounds for disownment."

Seriously? "That seems a little extreme."

"Like I said. You don't know our dad." He pushed back the hair that had flattened onto his forehead. "Business first, family second. He raised us to follow suit—apprentice under him, stake our lives in the company, the whole nine." His long exhale bore the weight of shouldered expectations.

Ainsley tugged her charm back and forth. "I doubt you're as different from your brother as you think you are. You're here right now, not in your dad's practice. Sounds like you did some standing up too."

"I'm not sure running away classifies as standing up."

"I thought traveling is what you wanted to do. See the world. Explore."

"It is—was. Sort of." He craned his neck back. "I don't know. My dad's probably right. Chasing the highway won't ever get me where I want to go."

"Maybe you just haven't found a place that feels like home yet."

His eyes gravitated to hers, soft and broken. "I'm more afraid I already have."

"You're afraid of staying." It wasn't really a question. More a heartache from experience.

"I'm afraid of leaving."

Her pulse raced at the way he looked at her. At the torment, the longing.

"You don't like what you do?" Her voice held the faintest tremble of hope.

He stared at the ceiling as though he'd find a map of answers if he strained hard enough to see it. "I never used to hesitate to answer that, but then I started wondering if that's only because my dad programmed me to think it's what I always wanted for myself."

"Just because he wants you to love being a chiropractor doesn't mean you can't."

Connor angled slightly to face her, mindful not to jostle Josiah.

She breathed in at his pause, afraid she'd overstepped.

"I know," he said. "I guess I wanted to figure out if it was really his love or mine. I've never worked outside of his practice. Living it in a different context, getting out from under his shadow… I needed to find out how I really felt about it on my own."

Ainsley pinched her bottom lip but couldn't keep the question from coming. "And now?"

He didn't have to answer. She could see it on his face. He loved what he did. Who wouldn't with his talent? She'd experienced it firsthand, knew it was something he was made to do.

"I've always enjoyed the work. Helping people overcome chronic pain is pretty rewarding. And consulting's expanded that impact beyond my own patients." His reflection on the role his profession played in his life led to a pensive smile. "It's actually a real privilege."

Ainsley coiled the hem of her shirt around her finger. "Sounds like you found your answer."

"Answers are never that easy."

"Maybe we overcomplicate them." The same way her heart overcomplicated feelings it knew better than to welcome in again.

"I suppose we do," Connor said without releasing her gaze. She couldn't tell exactly what thoughts lay behind those green eyes, only that she could relate to the turmoil they battled.

A dozen heartbeats passed before she could look away from him. "For what it's worth," she said with far more lightheartedness than she felt, "I'd say you can at least be sure of one thing. You have a gift for helping people, Connor Allen."

He laughed softly. "Even when they don't ask for it, right?"

"Even when they don't realize how much they need it." Ainsley risked looking up again, hoping the impulsive admission didn't reveal as much as it meant.

She should've known better. Connor was still inches away yet managed to embrace her without a single touch. The connection beckoned her heart past the cushion edge between them. Another swallow, another exhale. Her lashes fell.

A soft whimper jolted her attention back to Josiah. He'd turned his head in the opposite direction but still looked at peace—something Ainsley hadn't known in so long, she'd forgotten what it felt like.

"I should go put him down. I'm sure your arms are tired, and we could all use some solid sleep."

Connor moved to hand him over but froze when Josiah squirmed. "Maybe I should take him back so we don't risk waking him."

Ainsley nodded and motioned for him to lead the way. She couldn't deny how well he'd done with him so far. Nor could she deny how much seeing them snuggled together was making each step down the hall harder to take.

Once in his dark room, Josiah barely stirred as Connor slowly transferred him to his crib.

Moonlight cast enough of a glow over his face to undo Ainsley's heart as it did every time. She lifted two fingers to her lips and softly pressed them against her son's forehead. "Love you to Neverland and back, sweet boy," she whispered.

When she looked up, Connor's eyes held the same level of awe they'd held earlier in the barn. She was tempted to peer behind her, certain the Monet piece had followed her inside, but gestured to the door instead.

He turned without uttering a word. It wasn't until they'd spanned a safe distance from Josiah's room that Connor finally met her gaze again.

Ainsley looked away when he still didn't say anything. Thankfully, a quick glance into the living room gave her a momentary reprieve. With Daphne burying her face into the crease of the couch now, and Matty zonked out at her feet, at least she and Connor wouldn't have to worry about waking those two. Assuming either of them found their voices again. They both dawdled near the door—Ainsley with her hands in her back pockets, Connor rubbing at a callous on his thumb.

"Thanks again for sticking around and helping out," she finally said. "It meant a lot to Josiah. And me," she added softly. Clearing her throat, she freed her hands from her pockets. "After working here all day long, I'm sure you had other places to be tonight. So, really, it was sweet of you to stay."

Chin down, smile unreadable, Connor shook his head. "There's nowhere I'd rather be, Ainsley."

Except on the open road calling him to what he loved to do. He'd just finished telling her how much his job meant to him, for goodness sakes. Why was she letting herself wish he wouldn't leave?

He found her eyes again. And without so much as a single breath passing this time, the answer stared back at her as clear as day.

She was falling for him—despite every single reason she shouldn't.

She brought her hand to her necklace, but her lips weren't anywhere near as obliging in following orders. They tipped to the side, failing to conceal the reaction he spurred.

He pointed behind him. "I should head back to the loft before the sun comes up. I told Herald earlier I was gonna beat him to the punch this morning."

"You did, huh?" A chuckle nudged its way past her still-insubordinate lips. "I didn't know it was a competition."

He laughed. "Never underestimate a male's ego."

"Oh, trust me. I don't."

He ran his fingers through his hair and down to the base of his neck. Her eyes clung to every movement, every muscle. When she finally convinced them to steer clear of his arm, they traveled back to his smile, which only made things worse. *Way* worse. Warm and captivating and knowing, it matched dimples capable of saying more than she could probably handle hearing.

Connor hooked a thumb over his shoulder like it was a knee-jerk reaction. "I should get up to the loft."

"You already said that."

"Right." He jutted a finger in the air, grinned sheepishly, and reached for the doorknob. "And this is me actually leaving this time."

"Wait."

He turned.

Inhaling, Ainsley strode forward and lifted on her toes to kiss his cheek. "Thank you again. For everything." She dropped back on her heels, a little too nervous to look up until the feel of his fingers settling behind her ear lured her eyes to the ones locked on hers.

His chest moved in step with the pulse drumming against her skin. He smoothed his thumb over her temple, swallowed, and brought his lips to the edge of hers as though torn over crossing an invisible line. "Good night, Ainsley Grace."

Putty. One hundred percent putty. Her legs couldn't move. Her arms were goners. Never mind the state of her mouth.

He reached behind him for the doorknob again. "Going for real." He glanced across the room. "Night, Matty. Night, Daphne," he whispered even though they were asleep.

When Ainsley's body finally solidified, she caught his hand midturn. Everything she wanted to say pounded through her tendons until reason gained enough ground to make her release his hand. She stepped back. "Good night, Connor."

"Night, John Boy," Daphne mumbled away from the couch cushion.

Connor and Ainsley both laughed.

"Sorry," she whisper-hollered across the room, to which Daphne waved a forgiving arm behind her.

Ainsley made a face at Connor. He smiled again, looked down like he was wavering over whether to say more, then turned and made it all the way outside this time.

She caught the screen door before it closed. "Hey."

Sweet heavens, why couldn't she let the poor guy leave already?

"Are we gonna make it?" she asked in spite of herself.

If the cold, late night air chafing her flushed cheeks didn't paralyze her, the mixed emotions racing across Connor's face were about to.

"Through Thanksgiving, I mean," she hastily amended. "Convincing everyone you're a country boy, and we're…" She couldn't bring herself to finish.

"Nothing a worn pair of cowboy boots and hat can't handle."

If only they were tailor made to protect her heart.

She knew he was keeping things light. Honestly, right then, she appreciated it. They'd need every tactic they had to survive the holiday fiasco waiting to happen. But even then, would it really be enough?

"You can still back out, you know. I can make something up." She huff-laughed at herself. "Apparently, I'm pretty good at that." Usually. She dodged the look on his face as he started toward her. "Really, Connor. I mean it. All your help around here has been amazing, but I don't want to ask more of you than is fair."

"You seem to have this stubborn habit of forgetting I'm the one who volunteered for this."

"That was before you really knew what you were getting into."

His grin didn't argue, only inched that much closer.

"Thanksgiving's almost here. Are you absolutely sure? I mean, *one hundred percent*. Because if not, I can—"

"Ainsley." Right in front of her now, Connor cupped the back of her hair, kissed her forehead, and closed his arms around her. "I'm sure."

She sank into his words—into him—not caring how long the moment would last or how much it would reveal. Her fingers clenched the back of his shirt as she allowed herself to trust a man's embrace again.

"Besides, a girl brave enough to save a worm's life can handle anything."

She laughed into the flannel warming her cheek. "You're never gonna let that go, are you?"

"Not if I can help it." He let a quiet moment lapse, then lowered his lips to the tip of her ear. "We'll take it moment by moment, okay?" he whispered.

Her lashes squeezed together. Moments were beginning to scare her the most.

Chapter Seventeen

Connor's eyelids flew open four hours after he'd collapsed into his bed. He'd never loved and hated the alarm on his phone more in his life. He slid his legs over the mattress and patted both cheeks a dozen times. Today was the day. One way or another, that rooster's joyride of waking him up each morning was going down.

A flicker of the sunrise weaved into the loft.

No, no, no. Not yet. Connor wheeled around the doorway to the stairs with only one arm through his shirt. He'd come back for his boots. And his pants.

The smell of dawn greeted him past the barn doors. He tugged his other arm through his shirt sleeve and pulled it over his head while jogging across the dew-covered grass. His toes squished over twenty things that'd probably turn his stomach if he could see the color they were, but he didn't care. He was making it to the rendezvous point on time.

Across the way, Billy the Pig did his usual awkward dance of trying to lift his stubby front legs in the air like his round ol' belly weren't weighing him down. He might be more than a little confused, but he was steadfast and determined. Connor would give him that.

"Way to persevere, Billy," he called as he passed the pig's favorite stump.

Billy stared at him like he was the crazy one.

He glanced down at his boxers. Okay, so maybe he was. He kept jogging anyway.

He skidded in the mud and slid into the doghouse at the same time Herald hopped to the top. Connor slapped both hands on the roof. "Ha! Made it."

Unimpressed, Herald stared at him blankly.

"Crowing isn't so fun when you can't taunt the new-comer, is it?" He jutted gun-shaped fingers at his nemesis. "Uh-huh. *That's* what's up. You like that? Boom."

One blink. That's all he got before Herald strutted to the roof's pinnacle. With his beady eyes dead on Connor's face, he stretched his neck and crowed straight at him.

Unbelievable. Connor's arms fell to his sides, and full-on laughter spilled from somewhere behind him. He turned to find Ainsley and Matty as their attentive—and highly entertained—audience. Even the dog was grinning.

Smiling himself, Connor pointed one last time at the rooster. "This doesn't change the fact that you didn't wake me up."

Herald flapped to the ground, waggled his red comb close enough by him to graze his leg, and went on his way.

Connor looked at Ainsley. "And you think *I'm* proud?"

"Well, considering you're standing in the mud in your underwear, I guess I can concede to notching that stigma down a level or two."

His boxers. Right. A self-conscious laugh warmed the cold air. "As long as you don't start calling me Calvin Klein Connor, I'll take it."

Her grin latched onto the nickname a little too fast.

"Ainsley…" he warned.

"What?" She raised one sassy shoulder, and that was it. Connor took off after her, Matty running interference between them. If any of the animals had managed to sleep through Herald's wake-up call, they were surely up now. Ainsley's squeal almost topped Matty's nonstop barking.

Connor caught her at the waist just short of colliding with the fence bordering the paddock. She turned in his arms in time to drag him against the rail with her. Still laughing, she landed one palm to his chest, the other to his waist.

Matty's bark fest kept him jumping up and down beside them. No one could blame him for staying caught up in the moment. Connor was too. Grass swayed behind them. Leaves rustled in the wind. But with the girl he'd fallen for in his arms, he couldn't hear anything above the urge to draw her to him.

Her eyes slowly lifted the way they'd done a number of times last night. He'd managed to hold onto his willpower then. Right now, though, he had no idea how.

The sunrise cast hints of orange over her hair and across the smatter of freckles he couldn't unearth the strength to pull away from this time. He glided his fingers across her cheek. He took in every inch, every pulse and flutter matching his own urgency.

Ainsley slipped her hand over his. Rapid breaths invited him closer. Her lashes dipped, rose once more, and left Connor more undone than he'd ever felt in his life.

He swallowed hard. Yearning heated through him—desire, fear... love most of all. He brushed his thumb alongside the blue eyes that had anchored him from the beginning. Slow and sure, he removed her straw hat, threaded his fingers into her hair, and didn't release her gaze until his lips met hers.

Ainsley melded against him, nothing withheld or hidden or carefully guarded. Connor dropped her hat and curled his arm around the small of her back. Their fake relationship faded in the sunlight. And in that moment, nothing stood between a lost boy chasing answers and the girl who'd shown him the only ones that mattered.

Connor clutched the splintery rail beside her. If he didn't grip something, he'd lose his grasp on all he'd been withholding. A breath from somewhere deep within slowed his lips. His heart was another story. It kept pounding as he rested his forehead against hers. "Ainsley..."

Her fingers curled around his sleeve. "Please don't tell me you're sorry." Soft and vulnerable, the quiet plea barely rose above the wind.

Connor brought his palm to her neck and leaned back. There were many things he grappled with in life. Questions he still wrestled, doubts he still fought. But regretting this moment would never be one of them.

He searched her eyes, prayed she could see the certainty in his, and kissed her once more. "I'm not sorry."

Her grip on his sleeve tightened.

A notification from her phone played into the silence before she could say anything.

Ainsley shook her head at the sky as though amused at life's inevitable timing. "That's the baby monitor app. Josiah's up."

"Does that mean he slept the rest of the night?"

"Soundly," she answered with relief.

"That's great."

"Yeah." She faced the sky again. "It is." Even with her eyes closed, gratefulness emanated from every inch of her. "I probably worried more than I should've."

"You're his mom, Ainsley. You get to worry as much as you need to."

She raked her hair off her forehead. "Even when I turn into a psychotic, frantic mess of a mom?"

He slipped her hand free from her hair. "Even then."

Her chin drifted to her chest. "Still, I'm glad you were there with us last night." After keeping her head lowered a moment longer, she aimed her phone over her shoulder. "I should get in. Kate said I need to make sure he stays hydrated today."

"Sorry." He let go of her hand and motioned to the house. "Of course. Please."

"We'll connect later?"

"Definitely."

Nodding slowly, she tapped her cell against her thigh in a call for Matty to follow.

214 | CRYSTAL WALTON

They didn't make it more than six feet toward the house before Connor pushed away from the fence. "Ainsley?"

She spun around, and the look in her eyes made him wish he still had the rail to hold onto.

"Can I take you to dinner sometime?" he asked out of nowhere. "A real date. Promise. Just the two of us."

Her hidden smile pushed past its borders. "I'd like that."

He exhaled on the inside. "Good."

"Good." With her bottom lip twisted in her teeth, Ainsley lingered a minute more.

If she stayed any longer, his pulse was going to race him straight to her again.

"You know," she said after starting and stopping again. "You could come inside in a little bit. Hang out with Josiah for a while. If you want," she added.

His heart swelled. For her to ask that—to trust him enough to invite him into her son's life—was a big deal. And an honor. "I'd like that."

"Good," she mimicked.

He dipped a grin at her. "Good."

They hovered in the lawn, connected by smiles having an entire conversation of their own.

"But..." she said midturn. "You might want to put on some pants first."

He looked down at his stark white legs glaring in the sunlight. "Pants. Right." He laughed. "That's probably not a bad idea."

She swayed her head like that was debatable. "See ya in a while… Calvin Klein Connor." A trail of laughter followed her to the house while he stayed in place—pantsless.

When he turned back to the fence, he found Shiloh had approached sometime during their interlude. Probably to check up on him. In all honesty, he didn't blame him.

Connor leaned against the rail and rubbed the horse's nose. "Wish I could tell you I knew what I was doing, bud." He cast a glance over his shoulder toward the last glimpse of Ainsley and Matty disappearing around the bend. He'd told her they'd take it moment by moment. Not because he was trying to operate off the cuff for the sake of being smooth or spontaneous, but because his heart kept him savoring one moment at a time.

A nicker behind him brought him back around to her best friend staring longingly at the house. "You really love her, don't you?"

Shiloh neighed his obvious answer, and Connor couldn't deny his own.

"I think I do too, boy," he whispered. He just had to figure out if he should tell her before the last of their moments together ran out.

Chapter Eighteen

Spending the past week alongside Ainsley and Josiah had been some of the most fulfilling time Connor had ever spent, even if their sprint to finish up projects had pushed the dinner date he'd promised her back further than he wanted. That didn't mean he'd stopped thinking about it. Nor had he stopped waiting for the next moment he could kiss her again.

Even now, he could hardly look at her without communicating the restraint it took to stay seated on the floor in front of Josiah instead of sweeping her outside.

An eerie noise shook him from thoughts probably better kept under control. Connor looked around the living room for whatever it was that needed to be put out of its misery. "What *is* that?"

"Sorry." Ainsley crossed the room to the coatrack and rifled through her purse. "It's that stupid toy my mom bought for Josiah. The creepy thing starts playing music on its own."

"That's supposed to be music?" It sounded more like a Halloween soundtrack.

"Don't get me started." Ainsley pulled out one of those long plastic toys that strap across a car seat. "The batteries are dying, but I haven't had time to figure out how to change them. There's no battery section." She opened the front door, dropped the toy, and turned with pure innocence.

Connor grinned at her. "Did you just toss that toy outside?"

"You'll thank me later. Trust me."

He laughed. "Why don't you throw it away?"

"That's what I've been saying," Daphne interjected from the kitchen.

She pointed at Connor. "Okay, *you* I can understand asking. But *you*…" She tipped her head at Daphne. "You know full well my mom would call the instant I walked it near the garbage can. That woman senses all things. I have no clue how, but she does. And frankly, I'd rather put up with the sorry thing than never hear the end of how we don't appreciate her gifts."

That made one of them. Even Josiah looked traumatized over the horror movie music.

Connor would have to figure out a way to ditch the toy for Ainsley at some point. For now, he was set on making Josiah smile. Determined, Connor went back to flapping his hands open and closed in front of his face. "Peek-a-boo."

No response. Not even a twitch of a grin.

"Nothing? Really? I've seen you crack up over this with your mom, big guy."

"You gotta use a girl's voice," Ainsley said from the edge of the kitchen.

"A girl's voice."

"*Extra* high-pitched," Daphne piped in.

Connor knew that exaggerated inflection meant they were messing with him, but with Stone Cold Face of the hour staring blankly at him, he wasn't beneath trying. He covered his face again, flung his hands apart, and… "Peek-a-boo!"

The girls' laughter topped Josiah's, but who cared. The kid was finally amused. Mission accomplished. Validation reached. Connor could officially wield business deals at the drop of a dime *and* make a baby laugh by the seventh try. Life was good.

Daphne raised her coffee mug and a wry grin at him. "I knew you had it in you to be girlie."

Connor cocked his chin at her. "One of my newfound talents."

"Meh," Daphne countered. "Talent's a stretch." Not missing a beat, she pulled out her cell. "I can download a Celine Dion track for you so you have an octave to match if you want."

This girl found way too much enjoyment in making him squirm.

"I think I'm good. At least *you* think so, don't you, kiddo?" He clapped Josiah's pudgy hands together. "Mr. Connor's a pretty funny guy, isn't he? Yep, see, *there's* another smile." He brought Josiah's hand to his in a fist bump. "Boom. We guys know what's up, don't we? Isn't that right, Matty?" At this point, he wasn't beneath soliciting backup either.

Lying beside Josiah, Matty lifted his chin off his crossed front paws and barked in solidarity.

Connor had to laugh at the whole thing: his girlie voice, the googly-eyed faces he'd been donning at Josiah all morning, his bond with the dog. His brother would never let him live it down if he could see him now. Not to mention what his father would think of him.

The uninvited thought stormed in and clouded the carefree moment. Nearly five hundred miles away, and the rain of Pop's disappointment still reached him.

"Hey, you all right?"

Ainsley's thoughtful voice drew him from his reverie. With her mug of barely sweetened Irish cream between her hands, she looked at him the way few people did. As if his heart had no borders, and she not only saw the ache lying beneath, she felt it.

It took his phone ringing to break the connection. He checked the screen. Flynn. Again. He wasn't looking forward to the flack he'd catch for ignoring his buddy's calls, but the timing had always been bad. At least, that's what he'd been telling himself. But as he peered toward Ainsley again, he knew better. Time had to do with it all right—the fact that he was running out of what he had left in Whispering Pines.

He tucked his unanswered cell into his pocket, still not ready to deal with where his original plans would be taking him next. Right now, he wanted to be fully in the moment. Starting with sweeping Josiah into the air like a plane above his head.

"Um," Ainsley cautioned. "You might not want to—"

"Aw, man…" Connor lowered Josiah back to the floor and wiped his face on his sleeve. "I think he drooled up my nose."

"I tried to warn you."

He turned toward her grin beaming from the adjoining kitchen. She'd tried to warn him about a lot of things, none of which his heart had been listening to. Including his own warning to look away right now. Instead, he held on to the softness in her eyes, their kindness, their draw—things that were becoming impossible not to fall in love with.

"Be glad it wasn't spit-up," she added. "You'd never get that smell out of your nostrils. Trust me."

Speaking of smells, a horrid stench hit Connor's nose five seconds before Josiah's squeals struck his eardrums. He broke eye contact with Ainsley in time to see Matty dragging the kid across the floor by the back of his diaper.

"Matty." Ainsley scurried over to cut them off at the door. If she hadn't, Connor wouldn't have been surprised if Super Dog found a way to twist the knob and get that diaper bomb outside.

Josiah gleefully slid along the floor as Matty swung his head back and forth like he had hold of a chew toy.

"Will you stop that? Let go. Matty, no." Ainsley lost her grip on his hind legs, fell back on her rear, and whipped a glance at Daphne. "Little help here, please."

Her cousin grabbed a Milk-Bone from a bottom cabinet to lure Matty away from the offensive diaper he was on a mission to destroy.

Connor echoed Josiah's laughter. "Is there a county fair coming up? 'Cause this event would definitely sell out." As could any event that showcased the sexy—and somehow daunting—side-eye Ainsley could dish out like nobody's business.

"Not as fast as the Connor Is About To Change His First Dirty Diaper event." She walked her little stink bomb straight for him. "Tickets are already flying out the door."

Could he fly out too? Connor sprang up from the floor and shuffled backward. "Now, let's not go getting crazy here."

"Crazy would be my boyfriend not having experience changing Josiah's diapers. You don't want another episode like last time to expose us, do you? One day left to practice making it believable," she nearly sang. "Besides, you *guys* know what's up, right?"

Talk about being cornered. She held her son out to him. Happy babbles and bright-eyed smiles landed their mark. Done. Toast. Connor didn't stand a chance. He grasped Josiah under the arms, turned his head the second the smell punched him in the face again, and offered a non-convincing, "We've got this."

He managed to make it down the hall and into Josiah's room without a gas mask. But once he unclasped the diaper, a full-on hazmat suit wouldn't have saved him. "Aw, dude." He buried his face in his elbow. "That's messed up, bro."

"Use the diaper to get most of it off," Ainsley said from beside them as if utterly immune to the sight and stench of a blow-out mess climbing halfway up the kid's back.

Connor sucked in a breath, raised his shirt over his nose, and proceeded Operation Don't Gag, which lasted all of three seconds.

Josiah almost squirmed off the changing table. Legs and arms flailing, he swiped his fingers in the diaper. Connor had no clue poop could smear in so many directions.

Ainsley wrestled to still the Kung Fu artist's hand. "Grab the wipes. Grab the wipes!"

"Where?"

"On the side."

Connor frantically jerked a plastic container out of a basket attached to the changing table and banged on the little lever like he'd just stepped up to a strongman carnival game.

Evidently, he wasn't fast enough.

With his mustardy colored behind exposed, Josiah decided it was the right moment to relieve his bladder too. A fountain of pee shot clear across Josiah's chest, skimmed his face, and splattered onto the wall with audible force.

Once shock gave way, reflexes kicked in. Connor yanked out one wipe after another until he had enough piled on top of Josiah to crochet a full blanket out of. A very cold, cry-inducing blanket. Bad idea.

The wipes fell to the floor as Connor instinctively scooped him off the table and held him in the air.

He obviously hadn't thought that move through either.

The firehose, now free of its wipe barricade, sprayed straight onto Connor's shirt. The warm liquid soaked through the fabric onto his torso while he stood there, waffling over which was more disturbing—watching pee race down the wall or feeling it run down his chest.

Josiah cooed happily when his never-ending reservoir finally tapped out.

At least one of them was content now.

Connor looked from Josiah's smile to the one Ainsley was painfully trying to keep covered behind the hand clasped over her mouth.

"I'm so sorry," she said through her fingers.

"Is that why you're laughing?"

The answer flew out in a series of snorts. She pulled herself up from a doubled over wheeze and extended her hands. "Sorry. No really, here. Let me take him."

More than tempted to pass off the little missile launcher, Connor brought him to his sodden shirt instead and braced an arm under his cold, gooey tush. "We're good." He flaunted Ainsley's side-eye back at her and followed it up with a wink. "We guys stick together." Literally, at the moment. "Right, buddy?"

Clearly relieved, in all ways possible, Josiah climbed up Connor's stomach like he usually did with Ainsley.

"Hang tight, Ant Man. We've gotta get you cleaned up first." He rushed him to the kitchen, where Ainsley had the sink filled and bath supplies in hand before Connor could say the word.

Once all their skin was back to a non-gag-inducing color, and Josiah was happily cloaked in a hooded towel like a caped crusader, Connor gave Ainsley a high five. "And that's how it's done."

"Boom," Ainsley added in a husky voice meant to mimic his.

His eyes gravitated to her lips caught up in a smile he could spend every day savoring.

Looking down, she opened and closed the cap to the baby wash. "We make a great team."

"We sure do," he said slowly.

"And you guys think Josiah's diaper was gag-worthy?" Daphne strolled in with her empty coffee mug and set it in the sink. "Seriously, you two are sickeningly adorable." She picked up a biscuit and napkin off a plate, backed against the counter, and took a bite. "What?" she said when their blank stares must've registered.

Connor laughed. "You don't believe in filters, do you?"

Her slanted grin answered that one. "You should try it sometime." She tossed the balled-up napkin for him to catch. "Never know what you'll find out."

Finding out wasn't what had his heart in knots. Being able to walk away afterward was.

Chapter Nineteen

Their little diaper marathon had kept Ainsley entertained throughout the afternoon until Connor had brought up the date she was starting to think he'd changed his mind about.

"Don't even think about it."

Ainsley startled at the sound of her sister's voice coming from the bathroom doorway. "Jeez, Kate. Just 'cause you know how to resuscitate someone doesn't mean you should walk around giving people heart attacks." In front of the mirror, she lowered her hands to the sink. "Welcome to the land of the living, by the way."

She yawned. "Coffee first."

Ainsley couldn't argue with that. "I don't know how you survive those twelve-hour shifts."

"One of the many glamorous perks of being a nurse." She slumped a shoulder against the trim and ruffled her bedhead. "Give me that hairband."

Ainsley glanced at the elastic around her wrist. "I'm about to use it."

"No, you're not."

"Excuse me?"

"I just told you not to think about it."

"About using it as a slingshot?" Because that idea had already crossed her mind at least five times since Kate barged in on her.

"About putting your hair up." Kate snagged the brush off the counter and stood behind Ainsley like they were seven again, playing beauty parlor. She stroked it through Ainsley's long hair. "If you're going on a date, you should wear it down."

Ainsley turned. "How did you—?"

Kate's single eyebrow raise cut off the need to finish her question.

"You know, the whole telepathic thing you have going on lately is really starting to freak me out."

"I was standing in the doorway a good five minutes before you even noticed. I know what your fretted tics mean. No mind reading necessary."

"They're not fretted." She yanked the brush back. "They're... deliberate." And antsy, maybe. Anal? Good grief. Why not grab her lipstick and scribble *Lame* on her forehead before going to meet Connor, for crying out loud.

Head down, Ainsley picked at the bristles. But when she felt Kate's telepathic force encroaching on her again, she unearthed as much humor as she could muster. "Trust *me*, girl. You don't need to be talking about anyone else's hair."

Kate looked in the mirror and laughed. "Considering my only date today is with an adorably oblivious seven-month-old, I have a feeling I can get away with it." She tugged the brush back anyway and attempted to tame the Medusa curls her pillow had done a number on. "Now, stop your sidetracking and catch me up on what I've missed. Where's he taking you?"

"I don't know, to be honest. He didn't say."

"A surprise date," she said like a dreamy tween.

"I'm sure it's no big deal."

"Right." Kate perched a hand on her hip. "Which is why you've changed your outfit no less than four times already."

Ainsley stopped herself from pointlessly asking how Kate knew what she'd been doing. "Can't we talk about something else?"

"Like what? The catheters I've been putting in all week? C'mon, Ains. We haven't even had a chance to talk about that night Connor stayed over yet. I'm dying here, girl. I need the details. What happened?"

"First of all, he didn't *stay over*. And second of all, nothing happened." Not exactly anyway. She glanced at her obstinate sister, knowing she couldn't get away with downplaying.

Sure enough, Kate's expression demanded more.

"Fine. He was incredible, okay? Steadfast. Supportive. *So* good with Josiah." Every moment from that night and each day since rushed in on a wave of feelings that hadn't freed her to the surface yet. "You should've seen him. The way he cared for us. It was…"

"The way it should be."

The way she wished it could be, maybe. "I don't know—"

"Well, I do." Kate leaned against the wall. "He got you reading again." She shrugged when Ainsley slanted a brow at her. "I've seen you curled up on your bed with your *Anne* books, and I'm sorry, but it's sweet."

"The fact that you're stalking me in my room?"

Kate shoved her. "The fact that he's bringing joy back into your life. I haven't seen you this *alive* in a long time."

Ainsley could deny it, but what was the point? "It's ironic, though, isn't it? The country girl's supposed to teach the city boy how to appreciate the little things. Not the other way around."

"Daddy always said God has a sense of humor."

"So now our relationship isn't only sweet, it's a divine intervention?" Mama must've been rubbing off on her.

With one foot lifted to her opposite leg, Kate wound a curl around her finger. "To get through to a girl as stubborn as you? I wouldn't be surprised."

Ainsley knocked her off balance.

"Hey, I'm just being real."

A little *too* real. Just like Daddy always was.

Memories swelled to mind without warning, the ache of missing him close behind. She'd never understand how humor and hurt could coexist in the same broken world.

She plucked the hair band against her wrist. "Yeah, well, I'm being real too. And the reality is, Connor's not staying."

"There's still time."

"To what?" Ainsley looked up. "Convince him to leave a job he loves, uproot his whole life, and take up farming instead? C'mon, you know I can't ask him to be someone he's not." Ainsley pulled the elastic to her fingers and gathered her hair behind her neck. "I've been down that road once already, remember?"

Kate turned Ainsley toward her. "You mean, the same way we've had this exact conversation already? Connor's not Jonathan."

"It doesn't matter."

"Of course it does. How can you say that?"

"Because." She whirled around. "Jonathan and I were friends since we were kids. We dated since high school. No one knew me better." Her arms drifted to her sides, the hairband to the floor. "I gave him every part of me. *Every* part. No blinders. He saw everything. All that I am. It was his, and it wasn't enough to keep him here. He left, Kate." A deeply embedded hurt wrapped around her lungs. So invasive, it hurt to breathe, to remember. "He left me."

Kate pulled her close. And for an unguarded moment, Ainsley simply let herself be held.

"If someone who's known me all his life could leave, how can I expect someone who's only known me a month to stay?"

"Ains…" Kate stroked her head. "This isn't about you being the wrong girl. It's about Jonathan being the wrong guy." She leaned back, swept Ainsley's hair off each shoulder, and tilted her head at her. "Listen, I think there's something special between you and Connor. I have from the beginning. Honestly? I think he's the right one for you. But regardless of what does or doesn't happen with him—or with anyone else for that matter—you already have the *best* guy in your life who knows your true worth." With a sheen in her eyes, she straightened the baby feet charm around Ainsley's neck. "And he's not going anywhere."

Ainsley clutched her necklace, her tears impossible to restrain.

"You're loved, Ains. *So*, so loved."

"I know," she barely managed.

Kate slid her hand down to Ainsley's and looked her square in the eyes the way only a sister could. "Then don't be afraid to start living like it."

A full-blown blubbering mess now, Ainsley tugged Kate to her. "I love you. You know that? I wouldn't make it through any of this without you."

"As long as you love me for more than my hair, we'll call it even."

Ainsley snorted.

"I'm serious." A teasing grin chased runaway emotions into her curls. "Don't be jealous of these beauties."

Ainsley shook her head at her, overwhelmingly grateful for all that made up her amazing sister—corny distraction tactics and all. "As long as you're not jealous of my boobs, you have a deal."

Kate gasped and swatted her in the shoulder. "No, you didn't."

"Had to."

Kate folded her arms over a chest she'd inherited from the smaller side of the family. "So wrong."

Ainsley laughed. "Just be glad yours aren't assaulting you in the middle of the night."

"How does that even happen?"

"Don't ask." She still hadn't figured that one out. "But you should be thankful that—"

"Enough about my boobs already." Kate turned her toward the mirror. "You have a date to go on, *remember*? Now, hair stays down." She wielded the brush at her like it was an ominous threat.

"Yes, ma'am."

"And you better kiss him if he makes a move."

Ainsley stared at the ceiling and chewed on the edge of her thumb nail.

"Ains."

"What?"

Kate gasped again, this time with all the subtlety of an eighth grader. She even tented her hands over her mouth. "You already kissed him, didn't you? Spill it. Right now. All of it."

If she sat cross-legged and grabbed a giant bowl of popcorn next, Ainsley wouldn't have been surprised. She cracked up. "Do you see yourself right now?"

"Do you know the last time I've been kissed? C'mon. Don't hold out on me."

Ainsley hoped she didn't look as starry-eyed as Kate did. But the minute she thought back to the kiss, she sank headfirst into the feelings that hadn't stopped turning her stomach inside out since she and Connor were by the fence that day. "It was tender and heart-racing and perfect. Everything I was scared it would be. He has this way about him. This tenderness. I can't help getting caught up in the way he looks at me, in the things he says." Even more in the things he didn't have to say.

"I feel valued with him. Like he *sees* me, you know? Like *really* sees." Which scared her beyond belief. "I don't know. Maybe it's naïve to feel like I can be so real with him already, but I do. And with all those feelings leading into a kiss, it was... magical."

She rolled her eyes at herself the second the word left her mouth. "Wow, I can't believe I just said that."

"Why?"

"Why?" She glared at her sister. "Because I sound like a giddy teenager playing her first round of spin the bottle. That's why." She craned her neck back. "I really do, don't I? Like a smitten thirteen-year-old writing some kind of gooey fan fiction." Her hands fell from her face. "Oh my stars. It's finally happened. All those books I've read, all those love stories I've daydreamed about... I've officially deluded myself into believing *I'm* one of those heroines."

"All right, A, there's nothing wrong with being giddy *or* gooey. And B... okay, delusional might be debatable." She backed up from an incoming swat to the arm. "But C," she quickly added. "You don't sound like a kid, Ains." Her smile sobered. "You sound like a woman who's falling for a man she never expected to."

Ainsley cut a glance her way without straightening her neck. She wasn't ready for the L word. She'd reminded her heart of that a million times over the last month. Even now, she could halfway talk herself out of believing it. But when she was with Connor—when his eyes spoke before any words, and hope reached places she hadn't known needed to be healed—her heart couldn't hear anything but the tender whisper inviting her yet again into the vulnerable, messy, beautiful risk of falling in love.

She smiled through even more tears. "You're right. I'm falling head over heels for my fake boyfriend." She laughed at the irony. "He's still all wrong for me. Still can't walk in cowboy boots to save his life. Still says coffee like he was born in Brooklyn. Don't get me started on how much the guy drives me up the wall with his stinkin' perfect dimples."

She shook her head. "I mean, really, thinking *any* of this would actually work is flat-out crazy talk. And yet, I still want him *exactly* as he is—here, with me. I want to relive that kiss every day." She bit her lip and turned. "I want to be with him, Kate. He's kind and courageous and bull-headedly hard-nosed." She laughed. "And—"

"Presumptuous?"

One word. One voice. One heart drop.

Ainsley spun toward the bathroom doorway and sucked in a breath. "Connor."

Chapter Twenty

Ainsley snuck a sideways glance at Connor walking alongside her behind the house. His even-keeled expression didn't show the slightest hint of how much he'd overheard of her and Kate's conversation back in the bathroom. She wasn't about to ask. She'd play it cool. Divert, sidetrack, do karaoke if she had to—anything to avoid putting him in the insanely uncomfortable position of admitting he'd heard her say she wanted to relive their kiss every day.

Something snagged the tip of her boot. She stumbled forward, thanking the heavens she chose not to wear a dress for their date this time.

Connor caught her arm. "You all right?"

"Mm-hmm," she squeaked. "Fine." She tugged on the ends of her sleeves like she could yank that telltale inflection out of her voice. With no chance of that happening, she had only one option. *Move. Just keep moving.*

Connor's longer strides easily caught up to hers and directed her toward the barn.

Stopped in front of the doors, Ainsley studied the sky to avoid looking at him and making the awkward silence even worse. But when he still didn't say anything, she broke.

"So, a minute ago... in the house... how much did you overhear exactly?"

There went her resolve not to ask. Honestly, what kind of sadist was she?

Connor's smile answered before he did. As usual. Meanwhile, she continued to stand there like a mortified Gumby doll. As usual.

"I walked up when you were saying..." He scratched the back of his head. "Bullheadedly hard-nosed, I believe was the phrase. I assumed you had to be referring to me."

A mix of relief and chagrin trickled out of her. "Not saying you are or anything, but if the boot fits..." *If the boot fits*? What *in creation*? She turned, cringed. *Shoot me now. Someone. Anyone.*

Connor laughed. "I guess you'll have to tell me if it does. I'll be right back. Hang on."

To what? Dignity was clearly a lost cause. Sanity had drifted to the fringes some time ago. She'd have better luck holding on to a bronc's saddle horn than to anything halfway resembling composure. She needed to get her conversation with Kate out of her head.

Watching Connor strut through the barn doors did the trick. Between a belt buckle the size of Texas and actual spurs on his boots, he'd be lucky if he made it two more steps without teetering over. He spaced his feet apart and tipped his hat at her. "Ma'am."

She should've known he'd find a way to put her at ease. "Look at you, cowboy."

"Told ya you had nothing to worry about." He winked. "Some things are meant to be."

There was that phrase again.

Ainsley ignored the prick in her chest those words always brought on and crossed her arms. "Looking the part is only half the battle."

"Don't you worry, darlin'. Acting's my middle name." Connor stuck a piece of straw between his teeth and strutted back and forth like a chicken on steroids.

She flung a hand over her mouth. But when he grabbed his giant belt buckle and adjusted his jeans like he had a pistol weighing down one side, she literally had to bite her skin to keep from dying. "Better be careful swaggering around like that, or Spock won't be able to keep his hooves off you."

"You sure he's the only one?"

She rolled her eyes. "Positive." Or she *was* anyway, before his strides kept bringing him closer. Flush with the barn door, she had nowhere to go, nowhere to look but at the eyes draining every certainty she had into a mud puddle at her feet.

He flexed a palm against the wood. "I've been known to be fairly convincing."

Then maybe he could convince her lungs to work again.

"I don't know, Lone Star," she teased. "You might've met your match on this one."

Head down, he wrestled a grin. "No doubt about that." When he looked up again, something had shifted in his eyes. "You know I'm just messing around with all this cowboy stuff, right? You seem like something's on your mind. If tomorrow has you concerned, don't worry." He lifted three fingers to salute his scout's honor. "I promise it's going to be okay. No howdys. No *straw*." He flicked the piece he'd been toying with to the ground. "No trying to give Billy the Wannabe Goat a spinal adjustment."

Ainsley's worry tumbled out in a laugh.

"I'll play as convincing a true country boy as I can."

"And a boyfriend?"

Whatever possessed those whispered words to escape her mouth kept her eyes glued to her feet until Connor raised her chin.

"I don't think you have to worry about anyone doubting that part."

Even her?

"Hey." He brushed back the hair sweeping across her cheek. "You sure you're all right?"

She blinked away from his genuine concern and somehow convinced her noodle arm to bend. "Yeah, fine. It's just... this hair," she rattled off. "I'm not used to having it down. Josiah's forever grabbing it. Never mind the spit-up. So, it goes straight in a ponytail now without me even thinking about it." Which was definitely true. "I guess it's kind of throwing me off. That's all. Sorry. It's nothing." Which wasn't exactly—*anywhere*—near being true.

Ainsley ducked under his arm and motioned to the barn. "Did you, um... Did you need to run inside to grab anything else before we leave?"

"Only the horses."

"Horses?"

"Daphne's loaning me Phoenix for the evening." He laughed when Ainsley stared at him. "I know. I was shocked too. Guess that girl voice earned me more merit with her than I thought."

"It *was* rather impressive." She scratched the skin under her nose. "Almost as much as your cowboy strut."

He countered her grin, grabbed her hand, and led her inside the barn. "Wait 'til you see me ride."

"Oh, believe me. I'm counting down the seconds."

Even the shade from the trusses couldn't dim his charm. "Well, wait no more, my lady."

Two horses already tacked up and ready to ride stood before them.

"Wow, you really are impressive, aren't you?"

"Told you I might surprise you."

When Connor mounted Phoenix with unexpected skill, Ainsley couldn't help wondering how many more ways he could prove that statement true.

Thankfully, the beauty of her property stole her focus not long into their ride. She breathed in the scent of autumn. Sometimes, the wind was the only thing capable of reminding her that the great vistas surrounding them were more than vivid paintings.

"It really is something."

Ainsley turned toward a look of enamor wrapped around intuition. He was getting to be as good as Kate was at reading her thoughts.

"We've lived in the city so long," he continued. "I almost forgot what it was like to live in a place this peaceful."

"I didn't know you lived anywhere else."

"When I was a kid, yeah. Upstate New York. We didn't have anywhere near the acreage you've got here, but I remember the open space, the fields Reed and I used to play in." A look of nostalgia colored his eyes. "Even fishing down by the creek."

"Fishing. Wow."

He laughed. "Like I said, it was a *long* time ago."

"Still, sounds like it stayed with you."

A slow blink brought his eyes to hers again. "Places like this have a way of doing that."

They weren't the only thing. Ainsley tightened her grip on Shiloh's reins. "Upstate New York's similar to here then?"

"It is, actually. Away from all the light pollution and constant noise, you can hear yourself breathe, you know? Hear your own heartbeat for a change."

Ainsley looked around the massive pine trees she'd grown up with all her life—trees that had seen her in every stage, listened to every question, heard every cry. "Hearing your own heart isn't always as peaceful as it sounds."

Her mind raced for a way to skate past that unintentional confession. She didn't want her past to dampen the moment. Their date was supposed to be fun.

"But what you really have to worry about," she blathered off, "is if you start hearing the trees whisper back. *Then* you know you've got serious problems."

He didn't return her laugh, didn't even so much as blink. A look of sheer panic kept every muscle frozen in place.

"Connor?"

"Don't move."

Okay, now *she* was starting to panic. Tingles rushed up her body as he inched Phoenix toward her.

"Easy," he whispered. Whether to her or the horse, she wasn't sure. Either way, easy was about to be thrown off the table if he didn't hurry up and tell her what the heck was going on.

"Connor, you're starting to freak me—"

He grabbed hold of Shiloh's reins. Thrown off balance, her horse neighed and lifted on his hind legs to regain control.

Ainsley didn't have time to grab anything to keep herself from falling. Her back landed on a pile of fallen pine needles, dead oak leaves, and random clumps of hay that had ended up out here from who knew where. She didn't want to think about it. Especially when the cold, moist earth bled through the back of her shirt onto her skin. Oh, he was going to pay for this.

"Stay still."

A hundred and eighty pounds of solid muscle, adrenaline, and apparent chivalry pounced over her like a shield. From what, was anyone's guess. An incoming missile strike? A loose grenade?

When no imminent disaster struck, Ainsley lifted a hand to his chest. "Is it safe now?"

His head, tucked beside hers, hovered close enough for her to feel his eyelashes brush her cheek. With his face now directly above hers, it took less than ten seconds for his entire demeanor to change. "Sorry," he said through a lingering smile that said otherwise. "There was a snake."

"A snake."

"A huge one. Looked like a rattle snake. It was right there—" Connor whisked her away from the leaf pile in a full-on roll like her clothes were on fire. Hunched above her again, he shot another panicked glance at a giant rock beside the leaves. "Did you see it?"

"Considering your heaving chest keeps blocking my view of anything else, I'd say not likely."

His eyes swept back to hers. A slow grin crept up his cheek in response to the one she couldn't bring herself to shake. His fingers grazed her forehead as he drew a crumpled leaf from her hair. "Sorry," he offered again. And this time, she hoped he truly wasn't.

He had to feel her heartbeat thundering against her rib cage. Even if he couldn't, her eyes no doubt told him all he needed to know.

"It was probably a milk snake. They look strikingly similar to rattlers," she blabbered as if it were the most appropriate moment to insert that random tidbit of information. Sweet mercy, she sounded like Hairpiece Hank.

Connor didn't seem to notice. "And milk snakes are safe?"

Safer than having him this close to her right now was. She swallowed. "Mm-hmm."

"Well, then." Connor pushed off the ground into a sitting position. "Guess that means I'm not nearly as smooth as the noble worm saver."

Ainsley shook her head as she pulled herself up by her knees. "Speaking of creepy crawlers, you have a little something…"

He didn't give her the chance to finish reaching for his neck. He propelled to his feet and hopped around like a river dancer with fleas.

A meow brought Sox into view out of nowhere. Truth be told, Ainsley couldn't blame the cat for being drawn to the show. Connor was squirming more than Josiah trying to get out of being dressed.

"I was just kidding, Connor. There's no bug."

"No, something's definitely crawling on me." He hitched his arm over his shoulder to his back. "It feels like a—"

"Mouse!" Ainsley scrambled backward in the fastest crab walk ever. Snakes were one thing, but mice… She shuddered.

The little rodent froze on top of his shoulder long enough for Connor's eyes to grow wider than a bale of hay.

"Ainsley," he said through gritted calmness. "Do something."

Like what? She pushed up to her feet and shuffled in a circle. By the time she faced him again, his river dance jive had kicked back into full swing.

"Ainsley," he called louder this time.

Not knowing what else to do, she scooped Sox off the ground and launched her at him. An offended meow soared through the air in what felt like slow motion until her claws were hanging in the front of Connor's shirt.

A deadpan stare landed on Ainsley. "Really?"

"Sorry." She bit her lip. "Reflex."

Evidently, she wasn't the only one with them. The cat must've spotted the field mouse. She scurried up Connor's stomach, across his shoulder blades, and down his pant leg to the grass.

Ainsley lifted both shoulders when Sox finished chasing the mouse into the pile of leaves. "At least it worked, right?"

Oh, that look couldn't be good.

One intentional step bounding for her led to another.

"Connor." She backed up, trying not to laugh again. "Don't you dare—"

He had her up in the air and over his shoulder before she could finish her baseless threat. The world spun, her heart most of all. Even when he finally returned her feet to the ground, her pulse didn't slow.

She slid a patch of fur out of his messy, post-animal-dance hair that had succeeded in making him even sexier than usual. "They didn't scratch you, did they?"

"As long as neither has rabies, I think I'm good."

She picked the fur apart a piece at a time. "If they did, I happen to know a vet on the premises. I'm sure he'd know *exactly* what to do."

244 | CRYSTAL WALTON

Connor rubbed a finger under his bottom lip. "He sounds mighty presumptuous to me."

"One of his most endearing qualities."

"Really?"

"Of course, I'd never tell *him* that." She made an inflated head gesture and whispered, "You know how those doctor types are."

He laughed. "Especially chiropractors."

"They're the worst."

"Mm." The look in his eyes deepened. "I guess that's why those types need someone to keep them grounded."

"Not even love can do that."

Ainsley immediately regretted the automatic remark. Regretted the way the jaded scars left in Jonathan's stead flared up every time she thought she'd put them behind her.

She fluttered a glance away from Connor but couldn't wave off the reaction his words had stirred. *Those types.* Not the haughty ones. The ones whose spontaneity and hunger lured them past borders too small to contain them. She wouldn't try to cage another one in again. As much as Jonathan's abandonment stung, remorse for pushing him to stay never lagged far behind.

Her lashes fanned Connor's way. One connection with those green eyes told her this was no longer about Jonathan. It was about him. His dreams, passions. She wanted him to be happy doing what he loved, where he loved it, no matter where that took him. That need to wander was what drove him away from his home to begin with. He'd said it himself when she met him.

Yes, something had changed since that first day. She'd sensed it in his eyes, heard it in his voice. But asking him to sacrifice what made him who he was at the core wouldn't be fair to either of them.

Down to only five strands left of the fur patch she'd been picking at, Ainsley rolled them between her fingertips and stared at the shriveled leaves by her feet. "I'm not sure it's right to try to ground someone who thrives on flying."

She didn't have to look up to know he'd heard what she hadn't spoken. He always heard.

Slow footsteps brought him near. "What if that someone never felt more like he was soaring than when he was standing right in front of you?"

Ainsley's pulse rocketed at his words.

His fingers found hers. He didn't say more at first. Didn't need to. She felt everything in his touch. So much so, she couldn't voice a single word in return. Her throat turned drier than hay chaff.

"'Cause if I were that person, I'd—"

"Connor?" Aunt Penny jogged toward them on the tail of Mr. Tumnus jumping in a sporadic pattern ahead of her.

The goat slid to a stop at the sight of Connor, froze, and tipped onto the ground.

"Aw, it's okay, baby." Aunt Penny knelt beside him. "It's just Connor and Ainsley. Nothing to be scared of." She rubbed his side. "Shake it off. There we go."

Mr. Tumnus stirred to his feet a few seconds later but continued to hesitate in front of them like he wasn't sure what move to make next.

Connor's brow pinched. "Sorry, Penny. I thought I did everything right to reinforce their pen. I'll check it again when we get back. See what went wrong."

"Oh, no, hon'. Their pen's fine. We were in the field for class." She cradled Mr. Tumnus close. "This little booger took off out of nowhere, running catawampus across the pastures like someone'd lit a fire to his cute furry backside." She ruffled the top of the goat's rear. "I don't know what's gotten into him."

When Connor nodded like he had the slightest clue what catawampus meant, Ainsley had to shield her grin with her hair.

The corner of his mouth hitched, because of course he'd noticed her reaction. He lifted a feisty brow her way, turned, then cautiously inched toward Mr. Tumnus. The goat didn't faint this time, but he did cry. At first.

Little by little, Connor stretched out a hand for him to smell. "There we go. Nice and easy. See? I'm not so bad."

Ainsley pressed her lips together when he almost didn't stop himself from automatically assessing Mr. Tumnus' spinal alignment. He rubbed the side of the goat's neck instead, and the little guy surprisingly looked relaxed.

At least one of the four of them was.

Ainsley was going to need an adjustment herself if Aunt Penny kept looking at her and Connor like they were standing on a Jane Austen film set.

She saw it on Penny's face the minute she'd walked up. The joy. The expectancy. She'd always wanted Ainsley to find happiness.

Guilt tanked hard and fast in her stomach. The thought of playing out their breakup plan in front of her family this weekend sank in. How could she hurt them? Herself? Josiah, most of all?

Unless they didn't have to stage a breakup. Unless they didn't have to act at all. A moment ago, it'd felt like Connor wanted it all to be as real as much as she did.

She let go of the necklace she'd brought to her chin. It fell to her chest, clanging against the hope beating from the opposite side. Could she truly, unrestrainedly give her heart away again?

Aunt Penny scooped Mr. Tumnus up in her arms. "We should get back to class and leave you two to keep frolicking."

Frolicking?

Ainsley cringed. Unlike Aunt Penny, who gushed enough to nearly tear up. "The two of you together... You're just as sweet as a summertime pie. I could eat you up, the both of y'all."

Mr. Tumnus took advantage of the distraction to finagle a way out of her arms. Free, he catapulted from one imaginary springboard to the next on his way toward the pasture they'd come from.

Aunt Penny hustled backward and motioned to Connor. "If you want to tighten up those muscles before the wedding, you come on out to my yoga classes. Mr. Tumnus and I will whip you right into shape."

He choke-wheezed when he must've realized she was serious. No doubt, the word "wedding" had something to do with it.

"Think about it," she called with a boisterous wave goodbye.

Once the entertainment duo had trailed far enough out of view, Connor faced Ainsley. "Was it me, or did your aunt just insult me? Because I'm pretty sure my muscles shrank a size or two."

"What muscles?"

Connor ran his tongue along the corner of his mouth. "The whole family's got jokes, is that it?"

"Maybe. But I'll tell you what. Nothing could top you doing goat yoga." She tapped him in his definitely-not-deflated bicep. "I'd pay a pretty penny to see that go down."

"Luckily for you, you won't have to spend a dime. 'Cause that ain't never gonna happen, darlin'."

She tossed her head back at his nonsensically adorable attempt at pulling off a southern accent. "Oh, c'mon. What happened to no fears?"

"There are limits."

"Only fair since you've been pushing my diaphragm to its limit all day. I haven't laughed like this in a long while." Sobering, she set a hand over his sleeve. "Really, Connor. I can't remember the last time I've had this much fun." Not only over the last hour, but since she'd met him. She hadn't wanted to admit it at times. And they'd certainly had their fill of intense moments too. But the truth was, Kate was right. He'd helped her remember how to live in the present again.

The awareness of how much that meant swelled inside her. She stared at the bottom of her shirt twisted between her fingers. "Thanks for taking me out tonight."

"Who said the night was over?"

Definitely not his dimples. If those blasted things had a say in it, their date was only just beginning.

Chapter Twenty-One

Ainsley pulled up on the reins as they trotted into the tree-covered alcove she hadn't visited in three years. Connor had already dismounted Phoenix and tied him to the fence before Ainsley moved a muscle. The rope swing, the ivy-twined bench, even the rusted bucket of whittling tools were still here, exactly as she remembered.

She clutched the leather under her fingers. "How did you...?"

With what looked like relief, Connor stopped in front of them and petted Shiloh's nose. "The girl voice might've worked with Daphne, but I'll tell you what. Nothing was impressing your horses enough to get 'em to confirm if this was the right spot. But when I found it, I hoped it was the place you'd told me about."

"Found it?"

"I've been riding in the evenings. Getting some practice in and—I don't know—getting away, I guess." He cast a reverent glance around the childhood treasure she'd tucked away when she'd lost her father. "Your land, Ainsley. It really is something special. I always knew it was, but after coming out here..." An exhale finished a sentiment beyond explanation.

He reached up to her waist to help her off her horse. "I hope this is okay. After my last date mess-up, I know I probably shouldn't have sprung anything on you again, but I figured you'd be more comfortable here than in a stuffy restaurant." He winked. "No flash card studying necessary. And this way, you're nearby if Josiah needs you." He rubbed his thumb over a spot of mud she'd felt dry on her face earlier.

His touch made her want nothing more than to bring his hand to her lips. To show him how much his thoughtfulness meant to her.

A little overwhelmed, she backed away instead and cast a long look around the small corner of her property. Though vines now resided were Daddy had always sat, she could still see him on that old bench, as much a fixture of the land as the towering pines. Time and the elements had deteriorated his tools but not his memory. It was here. Alive. Palpable. Every scent, every sound—they wrapped around her with the strength and tenderness of her father's arms.

With her back toward Connor, Ainsley lowered her lashes and let the memories brim from inside her. "Thank you for knowing," she whispered.

"I only guessed it was the right place."

"No. Not for that. For knowing I needed to come back here." She turned, unafraid to let him see her tears, and rushed toward another embrace she didn't want to lose. "Thank you," she said again.

He didn't answer, simply held her close.

When it registered that she was probably cutting off the poor guy's circulation, she loosened her hold around his waist. "Sorry."

"For what?"

"For practically tackling you, for starters."

The amusement she expected to see dimmed far behind something much less readable as he kept his arms around her. "If it leads you here, I'll take a running start any day, Ainsley Grace."

The way he said her name melted her every time. But something about being here—in this place, this moment— amplified everything she'd been scared to let herself feel for him.

A nicker from behind reminded them that they hadn't tied up Shiloh yet. While Connor quickly attended to that, Ainsley noticed a picnic set up on the bed of the antique Chevy Daddy had refused to part with. The heap of metal should've been in a garage somewhere. Maybe even in a junkyard, to be honest. Yet somehow, the out-of-place truck, canopied by tree branches and bordered by over-grown grass, was exactly where it belonged.

"Don't worry," Connor said on his way back over. "It's all meatless and sugar-free."

She raised an unconvinced brow at him.

"Just 'cause I'm a bachelor doesn't mean I don't know how to cook." He ran a thumb along his scruffy jawline. "Or that I don't know how to order good takeout."

She looked from his wry expression to the picnic basket. "Yeah, still a little worried."

He laughed. "Don't be. It's all Ainsley approved." He led her toward their informal—and utterly perfect—dining arrangement. "I promise it's safe."

For the first time since she could remember, she believed it was. Not for her taste buds. For her heart. To open up again. To trust, risk. With her hand in his, she felt seen. She felt known. Even... loved.

"Connor, thank you for doing this. Really, it's all very romantic."

"More romantic than a graveyard full of buried hopes?"

The shocked stare she whipped at him turned into a giddy grin half a second later. "You read *Anne of Green Gables*?"

"I might've caught a few movie clips on YouTube."

And she might've been tempted to start gushing as much as Anne would've right then. As it was, she was already squeezing his arm like she had hold of a teddy bear. She let go when it finally dawned on her that the series wasn't exactly guy material.

"You didn't have to do that, you know."

He shrugged. "I liked it."

"No, you didn't." She shoved him in the bicep. "I know it's more of a girl thing. And admittedly, Anne can come off a little over the top at times."

His grin didn't deny it. Yet instead of dishing out a comeback, Connor admired the trees surrounding them. "You know, I've never been to Prince Edward Island, but I bet Whispering Pines could give a Canadian fall a run for its money."

Pride in Ainsley's hometown warmed her chest. "It does hold a bit of romance to it, doesn't it?" Though halfway teasing, she truly believed that. The countryside that had taught her to hope for love was indeed romantic. Everything about this moment was—the way Connor was looking at her right now, most of all.

Before she could stop herself, she ran her fingertips through the hair between his ear and his cowboy hat. "I have to say, the country's starting to look good on you."

Feigned shock widened his eyes. "Why, Ainsley Grace, did you just admit I could fit in here?"

More that he belonged there. With her.

"I guess we'll find out this weekend." She hopped up on the Chevy's tailgate and twisted the fringes of the blanket he'd spread out over the truck bed.

"Piece of cake." He joined her a beat later and stretched back with his hands behind his head.

Ainsley followed suit, just as comfortable. She didn't doubt he was right about the weekend. Out here, anything was easy to believe.

The leafless branches swaying overhead opened up glimpses of the massive sky. She was accustomed to admiring views stretching to the horizon. But here... here she was used to the shelter that had made everything important to her feel close and protected. Maybe because she'd spent the most time here during the summer when the trees flourished as much as dreams did. Or maybe because she'd never been here without her dad until now. Whatever the reason, the unanticipated feel of the sunlight made her realize how much had changed. What surprised her more was how little that change ached now.

"I can see why this is your favorite spot," Connor said slowly. "There's a real peace about it. Beauty too." A deep breath added to the esteem in his voice. "Not many people could resist falling in love out here."

Heat tingled up Ainsley's body at his words. "Can you?"

He angled toward her, but she couldn't bring herself to do the same yet. She sat up, scooted to the edge of the tailgate, and curled her fingers around the cool steel.

The autumn breeze stirred furled leaves scattered on the ground. She knew how easy it would be to keep her focus on all that had withered and died. She'd done it for years, afraid to face the barren branches of how things used to be. But she knew better now. Though still not easy, she understood. Unless she fixed her eyes overhead, she'd miss all that was waiting above fallen expectations.

She peered toward the sky. Sunshine warmed over her, and the peace Connor spoke of met her right there on a broken-down truck surrounded by broken leaves she was finally ready to let go of. Life had a way of doing that—uncovering an unexpected view once she was willing to surrender the way she thought it should look.

Connor eased alongside her but didn't speak. She loved that about him. The way he rendered words unnecessary when he settled next to her. She could sense his consideration. At times, it stole her own words too.

Ainsley slid off the tailgate and wandered to her old, childhood rope swing. She ran her fingers along the frayed threads. "Could you really see yourself living in a place like this? Away from all the lights and hype?" She turned to the huge Cypress tree the swing hung from. "After the romance of the mountains fade, and everyday life anchors you to a small-town home…" Her hand trailed down the trunk to her side. "Would you still stay?"

Leaves rustled behind her in place of a response.

With one more inhale, she urged herself to turn. "Earlier, you said you can hear your heartbeat out here." Surely, he had to hear hers too. The sputtering, the hope. She balled her shirt cuffs under her fingers and clung to courage, no matter how small. "What's your heart telling you right now?"

Wordless, resolute strides continued toward her. His Adam's apple bobbed. His chest moved up and down. Through every motion bringing him closer, his eyes never once strayed from hers. Even from a foot away, Ainsley could sense his touch. The anticipation backed her against the Cypress. Each footstep, each breath took too long.

Still without looking away, Connor pressed one hand against the bark beside her and lifted the other to her neck. "I'd stay," he finally said. "But not because I've fallen in love with Whispering Pines."

Ainsley's marginal grasp on the tree was the only thing keeping her standing.

A stark ring from a pouch on Phoenix's saddle soared up into the trees and crashed back over the moment, but Connor didn't move an inch.

She looked from the horses to him. "You're not going to get that?"

"Wasn't planning on it."

"It could be important."

He brushed his thumb across her cheek. "Not more than you."

His words settled into crevices of her heart that'd once been pried open by rejection. "You don't have to say that because of what I told you about Jonathan."

"I'm not." His fingers stretched into her hair. "I'm saying it because—"

No sooner did his phone stop ringing than it started back up.

Connor hung his head, and Ainsley bit back a smile at his frustrated expression.

"At least go check who it is. I'm not going anywhere."

"Promise?"

She looked at him with the same assurance he always offered her. "Promise."

A resigned exhale backed him up and led him over to the horses and the persistent ringing.

Ainsley moseyed to the picnic basket in search of a drink. She did a double take at what looked like the corner of a book buried under the rest of the basket's contents. After a quick glance to confirm Connor was still tending to his phone, she slipped the book out far enough to read the title. One glimpse at the top was all it took. She peeked back at the man who kept surprising her and traced her fingers down the cover. "He *has* read it," she whispered to herself.

Footsteps announced his return. Ainsley tucked the copy of *Anne of Green Gables* back inside the basket and pulled out a thermos instead. "All good?"

"Yep."

The clipped word begged to differ.

"Who was it?"

"Someone who can wait." Connor gestured to the thermos. "Irish cream. No sugar." He fished through the basket. "I *did*, however, pack my own stash."

She laughed. "Of course you did. Tell me you didn't cram the entire bag of sugar in there. 'Cause if you did, that's just—"

Two seconds. It couldn't have been longer. Adrenaline whooshed to her ears and sent her hands flapping the spider or centipede or whatever creepy crawler had chosen this moment—of all times—to decide her hair looked like a place to make a home in. She screeched as she flailed. "Get it off. Get it off."

"Whoa." He reached for her. "Get what off?"

"I don't know." She shook out her shirt another dozen times. "But whatever it was, it had legs, and it was fast, and I'm pretty sure it needs to die."

Connor scratched behind his ear. "You're afraid of a bug?"

"It was *in my hair!*"

"Right. Sorry," he said with too much amusement to be true. "It's just… You grew up *on a farm*," he said as though the short statement needed no further justification.

Ainsley tried not to acknowledge his logic. She slumped against the tree trunk, laced her arms, and tilted her chin at him. "There are limits."

Grinning, he hung his head again. "And you have no idea how much you're testing mine."

"I didn't think your patience had any limits."

Slow and way too alluring for such a simple movement, Connor raised his eyes to hers again. "I wasn't talking about patience." He edged toward her until they were in the same position they'd been in moments ago with his hand pressed against the tree, her heart beating through it. "I was talking about the self-restraint it's taking me to resist kissing you right now."

Blood surged to her cheeks without relent. But as she stood there with him, a boldness took hold. Whether she'd found her own courage or was still borrowing it from Kate didn't matter. The yearning to take a risk kept her from shrinking away this time.

"You know, it probably wouldn't be the worst idea if we practiced a bit more. In case someone puts us on the spot this weekend," she added with a barely straight face.

"Mm." Connor matched her pretend seriousness. "You think that's wise, do you?"

"I do."

"For your family's sake."

"Exactly."

"In that case..." He inched even closer. "We should probably practice *a lot*."

Forever sounded pretty good to her.

Overhead branches swayed in the breeze. Without needing to look around, Ainsley could picture the fireflies beginning their dance with dusk just as she remembered. But instead of clinging to memory's grip of the past, she clung to the arms of the man she longed to build a future with.

Connor's gaze made a gradual trail to her mouth, and Ainsley would've sworn he was already kissing her. He brushed back the hair every bit as tameless as the hope mounting inside her. His lips brushed hers. Soft, earnest. The tenderness of their first kiss melded into a reciprocated urgency. She wanted this. Wanted them together. No ruses or looming timetables or hesitancy. She wanted him to know—*needed* him to know—this was real. She lifted a thumb to the edge of his mouth. "Connor…"

Raspy breaths met hers. "I know."

She leaned back to search his face.

"Ainsley, these past few weeks…"

"I know." She brought her hand to his unshaven cheek. Somewhere in the process of trying to write off the man she assumed him to be, she'd fallen in love with the man who'd fulfilled his promise to surprise her.

He wove his fingers together at the base of her back. "You know, we don't *have* to go through with our breakup plan this weekend. Since I'm fairly certain we've already broken whatever rules we never actually established, we might as well rewrite the script altogether." He leaned in. "Bring that unavoidable truth into fiction. Make it real."

Real. She melted into him and into the happy ending she'd never thought could be hers.

His relentless cell blared again. This time, right between them—literally.

Connor's chin drooped as he hustled to yank the no-good phone from his pocket. He silenced the call but couldn't mask the turmoil his face now held.

"Who is it?"

He stepped back without answering her.

"Connor?" Ainsley pushed off the tree. "Who keeps calling?"

With his eyes on the phone, he kept his head down. "It's my dad."

Chapter Twenty-Two

Connor turned away from the windowsill in his loft. Staring at the chickens roaming the grass wasn't making time pass any quicker... or decisions come any easier.

He plopped down on his bed and picked up the open takeout container of pasta he hadn't gotten to share with Ainsley as planned. As much as he appreciated her thoughtfulness in wanting to give him the time and space he needed to speak with his dad, he might've loved her more for knowing how much a plate of Alfredo could soothe the soul.

At least, it would've soothed if his ignored cell sitting on the bedside stand weren't turning the pasta in his stomach into a rock. Pop had called two more times since interrupting another kiss Connor hadn't been able to get off his mind.

He'd almost told Ainsley exactly how hard he'd fallen for her. That he wanted to stay—for good. He didn't know how it'd work out, or if he could be all she and Josiah needed the man in their life to be. But he knew beyond anything else, she made him want to try.

The last of an amazing day's sunlight descended behind the roof across from his window. Shadows crept into the loft and clouded the peace that had felt unbreakable when he'd been with Ainsley earlier.

He snapped on the lamp. Of all the room's endless nooks and crannies the light could've chased, it seemed overly zealous to zero in on his phone. Figured.

He lunged off the mattress like he'd downed the entire thermos of coffee and paced to the window again. He gripped the trim and the words anchoring him.

"*Whatever your dad has to say, I'm confident it's rooted in love.*"

Connor wasn't as convinced, but something in him ached to believe her.

Casting reservation aside, he marched toward the nightstand and grabbed his cell before he changed his mind. No voice mails. He wasn't surprised. Leaving things that needed to be said directly to someone over a recording wasn't Pop's style. To be honest, calling several times in a row wasn't either. It could be that something had happened. That something was wrong.

He scrolled for Pop's number. A tingle of worry spread to his chest when the unanswered rings stretched longer than they should've. He was about to hang up and try again when another call beeped in.

"Yeah, Flynn, what's up?"

"What's *up?*" His buddy scoffed. "You better tell me you're in a hospital right now. Because if you try pushing any other excuse for blowing off all my calls, I'm gonna put you in there myself. Seriously, Allen. I know you wanted to go off the grid and all, but I didn't think that meant from me. I thought we had a plan."

"We did, but then Ainsley and I…" How could he explain everything that had changed since then?

"Aw, bro. Tell me you didn't fall for that girl for real?"

Though Connor hadn't filled Flynn in on every detail of his and Ainsley's relationship, his silence must've served as confirmation, because Flynn heaved a sigh. "What's up with you lately? I get the appeal of a cute farm girl, but are you really willing to give up everything your pop's done for you for—"

"She's more than that. And what's going on with *you*? Since when did you become Team Maxwell?" He'd never been a huge fan of Connor's father. Of the money, yes. The prestige, maybe. But not of the way Pop lorded the business over him.

When Flynn hesitated, Connor wished they were video chatting so he could read his face. "What is it?"

"Nothing. I just think you should consider going home. That's all."

Okay, something was definitely off. "He called you, didn't he?"

"Can you blame him?"

Yeah, he could. Unbelievable. "What'd he do? Offer you a bounty?"

"That hurts, bro."

Connor wasn't up for laughing.

"Look, I know it's not my place to get in the middle of it, but he's your old man."

"Then he should start acting like it."

"Allen—"

"I gotta go." Connor looked out to the empty spot where Ainsley usually parked. "Next time you have a one-on-one with my dad, do me a solid and tell him to back off."

"I feel you, man. You know I do. But if you're not gonna talk to him, at least meet up with me tonight."

"Meet up with you? You're here in Whispering Pines?"

"What'd you expect me to do? You won't take my calls. We're down to the wire on lining up your next gig. You're leaving me high and dry here. If you want me to manage this trip for you, you can't keep shutting me out."

Connor's free hand slid off the trim down to his side. Flynn was right. He *had* been shutting him out. But Ainsley needed him here, fully present and focused for Thanksgiving. "I'm sorry, man. I can't tonight. Can we hook up after the weekend?" He owed him that much.

A heavy pause filled the line.

"Flynn?"

"I'll stay if you need me to, but I gotta be honest, Allen. You're running out of time."

He looked at the farmhouse, never feeling the weight of those words more. "I know."

The turmoil compressed deeper once he hung up and scrolled to his dad's number again. His thumb hovered above the screen. Something about Flynn's call ate at him—something that would only worsen if he didn't get a hold of Pop and clear the air.

It took less than three rings this time for the voice he'd been avoiding to soar through the line. "Connor?"

He swallowed. "Yeah, hey, Pop. It's me. Sorry I missed your calls earlier."

"Are you?"

And *there* was the man he knew and feared. Cut to the chase. That was the Allen way.

"Not really, if you want me to be honest."

"Did I raise you to be anything else?"

Noise in the background indicated he was still at the office. No surprise there either.

At the sound of a door shutting, Connor could picture himself sweating in the overstuffed chair opposite his father's equally oversized desk.

"I'm really starting to wonder here, Connor. I thought I'd raised you to be a better man than this."

A slow burn built in his veins. "A better man than what exactly? One who makes my own decisions? Who has my own aspirations?"

"Aspirations?" Frustration drenched the word. "Leaving a secure future I built for you to go play farm boy in some rural practice? That's what your life goals have amounted to?" His voice shook. "I will not stand by and watch both my sons throw away everything I've done to—"

"Build your own kingdom." Connor's fingers dug into his palm. "Don't you get that? A life measured in high-rise condos and an all-consuming practice... That's *your* dream."

"And when did it stop being yours?"

"I don't know!" All gumption deflated out of him. "I honestly don't know." He raked his fingers through his hair and caved onto the sill again. "I used to think I wanted to follow in your footsteps, but something changed this last year, Pop. I felt like I was starting to suffocate. Like something was missing, I guess. And I thought if I had some distance... If I did something on my own, I'd be able to figure out what I was supposed to do."

"Taking up the mantle here is what you're supposed to do," he said, blowing right past the vulnerability in Connor's voice. "You're a sought-after chiropractor, Connor. I've made sure of that. The board's meeting on Monday, and I fully expect you to be present. I've covered long enough for this adolescent field trip of yours." The creak of his desk chair retracting forward added a rigid exclamation point. "It's time for you to come home."

Connor's neck tendons clenched. They weren't talking about some mid-life crisis or fraternity joy ride to sow his wild oats. Maybe in some ways it had started out between those two. As an escape. A chance to breathe, to search. He hadn't known what he'd been looking for, but now... He peered at the only house that had ever felt like a home to him... Now, he didn't want to lose what he'd found.

"I think I already *am* home. I know that doesn't make sense to you. If I'm honest, I'm not even sure it makes sense to me, but I've found something here. Something real." For the first time in his life, he felt exactly where he was meant to be.

"Your life here isn't real?" A twinge of hurt tore at his father's words.

"That's not what I'm saying."

"Then you better start clarifying, because I'm losing my patience here."

Matching exhales poured across the line.

A call beeped in the background, but his dad only sounded more focused. "If you think for a moment, I built any of this just for myself… That I didn't work hard every day for you and Reed…"

"I know you did, Pop, and I admire you for that. We both do." He tapped the side of his fist against the window-pane, wishing he knew how to get through to him. "But we want you to be proud of us for doing the same. Even if our goals differ from yours."

"Security begets pride, son. You're only fooling yourself if you think otherwise."

Connor shook his head. "You're right. I don't know what ever possessed me to think you'd see it differently." Ainsley's faith in his father's love crumbled under the cinder blocks of pride Pop had spent his entire life cementing around him. So single-minded, he never even realized he'd erected a wall between them.

"I'm sorry, Pop. I really wish you could understand, but I can't come back. I—"

"Enough, Connor. I will not have both my sons abandon me when…" He wheezed a cough away from the phone. The man hadn't smoked a day in his life, but you never would have guessed it from the sound of his lungs.

Concern sprouted through him. "Pop? You okay?"

"Of course I'm not okay. I..."

For the briefest of moments, Connor almost thought he'd sensed vulnerability from a man who'd never once shown any in his presence.

Pop cleared his throat, all-business mode resurrected. "Now, you listen to me, son, and you listen good. Your little trip is over. As are whatever ties you think you've built there. I've already booked you a flight home, and I—"

"What?" He propelled off the sill. "I'm not some runaway teenager. I have a job here right now. People depending on me. A proposal to finish. You can't just—"

"It's done, Connor. Your plane leaves at 10:00 a.m. tomorrow, and I expect you to be on it."

Heat teemed through every ligament in his body. Connor searched for the sound of Ainsley's calming voice in his mind before he lost control completely. "Where's this urgency coming from?"

"It's your responsibility to be here."

Responsibility? "You know as well as I do, I haven't made every single board meeting. I don't understand why you're being this hard-nosed. Why can't you let me—?"

"Because I'm naming you my successor."

His rushed words sank dead into Connor's gut. He reached for the wall and the footing his dad had just knocked out from under him. "What?"

"What do you think, sweet boy? Should we pick up some hamburgers for Mr. Connor just this once?" Ainsley wheeled her buggy around the aisle toward the section she never graced. She was either truly falling for Connor or plumb crazy.

Drool ran from a smile showcasing Josiah's two bottom teeth. He slapped his hands against the cart, his pudgy legs wiggling and waving.

Ainsley stopped to admire her son's excitement. "You like Mr. Connor, don't you?"

He flapped his arms with even more gusto.

Never had a cheesy grin melted her heart more. She squelched back an inopportune public display of tears and swept Josiah's fine hair off his forehead. "Me too," she whispered. "A lot." More than her heart could handle losing.

A pang of worry nagged at her. Connor had said he wanted to make things real. Did that mean staying for good? Trying long distance? She would've asked if his father hadn't called. Well, assuming her lungs still worked after that kiss.

A swell of heat raced up her cheeks until Josiah jabbed a finger into her arm. Ainsley quickly tucked all middle school reactions down—way down—and redirected her focus to her son. "What is it, buddy?"

"I hope that smile's for me," a woman behind her said.

A wave of fresh laundry fragrance hit Ainsley before ever having to turn around. Downy Donna. There were far worse things a person could smell like, but the sheer magnitude of the scent was strong enough to turn Ainsley's lips numb. It was as if the woman lived at a spa that specialized in fabric softener sheet body wraps.

"Donna, how good to see you." Though she held her breath, she really did mean it.

"You too, sweetie." Donna abandoned her buggy in favor of letting Josiah reach for her fingers first, then her long necklace. "And aren't you just darling, young sir. My, how big you've gotten. Are you helping Mama with the horses? I bet you're a good helper, aren't you?"

"The best." Ainsley gently freed Donna's necklace from Josiah's sticky grasp, exchanged it for a teething ring, and dug back through her purse. "Sorry about that. I have some wipes in here too." Somewhere.

"Oh, don't you worry about it, sweetie. I'm used to it with my own grandbabies." She rustled Josiah's hair. "They're only this little for so long."

Didn't she know it. As hard as these early months were, part of her wasn't ready to let them go.

She blinked toward Donna when she realized she must've missed something she'd said.

"Sorry. What was that?"

An understanding smile passed Donna's eyes. "I was just making sure crotchety ol' Mr. Hudson hasn't pestered you no more. My Charles gave him a good talkin' to about leaving your affairs to you and you alone." She tsked. "That man doesn't have enough sense to light a match, thinking you'd ever sell your daddy's farm. And to try to guilt trip you into it?" She wrung her dishwater-wrinkled hands. "I'd like to tell him where he can stick his offers."

Ainsley laughed. "You and me both, but don't worry. I don't think he'll be coming around again." Thanks to Connor.

"I'm glad to hear it, sweetie." She rubbed Ainsley's arm. "Your daddy would be awful proud of you for taking over the place the way you have. You've done mighty fine by him."

Her generous words tested the strength of Ainsley's ability to hold back her tears.

Donna must've noticed, because she quickly moved on to spare her the embarrassment. "Now then, update me about that empty stall you're needing to rent. No boarders yet?"

"No." One of the perks of keeping herself so busy working on the property this past month was no downtime to worry about finances. "I'm sure something will come along." Soon, she hoped.

"Good. Because I was going to ask if I could move Midnight in there."

Ainsley stared at her. "You have your own stable. I don't understand. Why would you need to board Midnight somewhere else?"

"I'm not as young as I used to be, sweetie. Or as fit." With a hearty laugh, she patted her round tummy. "It'd do Charles and me some good to start spreading out our responsibilities a bit. And that stubborn horse of mine could sure use some companions to teach him some manners."

She set her focus on Josiah again. "It'll be good for every-one, won't it, sugar foot?"

For Ainsley, most of all. She stared at the kindhearted woman, knowing full well half of what she'd just said wasn't true. She was offering purely to help Ainsley out. Her generosity tore through what was left of the flimsy veil holding Ainsley's emotions at bay. "Donna, I don't know what to—"

"There's nothing you need to say, dear."

Nothing that would be enough. She pulled the sweet woman into a hug. "Thank you. You've always been so kind to me." After Daddy died and Mama moved away, Donna had made it her business to check in on Ainsley like she was her own family.

"Aw, now, don't you dare make my mascara run." She gave Ainsley a squeeze and whispered, "A woman may lose her figure, but she always has makeup."

"You haven't been talking to my mom, have you?"

"If I could get the old geezer to return my calls, I would." She chuckled. "You tell your mama she better come see me while she's visiting. You hear?"

"I will." Why Mama had cut everything about Whisper-ing Pines—dear friends included—out of her life when she left, Ainsley would never understand.

"I best be getting on my way." After a grandmotherly pinch to Josiah's cheeks, she patted Ainsley's hand a final time. "You take care of yourself, and don't be a stranger neither."

"I won't."

274 | CRYSTAL WALTON

Almost back to her own buggy, Donna turned. "Oh, and Ainsley, dear? I'll have my Charles get in touch about boarding Midnight." She lowered her voice. "Men like to feel like they're in charge of these things."

Ainsley laughed. "So, I've been told. Thank you again, Donna."

"Of course, sweetie." She waved to Josiah. "Bye, sugar foot. Take care of your mama."

Ainsley faced her son's big smile once they were alone again. Where he'd gotten his extroverted personality from was still a mystery. "You don't even mind smelling like you just came out of the dryer, do you?"

"Excuse me." A guy about her age rounded the side of her buggy. "Sorry. I couldn't help overhearing that woman call you Ainsley." He looked from Josiah back to her, unable to hide the surprise passing his eyes. "You wouldn't happen to be Ainsley Jamison, would you?"

If his sharp business clothes didn't give him away as an out of towner, his northern accent sure did.

Ainsley hesitated to answer, then finally nodded. "Can I help you with something?"

"I sure hope so. 'Cause you might be the only one who can." He slid his cell into his pocket and extended a hand to her. "Flynn Bosco. I believe you know my friend Connor."

Chapter Twenty-Three

Ainsley parked Oprah in the same spot in her driveway as she always did, but the view to her front door seemed longer tonight. She clutched the steering wheel, waiting. For what, she still hadn't figured out. Everything she needed in that moment felt too far out of reach.

The motion light under the carport flipped on as Connor approached from the yard.

Ainsley's fingers balled at the sight of him—a sight she'd grown accustomed to seeing more and more each day. His stint on her farm had always had an expiration date on it. She knew that. Had from the very beginning. The thought of saying goodbye shouldn't have been blindsiding her like this, even if she'd temporarily lost herself in the hope of never having to.

Her conversation with Flynn pressed in. She knew what she had to do. She cared about him too much to do anything less. But as she looked at Josiah fast asleep in his car seat, her heart broke beyond words.

She inhaled, permitted herself one more moment to let her tears fall, then steeled herself and stepped out of the van. "Hey," she called before Connor reached the front door.

"Hey. I thought you were already inside."

"I was letting Josiah sleep another few minutes before stirring him."

He started for the side door. "Let me get him for you."

"No." She reached for his hand but quickly let go. "Thank you. I'll get him in a minute." Staring at the hen nestled on his shoulder, she tipped a genuine smile at the cute pair. "Looks like you could use a few minutes to let your dance partner down easy before going in yourself."

Connor looked at the hen as if he'd forgotten she was there and laughed. "Good call. I've learned my lesson about provoking the girls around here. Those side eyes they give you?" He shook his head. "They're somethin' else."

Ainsley gave him what he asked for, and he cracked another laugh.

"Yep, that'll slice through you every time."

No more than how deep his smile was piercing her right now.

He gently cupped his hands around his newfound friend and lowered her to the ground. "There you go, baby. We'll hang out tomorrow. Promise."

As he watched to make sure the chicken made her way to the coop, sincere affection filled his eyes. He'd fallen in love with Whispering Pines as Ainsley had warned him might. Why couldn't she have warned herself then that she'd fall in love with the city boy who was supposed to be completely wrong for her? Because right now, all she could see was everything that was right.

The tears she'd intended to leave in the van churned in her throat. "You're wrong, you know."

Connor looked at her, his face ridden with question. "About Nugget?"

The fact that he'd named the hen made Ainsley love him even more, which only caused the hurt to splinter deeper. "About becoming a father one day."

If her first statement had caught him off guard, the lines on his forehead left little doubt she was throwing him one curveball after the next.

"You're going to make a great one. I know you doubt that, but I don't. Not for a minute. You aren't destined to make your dad's same mistakes. I might not know him, but I know you. And the way you've cared for Josiah while you've been here… The way you've cared for me…" She swallowed hard. "You're your own man, Connor. A *good* man who has no reason to feel less than his brother."

He stared at her as though her words reached places she couldn't begin to see.

Ainsley cleared her throat. "I just needed to make sure you knew that." Needed him to know she meant it before the rest of what she had to say made him question everything else.

His eyes misted with emotion as he edged closer and brought his lips to her temple. "Thank you."

The soft words lingered as tenderly as he held her. Ainsley gripped his wrist, warring between the fear of holding on and letting go. Why did he have to be so perfect?

"Did you just come back from the laundromat?"

She sniffled through a laugh. But when he leaned back, there was no hiding what she knew he could see.

He brushed his thumb beside her eye. "You okay?"

"Fine," she said despite the quiver in her voice denying it.

"You're definitely not fine. Did something happen while you were out?"

Exhaling, she stared at his boots and another reminder that her time with him had always been on loan. "Do you really believe things are meant to be? That there's a reason for everything?" Providence, he'd called it—something her heart couldn't stop grappling with.

"You don't?"

"It's easy to believe it when something good happens. But what about the bad?" Her lashes creased together. "I can't reconcile that." She wouldn't accept that she and Josiah were meant to be fatherless. And what of love? Was she meant to find it only to lose it again?

"Ainsley…" He tilted her chin, and the look in his eyes didn't give her a chance to speak.

She shouldn't have brought any of this up. She stepped back, away from Connor and away from questions that were pointless to ask. Readjusting her ponytail, she kept her eyes averted from his. "Did you get a hold of your dad?"

"Unfortunately."

Her hope caved at the brokenness fracturing the single word.

He squeezed the base of his neck. "You don't know how much I wish you could be right about him. About my whole family. But we're not like yours, Ainsley."

"Doesn't mean you all love each other any less."

His expression disagreed. "You share more love with animals than I've ever experienced in my life with any member of my family."

It broke her heart to know he felt that way.

"I don't even have a dog waiting for me when I come home each night. You have your sister, your cousin—both who've been your best friends since you were in diapers. You have lunch with your grandparents every Sunday after church. I haven't seen either set of mine since I was in elementary school."

She couldn't imagine but understood much of their way of life was cultural. "It's a different mindset down here."

"That's one way of putting it." His forehead tightened. "Your family's been standing by each other for generations. There's not a doubt in my body that they would drop everything to be here for you when you need them." He shook his head. "My parents weren't even there for my brother when he lost his wife. Never once offered to help out with the girls. Worst part is, neither did I."

The ache he carried gnawed at her. The guilt, the loss—things she knew better than he thought she did.

"Our family isn't perfect, Connor."

"I didn't say perfect. Just that it's the way one should be."

She knew he was right about a lot of it. That she was blessed beyond measure to have such an amazingly supportive family. She had so much to be grateful for that sometimes she felt like she didn't have any right to grieve the losses life had cost them. Josiah, especially. Still, the thought of her son never knowing the selfless love of a father wrecked her heart. It had from before Jonathan had ever left. But right now, what hurt more was knowing what kind of dad Connor would make if he gave himself the chance.

She stared off to the neighbor's fence as if it could corral the words galloping inside her without beginning or ending. So many things she wanted to say—*needed* to say—trampled over each other in a stampede of emotions.

The front door opened. "Thank heavens you're back." Kate hurried outside. "Why didn't you answer my calls?"

Grateful for the interruption, Ainsley gathered her wits about her and motioned to the van where she'd left her purse. "Sorry. I didn't want to pick up while driving in the dark. You should've seen all the deer out. It's getting crazy this season."

"Forget the deer, girl. You have crazier things to worry about." Kate pushed her runaway curls off her shoulder. "Mama decided she needed to come early."

Ainsley's apprehensive glance bounced from Connor back to her sister. "What do you mean early?" She was already planning to arrive a day in advance.

"Early, as in she's standing in the middle of our kitchen right now."

Ainsley's stomach dropped. "What?" She spun around, only then noticing two extra cars parked along the far end of her front yard. Neither one she recognized.

"It gets worse."

"How can it be worse?"

Kate scrunched a sympathetic face at her. "She's not alone."

Connor took one look between them and hooked a thumb over his shoulder. "Should I go get Spock for back-up?"

Ainsley laughed softly, loving him for how easily he helped her to relax.

Kate nodded at the door. "Daphne's already in there, so…"

"Enough said." Chuckling himself, Connor gestured for them to enter first. But when Kate turned, he grabbed Ainsley's hand and brought her close. "I'm going to go get Josiah, but I'll be right beside you, okay?" he whispered.

As much as she'd leaned on his assurance before, this was one time she knew she couldn't. "Thank you," she whispered anyway. She clutched her elbows as he walked to the van. But the moment he lifted Josiah's car seat carrier out, and she caught a glimpse of the love reaching his eyes, no barricade could've kept her insides from unraveling completely.

Kate slid her a look that said she knew something was up.

Now wasn't the time to get into it. After another moment's hesitation, Ainsley breathed in and faced the door waiting for them.

Experience should've warned her there was no point in bracing herself. Wide-eyed, she jerked to a stop two feet inside. Mama's scalloped Dolly Parton apron was hard enough to look away from. Never mind that Set-up Steve and Hairpiece Hank were flanking either side of her like suitors who'd come calling for her eligible daughter.

Ainsley clenched Kate's sleeve. "Sweet mother of Pearl."

Connor leaned against the bedroom window and kept his back to the rocking chair Ainsley was nursing Josiah in. "You could've let me finish introducing myself properly before dragging me back here to hide out in Josiah's room."

"Hiding isn't the same as self-preservation."

"What about embarrassment?"

"I'm not embarrassed by you, Connor. I'm just…"

"Not ready for me to meet your mom?" He'd heard similar words before, about her grandparents last time.

"I'm not ready to battle with her is all." She sighed. "I don't know what she was thinking bringing Steve and Hank here. And did she seriously bake a pie for the occasion? I swear, the woman is relentless."

Connor ran his fingertip along the blind. "Part of her matchmaking ploy, I take it?"

"Imprisonment ploy is more like it."

"I thought she knew we were dating."

"She does."

He tapped the trim. "So… why bring them along?"

"Backup plan. Like I said. Relentless. I tried to warn you."

Yes, she did. It'd been mostly comical until now. How was he supposed to win over someone who'd assumed he wasn't the one for Ainsley before even meeting him?

"Then you should definitely let me get back out there so I can prove—"

"I need you here." Her voice sobered. "Please. Just a little longer."

The hidden tremble in her words left him little choice but to agree.

"And you don't have to stay over there by the window. I have a nursing cover on."

All the same, he'd rather give them the privacy the special bond between mother and child deserved. He tinkered with the blinds again. If he was being honest, he'd admit it was easier to focus on the darkness outside than to face the shadows that'd been clouding Ainsley's eyes since she'd stepped out of the van earlier. He still didn't know what had rattled her, but he sensed something had changed. Something that scared him.

He didn't turn until he heard her stand up from the chair. She burped Josiah, then gently lowered him into his crib. She brought two fingers to her lips, pressed them to her son's cheek, and whispered, "Love you to Neverland and back, sweet boy."

It could've been the hundredth time he'd watched her put Josiah to bed, and it wouldn't have lessened how much her tenderness made him fall in love with her even more.

Ainsley motioned for him to follow her into the hall. With her hand in his, she led him into her bedroom instead of back out to the kitchen as expected. She flipped the light on, wavered with her back to him for a minute, and hesitantly turned. Her beautifully broken smile speared into him like nothing ever had.

"You can make a run for it through the window," she teased. "I haven't done that since high school, but it's actually not a bad escape route. You just gotta mind your way around the chicken coop. You'd be surprised how noisy those hens can get when they're startled. They—"

"Ainsley." His heart wasn't going to take it much longer if she didn't tell him what was going on.

She cut a glance away from him to her worn copy of *Anne of Green Gables* on the nightstand. She'd started reading again. The knowledge renewed him with relief. He hadn't imagined the feelings they'd been sharing. It was real for both of them. He could sense it. And heaven knew, he wasn't about to lose it now.

Without hesitation, Connor wove his fingers through hers. "I'm not running away." Not tonight. Not tomorrow. "I told you once there's no place I'd rather be than here with you and Josiah. That still holds, Ainsley Grace."

She looked away again, but he wasn't giving up.

"I get things are rocky between you and your mom. And I'd be lying if I said the fact she brought two backup guys with her didn't gut me a little. But we don't have to go out there and be confrontational about any of it. In fact, we don't have to say anything about our relationship at all." He drew her closer. "We can just let them see us together. See that it's real, and it's going to last."

Her lashes fell.

"I know the plan was for me to leave next week, but I don't have to. I could stay." He lifted her chin. "For good."

Glassy eyes searched his for a mere second before she stretched on her toes to bring her lips to his.

Caught off guard, it took him a moment to settle into an embrace that felt different than the others. It wasn't that she was withholding something. The tenderness, the earnestness—he felt it in every movement. Yet it didn't feel like a kiss inviting him to stay. It felt like a kiss goodbye.

Connor waited for her to pull back, wanting to hold on as long as he could. A tear spilled down her cheek, and his chest nearly split in two.

"Ainsley, please." He wiped her face. "Please, talk to me."

"Tomorrow," she whispered.

When she struggled to look like she was holding it all together, he realized any front she'd planned to put up tonight wasn't for her family. It was for him.

She smiled away her tears. "That apple pie might smell good, but you'll regret eating it this late. You should go on to the loft. Get some sleep. We're all in for a long day tomorrow."

He tried to make sense of what she wasn't saying. "So, you want me to walk straight out the front door. Pretend your mom isn't even here."

"I want you to trust me. This is for the best. Really. We'll start fresh tomorrow." She looked up at him again. "Please."

Connor winced at the look in her eyes. He drew in a slow breath, exhaled, and stepped back. "If that's what you want."

He waited for her to say it wasn't. Prayed she'd say anything to let him know she didn't want him to leave any more than he did. But the truth was, she didn't have to say anything at all. Her eyes had already given him the answer he had no choice but to walk away from.

Chapter Twenty-Four

Connor took a sip of his third cup of coffee for the morning and tried another stab at carrying on a conversation with Hank. "Checking the stats on a game?"

Beside him on the couch, the dude glanced up from his phone. "A guinea pig race."

Connor almost spewed his drink. He laughed until Hank's straight face didn't budge. "Oh, you're serious. I didn't know that was a thing."

"Motion's their strongest problem-solving strategy."

Connor bobbed his head. "Wow, that's, um… I'm honestly not even sure what to say to that." He turned to his other couch companion. "Did you know that?"

Steve looked up from his book. "As a matter of fact, I did."

Of course he did. Connor wouldn't have been surprised if that fat book in his lap was an encyclopedia. And what was up with the off-white cardigan tied around his neck? Was the guy planning to play tennis with the goats after lunch?

Steve returned Connor's not-so-subtle appraisal. "What veterinary school did you say you attended again?"

Apparently, Ainsley hadn't yet informed her mom—and company—of the minor correction in medical fields.

"That's actually a very interesting conversation. One that Ainsley and I should probably share together." He balanced his mug as he scooted to the edge of the couch. "Speaking of which, I should go check in with her. Excuse me for a moment." He turned to Hank, who didn't glance up from his cell this time. Connor jutted his mug at him anyway. "Good talk, man."

He left his coffee on the kitchen table, strode down the hall, and turned to the bathroom after seeing Josiah's door was still shut. He could use a minute alone to regroup anyway.

Inside the bathroom, he skidded to a stop one step too short.

The door wasn't the only thing free and open. Ainsley's grandpa looked at him from in front of the toilet but didn't bother to cover anything up. "You just gonna keep staring, son, or do we need to settle this with a measuring stick?"

Connor finally slapped a hand over his eyes. "Nope, I'm…" Scarred for life? "I'm good. I didn't mean to barge in. The door…" He pointed behind him.

"Is letting a draft in."

"Right. Sorry." Connor backed into the doorknob and spun toward the hall. "I'm gonna go… unsee this now." He pulled the door as tight as it would shut and stared at the ceiling. Thirty seconds later, he pushed off it. "Yeah, that's not helping." He might have to go see Spock in order to blot one source of trauma out with another.

He hustled back to his coffee, fully intent on scouring the cabinets for some much needed Kahlúa… or eye bleach.

"You all right, dear?" Ainsley's nanna asked from the living room rocker. "You look like you've seen a ghost."

He wished that's what he had seen.

"All good, ma'am."

"Didn't I tell you to call me Ellie, sweetheart?"

Connor tipped his head in apology. "I'll remember next time." Assuming he'd have a next time. The unease left from his interaction with Ainsley last night worked up his muscles. He expelled a long breath. But when Ainsley came down the hall, his tendons tensed all over again.

With Josiah on her hip, she smiled warmly at him as she'd done all morning, and he couldn't decide which conversation she was pretending hadn't actually happened: the one in her bedroom last night or the one by the Cypress tree yesterday afternoon. Though, he supposed it didn't matter. She was acting either way.

Steve and Hank both rose to their feet when she reached the end of the hallway. From their reactions, she could've been a princess coming down a spiral staircase.

Her smile stiffened at the pair of them. She adjusted her hold on Josiah, who flapped his hand against the burp cloth draped over her shoulder while working his bare feet up her shirt.

The infatuation in Steve's and Hank's eyes dwindled, and something in Connor wanted to punch the uncomfortable look off both their faces. Especially when Ainsley ran her fingers over Josiah's hair in a protective motion.

Mrs. Jamison turned from the oven in her interesting choice for an apron. She took one look at them and clapped a flour-covered hand over her heart. "Gracious sakes alive. What in tarnation do you have around my grandbaby's neck?"

Ainsley impressively kept her eyes from rolling. "It's an amber teething necklace, Mama. They're supposed to help with teething pain."

Based on Mrs. Jamison's expression, Ainsley might as well have said she'd hung a noose around the kid's neck.

"A necklace on a boy. I ain't never seen the like." She scooped him out of Ainsley's arms. "C'mere, sugar plum. You come let Grandma get those juju beads off you."

Ainsley didn't resist. She simply rubbed circles across her forehead after her mom disappeared down the hall.

So much for everyone getting a fresh start this morning.

Connor's cell rang. Another call from home. He shoved his phone back inside his pocket, halfway wishing Ainsley's worn smile was as easy to ignore. Not possible. He set his coffee down yet again. Despite the turmoil he hadn't worked through from last night, he couldn't stop himself from wanting to be here for her today. No acting required on his part.

He turned her around and massaged her shoulders. Same as in the barn, her muscles melted as he worked out the knots. She lowered her chin when he moved on to her neck. With her hair pulled up as usual, it was hard to ignore how vulnerable the skin beneath her ear looked. Connor forced his eyes—and his thoughts—to the living room, where Ainsley's two backup suitors had returned to the couch in some kind of silent macho sit-off.

He leaned down to her ear. "If they whip out javelins here soon, my vote's on Bachelor Number One," he whispered. "Though, I don't know. Bachelor Number Two does have an impressive hair helmet on already."

She snuck a peek toward his insinuation and elbowed him from behind. "Hush." She turned, staying close enough for him to wrap his arms around her. He managed to refrain. But if she kept looking that beautiful trying not to laugh, all bets would be off.

Her blue eyes held his as always. His voice stalled, and he didn't know what else to do but pray that standing beside her would be enough to show her he wasn't going anywhere.

She flinched at the sound of the front door nearly slamming.

"Sorry," Daphne offered, though she looked far from it. She trekked into the kitchen and unloaded a bunch of fresh zucchinis into the sink.

Ainsley cast an anxious glance from Connor to her cousin. "You okay?"

"Peachy."

Connor raised a brow at Ainsley and whispered, "Better to not poke the bear."

Easton and Kate's entrance a minute later eliminated the need to probe anyway. Kate slumped into the closest kitchen chair and swiped a banana from a fruit bowl in the center of the table. "Remind me not to go riding after a week on third shift. I think Shiloh worked me more than the other way around."

"You did fine." Easton pulled out the adjacent chair and set his hat on the table. "You should've come with us, Daphne. We took the trail by the creek. Phoenix would've been in heaven."

Connor got the impression Daphne didn't want to turn from the sink, but her compulsive remarks obviously got the better of her.

"Only 'cause she would've knocked your butt into the water."

"Psh. You wish."

Both their smiles held an easy camaraderie. It might've been friendship only right now, but it was the kind that love could be built on if they were willing to let it. For Daphne's sake, Connor hoped they would.

"Punkin'?" Mrs. Jamison called on her way out of Josiah's room. "Where's that toy I got him the last time I was here."

Ainsley and Daphne exchanged a dreaded look.

"It's by the door."

Her mom rounded the corner with Josiah in a completely new outfit, sans the amber necklace. "I didn't see it on the floor."

"No, the *door*," Ainsley said louder this time. "By the coatrack."

"Now, why'd you go and take it back. He loves that toy."

Ainsley pinched the bridge of her nose. "Not back, Mama. *Rack*. It's in my purse on the *coatrack*."

"He can't play with a toy he can't reach, punkin'."

Exactly. Connor scratched the corner of his mouth to keep from interjecting. He handed Ainsley his cup of coffee. She needed it more than he did. "Let me get that for you, Mrs. Jamison." He retrieved the creepy carnival music toy and knelt beside Matty, curled up on the throw rug. "Want a treat?" he whispered.

Matty rose to attention in response to the trigger word.

Connor rubbed a Milk-Bone on the toy and let the dog sniff it, then casually dropped a calling card for backup out the front door. He ruffled Matty's ears and winked. Leaving their clandestine plan in Matty's paws, he crossed the hardwoods and held the toy out to Josiah.

The boy turned away from the scary thing and clung tighter to his grandma.

Mrs. Jamison looked like she assumed Josiah's reaction was directed at Connor instead of the toy. She'd been pleasant most of the morning. Southernly polite. But he sensed she didn't trust him as far as she could throw him.

He set the toy on the kitchen table and searched for the correct thing to say to change her mind.

When Josiah turned and saw Connor's hands were free, he reached for him. Mrs. Jamison raised a brow but said nothing until Matty started scratching at the front door like he was digging to China.

"Easton, will you let that blessed dog out before he has a dying duck fit."

Easton got up as told. "Yes, ma'am."

"Really, Ainsley, a house is no place for a dog." She patted Josiah's back. "Especially one bringing in who knows what from outside. You hear what they're saying about the tick epidemic this season?"

Ainsley sighed. "That's what we have the chickens for, Mama."

"The chickens?" Mrs. Jamison turned toward the table. "Katie Kat, please reason with your sister. And put that banana down and eat some grits. I swear, if you get any skinnier, you could use a clothesline as an umbrella."

"I keep a perfectly healthy weight, Mama." Kate set her almost-finished banana on the table nonetheless.

"Rubbish. You're working yourself to the bone at that job, is what you're doing. I told ya you can't let them run you ragged, suga'." She clucked her tongue. "At a hospital, no less. You'd think they'd know a thing or two about health. You come stay with Aunt Jean and me for a week. We'll fatten you up good and well."

Kate slid her sister a pleading glare for intervention.

"Mama?" Ainsley bumped arms with her cousin, who'd amazingly been playing silent observer in the corner. "Why don't we invite Mr. Finnigan over today? Daphne's pretty chummy with him. I'm sure she could swing a last-minute invite."

Daphne mumbled, "Well played," so her aunt couldn't hear her.

"Thomas Finnigan?" Mrs. Jamison fiddled with the oven while trying to balance Josiah on her hip.

"He's a very nice man, Mama." Ainsley peeked up from the mug handle she was picking at. "Not bad looking either."

"Not bad looking?" Pure shock, from the looks of it, whirled her mom around. "His buck teeth are longer than the hair on his head."

Daphne snorted out a sip of coffee.

"Mama." Ainsley fought to keep a straight face.

"Well, I'm sorry. But bless his heart, the man could eat corn through a picket fence."

For an isolated moment, the two shared a laugh reminiscent of a relationship they'd once had. One without strain or strife or disappointment. They both missed what they'd lost. Connor could see it on their faces.

His phone call with his dad sprang to mind and with it, the longing to remember a time when they'd ever shared a relationship built on family instead of on expectations.

The front door opened again. "Hey, y'all. Sorry I'm late." Penny strolled in with one of her recyclable bags in hand. "I stopped at a yard sale on the way. You should've seen the collection of CDs they had."

"Oh, Mom," Daphne whined. "You do not need any more CDs. You maxed out your quota two decades ago."

"There's no such thing as a quota on good music, baby girl."

The screen door shut, followed by the sound of scurrying feet tramping into the kitchen.

Mrs. Jamison turned with a cobbler in hand and almost dropped it. "Sweet heavens, how'd that pig get in here?" She clutched Josiah like she was protecting him from catching the swine flu or something. "Ainsley Grace, get that bottom feeder out of the kitchen this instant."

Matty chased Billy the Pig around the table as if it were a horizontal hamster wheel.

Easton's belly laugh added to the hysteria taking over the small room. "Looks like he's ready for the pig scramble next season."

Kate swatted him and lifted her legs out of the duo's spastic path.

"For crying in a bucket, will *someone* grab those rascals already." Mrs. Jamison shooed them with her foot. "Go on now. Get." Between carrying Josiah and the cobbler, she fully lost her grip on the dessert this time. Peach slices smacked onto the floor and slid every which direction.

The entire circus show paused. No one moved, including the animals. But the second Billy caught a whiff of the free for all, he slid snout first into the biggest pile of cobbler. Matty barked. Hank and Steve came running to the rescue. And Josiah giggled at the theatrics.

Connor couldn't have asked for a better setup. In the middle of the mayhem, he nonchalantly knocked off the creepy toy he'd left on the edge of the table. Matty's ears whipped toward the sound, his nose following. He took one sniff and abandoned Billy for the treat-smelling baby toy. He chomped at the thing, pawing and biting away.

Daphne slid Connor an approving look to which he claimed innocence with a shrug.

"Matty!" Mrs. Jamison passed off Josiah to Kate and went after the dog. "Give it here. Let go." When Matty refused to release his new chew toy, she ushered him to the door instead. "Out. Out you go." She prodded him over the threshold with her foot. "Go on now. The both of ya," she said to Billy as well.

Easton carried the cobbler-covered pig to the door, gently tossed him outside, and added a wave. "Happy Thanksgiving."

Mrs. Jamison glared at him.

"Come on. You gotta admit it was a little funny."

"Funny, my foot. How, pray tell, am I gonna have time to make another cobbler?"

"Oh, I'm sure Daphne would *love* to help you with that." He looked back into the kitchen. "Isn't that right, Daphne Duck?"

Based on her eyes-turned-daggers, the nickname alone was enough to land him in hot water, let alone tacking on the two-man baking event he'd just volunteered her for.

Connor didn't hear the comeback headed Easton's way. Caught up in his favorite smile from Ainsley, nothing else mattered right then.

"Thank you," she mouthed across the room.

He nodded, wishing that getting rid of the toy once and for all was enough to erase the unspoken strain her eyes still held.

"Ains?" Kate's chair screeched away from the table. She rushed Josiah over and brushed back the wispy locks of hair bordering his neck.

When the color in Ainsley's face drained, Connor's pulse jumped into high gear. Whatever Kate had just shown her, it couldn't have been good.

Chapter Twenty-Five

Ainsley cradled her son close as she hurried to the bathroom. Questions echoed off the hallway walls. How long had the tick been there? How could she not have noticed? She was his mother, for Pete's sake. The one who was supposed to protect him. Always.

The weight of neglect took Josiah's place as she set him on the bathroom sink. What if Mama was right, and she'd been so blinded by her own dreams of raising him here that she hadn't been willing to acknowledge the potential dangers?

Josiah looked up at her. No hint of accusation or question filled his sweet blue eyes. Only love.

"Ainsley." Connor rounded the bathroom doorway. "It couldn't have been there long. Don't worry."

The gentle touch of his hand on her back nearly unlocked the floodgates she'd been holding back since last night.

"It's going to be okay." He searched her eyes. "All of it."

The simple words undid her. She wanted to believe him—*needed* to—but couldn't. Not while faith the size of a Matchbox car stood against a pileup of doubts.

"I don't know what to do," she whispered.

Though she had a feeling he knew she wasn't talking about how to remove a tick, he had enough empathy to pretend she was. "Do you have any tweezers?"

"In the medicine cabinet," Kate said as she slipped in behind them.

"And alcohol?"

"Under the sink."

Connor fished both out, carefully removed the tick, and contained it in a Ziplock bag. After cleaning his hands, he rustled Josiah's hair. "There we go, big guy. As good as new."

Her happy boy, unaware of any danger, cooed at the man who'd found a place in his heart over such a short time. Her own heart cracked even more at the sight of them.

"Hey." Connor reached for her cheek. "This isn't your fault."

Mama appeared in the doorway. "She doesn't need to be coddled, Connor. If she's going to insist on raising a baby in this place, she needs to see the ramifications with open eyes."

"What she needs is support."

Oh, boy.

Ainsley clutched her imaginary rosary beads but doubted even a Hail Mary could get Connor out of this one.

Mama tilted her chin at him. "I'm sorry. Tell me again how long you've known my daughter?"

He didn't answer at first. Neither could Ainsley. The blood pumping double time through her veins pushed out all recollection of their fake relationship details. She turned to Connor, hoping he remembered.

His eyes softened. "Long enough to know she's one of the most capable, loving mothers I've ever met."

Ainsley's throat constricted at the power words had to touch places that felt beyond reach.

He turned toward her mom then. "And she deserves a heck of a lot more grace than you give her."

Yet again, Ainsley held her breath when Mama didn't so much as blink in response. She exchanged a nervous glance with Kate, then placed a hand on Connor's arm. "It's okay. She's right."

"No. She's not." He looked at her like they were the only ones in the room. "I understand you want to keep the peace whatever the cost, but I can't pretend about this."

"So, you're pretending about something else?" Mama stared at them, waiting for the confession she seemed to have been expecting all along.

Ainsley's pulse thundered. Her heart splintered. She brought Josiah close and breathed in. Seconds felt like minutes, but it didn't matter how much time did or didn't pass. She couldn't put it off any longer.

She focused solely on Connor and prayed with everything in her that he'd see how sorry she was. "We've been pretending to stay together for the holiday, but the truth is…" It took all her fortitude to keep her voice from wavering. "We're breaking up."

Ainsley rushed into the barn, grateful her tears had enough compassion to wait until she'd escaped the bathroom to bombard her bottom lashes.

"Ainsley, hold on." Connor caught up with her at Shiloh's stall. "Can we please talk?"

Talking would only make it harder. She lifted her eyes to the rafters. Grasping on to the strength she begged for, she inhaled from deep inside and turned. She'd tried to avoid being alone with him all morning, and this was exactly why. The confusion on his face roped around her chest until it choked out any hope of her getting through this in one piece.

His shoulders sank at the look she couldn't hide. She could pretend with her mom. Maybe even with herself. But not with him.

He started for her anyway but stopped within steps of her. His confidence waned under hesitancy, and the strain she'd created between them took another blow.

She grabbed her necklace, needing something—anything—to hold on to.

"What happened when you were out last night?"

Ainsley gripped her charm harder. "Nothing."

"*Something* happened. Something changed. I don't understand why you won't tell me what's going on."

Because she loved him too much. Because he'd stay for her unless she convinced him she didn't want him to.

"Did my dad call you?"

She glanced up from the ground. "I'm sure he doesn't even know who I am."

"The man has ways of prying." He released a hard exhale. "Trust me."

"He's your father."

"A lousy one."

"One who might need you to cut him some slack." She bit her lip and dropped her gaze right back to her boots. "I know things are hard between you two, but I'm sure he does what he does because he loves you. Even when it doesn't always feel like it."

"As sure as you are that your mom does the same?"

The question caught her in the gut.

"Sorry. That wasn't fair."

It was, actually. A little *too* fair.

Connor scrubbed a hand down his face. "Look, I know what you're saying, but I'm not so sure all fathers deserve the same grace."

It took little reading between the lines to know he lumped Jonathan into the less deserving group. Truth be told, she had too. The magnitude of her judgment swept in and pierced her heart with such force, Ainsley had to steady a hand on the gate beside her.

A breeze rustled the coat hanging on the wall where Daddy had left it. His faded scent curled around her. She closed her eyes. And with a strength she knew wasn't solely hers, she sought to pry free the arrow of unforgiveness she'd wedged into her chest the day Jonathan had walked out on their family.

Several breaths of assurance slowly steadied her in the embrace of a truth that had never stopped pursuing her. "None of us deserve it. That's what makes it grace."

Mixed emotions chased each other across his eyes until the overwhelming look of love he'd showered on her time and again drove him forward. "Do you have any idea how I feel about you?"

"Connor."

He crossed the barrier that'd kept him back a moment ago. "Yesterday at the picnic... I thought we..." He lifted her chin. "I thought it was..."

"It was." Her lashes squeezed back the pain of not being able to explain. "But it was a dream. A *beautiful* dream that would never work as more." She forced herself to face him. "Your life's in New York."

"Don't." He stepped back. Looking around the quiet barn, he fanned both arms out. "No one else is here, Ainsley. You can drop the breakup script."

"It's reality." Her almost inaudible response dropped to the ground under the hurt pouring from his eyes.

"All fiction has truth in it. Is that it?"

"Yes," she whispered.

"So, that's it?" A tendon on his neck flexed in and out. "We don't even try to make it work. We just give up. Walk away and pretend this whole thing was nothing but a charade the entire time." He strode right up to her then. "'Cause I'm sorry, but I can't do that."

Her chin quivered. "We had a plan."

"Screw the plan. I want to know what you feel right now. It's only you and me here. No acting." He clutched the top of the gate with one hand, brought the other to her cheek, and anchored his gaze in hers. "You asked me yesterday what my heart was telling me, and now I'm asking you. What do you want?"

What she couldn't have.

She closed her eyes. "Connor, please."

"I want you to look at me and tell me none of this is real."

This close to him, feeling his love... It was too much, too hard. "I can't."

"Can't what? Be honest with yourself?"

She winced at words she couldn't deny.

The tension lines creasing his forehead faded. Everything in him softened—his touch, his voice. "I want to be with you, Ainsley. Whether we're running through thunderstorms or running from Spock, I want to be right here with you. I want to watch your eyes twitch at how much sugar I put in my coffee each morning and see them light up every time you kiss your son goodnight." His fingers wove into her hair where they belonged. "I want to pretend I can wield a pair of pliers half as well as you can and rescue you from completely harmless snakes every chance I get."

A convoluted mix of tears and laughter stayed caught in her throat.

"But more than anything, I want the best for you and Josiah, even if I can't be a part of it." Smiling sadly, he brushed his thumb across her temple. "I've wished nothing but happiness for you since you got your hair caught in my adjusting bench. So, if having me walk away is truly what you want, then say the word, and I'll leave right now." The corner of his mouth hitched. "As long as you know I'm siding with Anne on her graveyard of buried hopes."

So was she. But unlike Anne, it brought little comfort to her soul.

Ainsley lifted watery eyes to the unexpected cowboy who'd turned out to be everything she didn't know she needed. He'd loved her sacrificially and brought healing to unreachable places. He deserved the same from her.

Without another thought, she drew herself to him and memorized the feel of being in his arms. When no one but the pine trees would be there to hear her cry, she'd release her pain. Right now, she held on to what would get her through it.

Ainsley lowered back to her heels far too soon, latched on to the resoluteness she had no choice but to show, and looked him head on. "Yes," she whispered. "I need you to leave."

He didn't move or speak. His eyes didn't release hers. Nor did the love they held.

Every muscle in her body trembled against the fight she was losing by the second.

"Connor?" Kate jogged into the barn. She looked at them and stopped. "Oh, sorry to interrupt, but there's a man here to get you?"

He turned. "Get me?"

"He said something about your father sending a car to take you to the airport."

Connor's chin sank to his chest. He raked his fingers through his hair and waited a minute before looking up again. "I guess some things are meant to be after all."

Ainsley's heart tore.

He stopped a few steps away, his pause unbearable. Her pulse pounded until he finally jogged back to her, closed her in his arms again, and pressed the softest kiss to her cheek. "I'll never stop hoping you get your happy ending, Ainsley Grace."

She couldn't say it in return. She couldn't say anything at all as she watched the man who was never supposed to be more than a temporary stand-in walk out of the barn he'd helped repair and out of the life he'd helped restore.

Shiloh nudged his nose to her neck from over the gate. Alone, Ainsley turned and held on to the one who'd seen her through every heartache, knowing she'd need him this time more than ever before.

Chapter Twenty-Six

Ainsley stroked Josiah's soft cheek while he nursed. It was a little early in his schedule to be feeding, but she needed the time alone with him. Needed to hold him tight. Just because he wouldn't understand why Connor was gone didn't mean he wouldn't feel his absence. It hadn't even been a full hour, and she already felt it herself.

"I'm sorry, sweet boy," she whispered. *For so much.*

"Punkin'?" Mama poked her head into Josiah's room, then let herself in the rest of the way. "You can't keep hiding back here. You have guests."

"No, *you* have guests." Ainsley fastened her nursing bra in place and lifted Josiah to her shoulder to burp. "You invited Steve and Hank, not me."

"And it's a good thing I did, now isn't it?"

Her eyes reached for the ceiling as she laid Josiah in his crib. "Not now, Mama. Please."

"You could at least be civil with them, Ainsley."

"I have been."

"Sending them to get your groceries from the van last night is not civil. You've been avoiding them like you're a long-tailed cat in a room full of rocking chairs."

If only she could do the same with this conversation.

"Hey Diddle, Diddle" played from the TV down the hall. As many times as Ainsley had endured listening to the nursery rhyme, she'd never been jealous of the lucky plate getting to run away with the spoon until right then.

"I don't understand you, punkin'. If you're going to insist on sulking over a fella you let hail a cab out of here before I even set the table, you can at least explain to me why you bothered pretending to be a couple to begin with."

Something in Ainsley snapped. She was tired of tiptoeing around the obvious. Straining not to raise her voice, she swung her pointer finger at the wall. "This. This is why, Mama. Two guys are sitting in my living room like they're on the *Bachelorette* show waiting to be handed a rose. What'd you do? Offer them some kind of dowry? 'Cause I'm pretty sure they're not going to be impressed when they find out Brie and Shiloh aren't worth as much as you promised them."

"Oh, Ainsley, please." She strode for the doorway. "I will not have you making me feel bad for wanting what's best for my daughter."

She headed into the hall after her. "And you think marrying me off to some uppity suit like Steve is best? You know I won't go down that road again. I want—"

"A cowboy rancher?" A look Ainsley couldn't read flickered in Mama's eyes. "You deserve better, punkin'."

"Better than what? A man like Daddy? A life like the one he gave our family?"

"That's enough." Face rigid, she looked Ainsley straight in the eye and lowered her voice. "We have a houseful of people and a dinner to finish preparing. We are not doing this right now." She fretted with the apron knotted behind her back while striding down the hall.

Ainsley followed her to the kitchen, too angry to drop it. "When exactly are we supposed to do it? This is only the second time you've come home since Josiah was born. Have you always hated this place, or is it just because I'm running it now? 'Cause if our whole childhood was a lie, I have a right to know—"

"I said *enough*." Mama whirled around.

Everyone in the living room froze with their heads turned in their direction. Ainsley didn't care if they heard. She was done with pretenses.

Mama yanked her apron over her head. "I poured as much heart and soul into this farm as your daddy did."

"Well, it sure was easy for you to walk away from, wasn't it?"

"That's not fair."

"And leaving your daughters here all alone was?"

Her mom turned for the sink so fast, Ainsley barely caught a glimpse of tears. "You think that was easy for me?"

"Running away usually is."

Mama slammed the balled-up apron down and spun around. "Dadgummit, Ainsley. You don't know what it's like for me to be here without your father. To see memories of him no matter where I look."

"You think you're the only one it's hard on?" Emotions soared. Her nails dug into her palms, frustration through her defenses. "Do you have any idea what it was like for me to take over this place alone? Constantly second guessing every choice, wishing he were here to tell me what to do? Wishing *you* were still here..." The harbored wound of abandonment wore through her voice. "Daddy was gone. Jonathan left. I needed you here more than ever, and you left too." Her chin trembled. "You left us, Mama." Couldn't she see how much that hurt?

Her eyes misted. "I didn't think you needed me."

"Why would you think that?"

"Because you're as strong as your daddy," she blurted out. Face and voice softening, Mama sighed. "You always have been."

Ainsley stared at her—at the love and admiration colliding with everything she believed her mom thought about her. "I... I don't understand. Running the farm... raising Josiah here... you always said I couldn't do it. That it was too much."

"Because it is. It *asks* too much. Don't you see what it's already cost us?" The tears she'd hidden earlier now spilled over wrinkles wrought by years of working under the sun. "I lost everything when your father died. This house, the property... it's nothing without him. He was my life, Ainsley. And this place took him away from me."

For the first time, Ainsley saw the reflection of her own sorrow in her mother's eyes. She knew that same hurt and resentment. Had lived with it for years.

Grandpa set his newspaper down and rose from the couch. "Fellas, what do you say we go take a gander at the work Ainsley's put into the old barn? I reckon Brie wouldn't mind the company either." He locked eyes with Nanna on his way out.

She reached for her shawl. "Daphne, sweetheart? I've been itching to see how your garden is doing this fall. Ladies?" She motioned for the rest of the women to follow.

Once alone, Mama picked up her apron again like she needed something to hold on to. "I just don't want you and Josiah to go through any more pain. If you stay on this farm and marry someone like your daddy..." She closed her eyes. "I want a safe life for you. Away from the heartache here."

"Oh, Mama." She crossed the invisible rift that had kept them from fully embracing each other for too long.

Her mom clutched her tight. "I'm so sorry, punkin'. I didn't know how..."

"I know. I didn't either." They'd both gone all wrong dealing with their grief, so much that they'd missed seeing they didn't have to walk through it alone. If it weren't for Connor, Ainsley still wouldn't have understood.

Mama rubbed circles along Ainsley's back. "For the record, I never actually thought you'd go for Hank."

Ainsley sniffled through a laugh. "Well, that's a relief."

"Now, Stephen, on the other hand..."

"Mama."

"Okay, okay." She stepped back with her palms raised. "You do know I only want you to be happy and cared for, right? You and Josiah both."

"I know." She backed against the counter and released a slow breath. "In all honesty, I probably shouldn't begrudge you for trying to set me up with someone. Turns out I don't have the greatest track record for choosing the right guys." Another breath escaped. "Jonathan—"

"Couldn't find his butt with both hands in his back pockets."

Ainsley gaped at her.

"Heavens to Betsy, child. Don't stare at me like I only have one oar in the water. I know what I'm talking about. And I'm telling you, that boy was always too big for his own britches. Running off for some highfalutin job like that." She wrung her hands together. "He best be glad he never came back. I'd tan his hide so fast his head would spin."

When her mom mumbled something she wouldn't be caught dead saying in public, Ainsley had to force her jaw to release. "I thought you were disappointed in me for not fighting harder to keep him from leaving."

This time, Mama was the one to gape. "No one could've fought harder to save a marriage than you did." She ran her hand down Ainsley's arm until their fingers connected. "As much as we want to change people's minds sometimes, it's up to them to use the sense the good Lord gave them to make the right choice."

"Yeah, well, the *good* Lord could've pitched in a little." The pain of abandonment Ainsley hadn't been able to reconcile dug into her side, and she knew right then. Jonathan wasn't the only one she hadn't forgiven. She stared at the tiles. "After all this time, I still don't understand how He could let him leave." Was he really meant to all along? How could she accept that?

"God doesn't break promises, sugar bunches. People do. And we make a right ol' mess of things, too, don't we?" Mama's sad laugh dwindled to a sigh. "Truth is, I can't tell you why Jonathan left any more than I can explain why your daddy died too young. I don't reckon it's something we'll ever understand, but heaven knows you've handled it better than me."

She cupped Ainsley's cheek, tears welling. "You've been through so much, punkin'. More than any mama should ever have to watch her baby face." She brought a hand to her nose and looked away until a loving smile slowly found Ainsley again. "I've gotten a lot of things wrong since losing your father, but raising a strong and compassionate daughter has never been one of them. I'm so proud of you."

Ainsley couldn't respond. She stood there, trying to process how her own guilt and disappointment had caused her to misread what her mom had truly thought about the situation, about her.

Mama reached for Ainsley's hands again. "Now, I don't know a lot about what is or isn't meant to be, but I believe that young fella of yours was right about grace. I should've given a lot more—to you and Jonathan both." She rubbed her thumb over the backs of Ainsley's fingers. "I know I can't undo what we've lost, baby. And I don't expect making it right to be easy. But I want to try... if you'll let me."

314 | CRYSTAL WALTON

Ainsley squeezed her mom's hands and let her tears for the unnecessary time and hurt that had passed between them fall freely. "Only if you let me try too."

Mama pulled her close. And there in her mother's arms, Ainsley remembered once again what it meant to live loved.

"Now then." Straightening, Mama dabbed under her eyes. "Enough blubbering over the past, especially over Jonathan. Tell me why you sent that other boy away." She placed her hands on her hips when Ainsley hesitated. "My hearing's going, sugar bunches. Not my sight. I don't care if you were pretending or not. It's plain as day neither of you wanted to break up."

Ainsley's brow pinched. If Mama was graciously going to change the subject, she could have at least picked a less painful topic. Ainsley turned toward the sink, and any response she could've given got lost in the sight of Connor's empty loft.

"If you ended things because you thought I—"

"I didn't."

"Then what? Was he not good with Josiah?"

She twisted around. "He was wonderful with him. Everything a son deserves in a father." The pain of Josiah losing that racked through her.

Mama stroked her hair. "Then I don't understand."

She wished she didn't either. Wished things could've been different. She faced the window again. Memories danced across the yard—from images of him running around like a banshee trying to get Nugget off his shoulder, to his painfully awkward strut in cowboy boots, down to the affection his eyes held every time he saw Josiah. Her chest constricted. "I let him go because I had to."

"Why?"

Head down, eyes shut, Ainsley breathed in the truth she'd been scared to admit aloud until now. "Because I love him."

Chapter Twenty-Seven

Connor's eyes hadn't budged from the last line of Dr. Southerland's email since he'd scrolled to the end. An invitation to return. An open door to work in Whispering Pines. He'd hoped to hear Dr. Southerland liked his proposal enough to implement it. But to offer him a permanent position at the small-town practice? He hadn't seen that coming.

"Sorry for the delay, Mr. Allen."

Connor quickly clicked his phone off and covered his coffee cup when Pop's secretary approached with a container of sugar packets. He sat up in the office chair he'd been slumped in. "You wouldn't happen to have any Irish cream around, would you?" Coffee no longer tasted the same without it.

The thought tugged at a smile that was getting harder to assemble in front of coworkers he hardly knew despite knowing them most of his life. Conversations carried on around him. Some alongside the rectangular table, others off by the floor-length window or the coffee bar. All business focused. All between associates who worked side by side regularly yet held no sense of community. Work here wasn't about pride and joy but climbing to the next title. It was a different way of life. One that had always been Connor's norm.

Until Jamison Farms.

"Irish cream?" Christen looked at him as if he'd exchanged bodies with someone else. "I'll see what I can find, Mr. Allen."

"Thank you, ma'am."

She shifted another dumbfounded look away from his out-of-place behavior and crossed the board room in her high heels.

Ma'am?

Connor shook his head in a pitiful attempt to shake himself out of one context and into another. Nothing changed. The board room he'd sat in a hundred times felt more confined than he remembered. It shouldn't have surprised him. Everything about his life before his trip now felt off. His apartment seemed abnormally quiet, his silent phone glaringly stark. His freshly dry-cleaned suit felt too binding, his shaven cheeks too smooth. Most of all, his heart felt emptier than ever before.

"Mr. Allen?" Christen stared like she must've said his name more than once. She held out a small container. "Your creamer."

"Thank you."

Her polite smile bore a hint of the southern pleasantries he'd come to love. And miss.

He added the cream to his mug but couldn't bring himself to drink it. His stomach churned as the noise around the room closed in on him. He needed some air.

Barely through the door, he ran into Pop's right-hand man.

Phil lifted his coffee mug away from his suit. "Whoa, easy there, champ. First degree burns wouldn't be a great start to your first day back." Once stabilized, he extended a hand. "Welcome home. I have to admit, I didn't expect to see you today."

More like he didn't *want* to see him there today. No one could blame Pop's longtime friend and employee for resenting being passed up for the position he was the most qualified for. Everyone in the room knew the man was better suited to run the company than Connor was.

He shook his hand nonetheless. "Good to see you, Phil."

"Quite the big day, huh?" He sipped his coffee. "Quite. The. Day."

When another board member joined them to engage in idle talk Connor couldn't have been less interested in, it didn't take long for him to tune them out. He looked around the office. *Pop's* office. He wasn't ashamed of what his father had built. In all fairness, he had to admit he was grateful for the trade his dad had passed down and the life it had afforded him. There'd even been a time when he'd thought it was the life he truly wanted. But now…

"You can't fight providence."

Connor's head flew up. He stared at the two older gentlemen continuing the conversation he'd zoned out of.

Phil gave him a pat to the shoulder. "You all right, champ?"

"Sorry, what did you just say?"

"Providence." He fanned his mug out in an all-encompassing inclusion of the business surrounding them. "I've built most of my career on the principle of investment, believing equity eventually yields a return." A plastic smile with no hidden façades turned to him. "But I guess we both know life doesn't always play by the rules." He switched his mug to his opposite hand. "No point in trying to fight it."

A tangibly awkward pause passed between them. The third board member casually excused himself, but the weight of Phil's words kept Connor in place. Every mishap that had led him to Whispering Pines, every obstacle that had kept him at Jamison's Farms, flooded to mind. His pulse raced.

Phil pointed to the room about to cast the fate of both their futures. "Shall we?"

Connor's cell graciously intercepted his chance to respond. "Excuse me." He turned to take the call. "Flynn, sometimes your timing is impeccable."

"Maybe you should hire me once you're running the joint."

"You knew about that?"

"Your pops might've mentioned it."

Of course he had. "A heads up would've been nice."

"Like you would've listened to me anyway. Shoot, if I hadn't run into your country girl, you'd still be digging your heels in that North Carolina red clay."

Connor's body tensed. "What are you talking about?"

"She didn't tell you?" Flynn sounded impressed. "Man, she must know you better than I thought. I gotta admit, I was a little nervous she wouldn't come through, but you're right about those sweet farm girls. One mention of your dad's state, and I swear the compassion in her eyes could've—"

"My dad's *state*?" Connor loosened his tie. "So help me, Flynn, if you don't start making sense…"

"Easy, bro. Just be glad the two of us got you back home before your dad ends up in the hospital again. I know you have your differences, but take my word for it. You don't want to live with the regret of not making peace before he dies."

Dies? Flynn's convoluted words spun through Connor's head. "He was in the hospital?"

Realization must've finally caught up to his buddy, because it took him a minute to respond. "I'm sorry, man. I thought he would've told you by now. Look, you know how hard it was for me to watch my old man go, so if you ever want to talk…"

Flynn's voice trailed into background noise as the elevator dinged open. Connor turned, lowered his phone to his side, and stared as his dad walked through the doors onto the floor.

His gait still spoke of confidence, his suit of authority. But for the first time, Connor didn't see the untouchable businessman he'd both admired and, on some level, resented. He saw a fallible father who'd kept a secret from him that could change everything.

When Pop's line of sight intersected with his, he stopped, knowing.

Connor's chest caved at the look in his eyes. "Why didn't you tell me?"

Ainsley nuzzled Shiloh a little longer than usual after un-tacking him. As soon as she slipped through the stall gate, her horse nudged her from behind. She turned, smiled. "I'm good. I promise."

His eyes said he didn't buy it.

"Okay," she admitted. "I *will* be fine." Eventually. She had to be.

Ainsley kissed his forehead. "Thanks for that ride, boy. I needed it." She needed the fresh air against her face, the feeling of gliding across the land. She needed the peace her farm kept offering her, even when she'd shut parts of it out of her heart.

She looked around the barn. Mornings seemed quieter than usual lately, slower. It wasn't as if time had stopped since Connor had left a week ago. Chores still needed to be done. The ebb and flow of days on the countryside carried on. But she couldn't ignore the lull left in the wake of his whirlwind through their lives.

On the other side of the stall, Ainsley folded her arms on top of the gate. Memories of the day they got caught in that storm played across the wall like a projected movie—scene by scene, feeling after feeling. She closed her eyes, breathed through it, and soaked in Shiloh's persistent nose nuzzles. She stroked his neck. "Love you too, buddy."

She gave him yet another kiss and turned for real this time. Eggs needed to be collected. On her way to the doors, something drew her to a stop in front of the narrow staircase leading to the loft. The *empty* loft. She hadn't been up there since Connor left. She had no reason to. Still, the urge beckoned.

She held her head back in defiance but knew her feet wouldn't listen. No surprise, they'd whisked her all the way to the top before hesitating. The old floorboards creaked under her footsteps when she finally brought herself to round the doorway.

He'd left everything as it had been before he'd arrived. Neat. Lifeless. Even the boots and hat she'd loaned him looked forlorn sitting in the chair, as though missing the cowboy they'd never anticipated getting used to.

It wasn't until she sat on the mattress edge that she noticed his copy of *Anne of Green Gables* left on the nightstand. After another moment of hesitation, she opened it to where he'd used one of her flash cards as a place holder.

"I went looking for my dreams outside of myself and discovered, it's not what the world holds for you, it's what you bring to it."

Ainsley traced her thumb over the quote, brought the book close, and shut her eyes.

A clatter of nails scurrying up the steps chased her tears away. Matty stopped inside the doorway and angled his head at her, then trotted over and lifted his paws onto her thighs. Music started playing out of nowhere.

Ainsley followed the sound to an mp3 player attached to his collar and shook her head. She knew what was coming before ever looking up.

Kate and Daphne slid into the room like Tom Cruise in *Risky Business*, except fully clothed, complete with the feather boas they'd played dress-up with when they were kids. Daphne pulled Ainsley off the bed, draped a boa of her own across her shoulders, and spun her around the floor while lip syncing to "Dancing Queen."

Her two best friends in the whole world smooshed their cheeks against hers and left her no choice but to belt out the chorus with them with every fiber of her eight-year-old self.

Even Matty joined them in their dance. Sort of. Either that, or he was trying to decide whether he should protect or attack the boas around their necks.

Ainsley cracked up at the whole scene. The mess, the randomness, the fun. Six minutes ago, she would've told anyone they'd all outgrown their cheesy ritual of cheering each other up any time one of them was down. Now, she was glad they hadn't.

All three girls fell backward onto the bed in a pile of feathers and laughter and a bond more sacred than any other.

"You gotta work on that bridge, Kate," Daphne said without sitting up. "You're a little sharp."

She swatted her cousin in the face with the end of her boa. "Better than being flat."

Daphne propped herself up on her elbow and cast a not-so-subtle glance below Kate's neck. "You really want to start talking about being flat?"

Ainsley clamped a hand over her mouth to keep from laughing.

"Really?" Kate sat up. "Why does it always come back to my chest size?"

"Because you're too fun not to tease." Daphne winked. "And because those push-up bras deserve some serious recognition." She reached over to Kate's shirt. "Let me see those things—"

"Will you stop?" Kate scooted off the bed. "Y'all are unbelievable. You know that? No boundaries. I swear, you're worse than Mama."

"Which is why you love us." Ainsley pulled herself up by her knees. Sobering, she looked between them. "And why I love you both so much."

Daphne scrunched her nose. "This isn't the gooey part, is it?"

Ainsley smothered her in a hug of confirmation.

"Okay, okay." Daphne pushed her off. "Gooey part's done. Check."

Hardly.

The stack of flash cards came into focus again. Ainsley twisted two feathers together. "Seriously, I don't know what I'd do without y'all." Her family was her bedrock. If she had any strength in her, it was built on that foundation. "I thought I'd been alone these last few years. But the truth is, I never have been." Not once.

"You still aren't." Non-gooey Daphne squeezed Ainsley's hand for the full ten seconds her affection meter could endure.

Ainsley laughed to herself until Kate stopped by the corner chair.

"Daddy would've been proud to see Connor wearing his hat, you know?"

Ainsley's fingers balled around the mattress edge, Kate's words around her heart. "You don't think I should've asked him to go, do you?"

"I think you should've given him the choice."

Ainsley turned toward Daphne whose expression agreed. Even Matty's puppy eyes added to the consensus. Heck, if she were to peek in on Mama and Josiah in the house, their faces would probably say the same.

"It wasn't that simple."

Daphne sat up. "No one said putting faith in love is."

Ainsley gawked at her. "I thought you didn't like him."

"The doc grew on me." She shrugged. "Anyone who concocts a scheme to destroy that evil toy your mom got Josiah can't be all bad." She smiled genuinely then. "And sometimes…" She lifted a shoulder again. "You just know when something's right."

"Not everything works out just because it's right. I mean, how do you know when to leave things up to fate and when to fight for them?" Would it even matter if she tried?

Kate crossed the room. "I don't know about fate, but I think sometimes love fights *for* you. And when that happens…" She swayed her head. "It's probably worth trusting."

Ainsley's tears ran into a smile only Kate had a way of bringing out of her. "You sound like Daddy."

"It must be my eyebrows talking." She exaggerated the quirky way he could communicate everything he didn't say solely with eyebrow movements.

Sobering, Kate sat beside her. A look of nostalgia wandered back to the chair where the hat and boots sat instead of their dad. "He had a way about him, didn't he? I don't know how he did it, but he never lost faith that things would work out for us." She laughed to herself. "Even when we swore up and down that everything in life was going to pot." Kate elbowed her. "*Some* of us more dramatically than others."

Ainsley shoved her back but couldn't deny it.

"Seriously, though. I know Daddy didn't usually say all that much, but he believed in your dreams, Ains." Kate leaned the side of her head against hers. "And maybe you should too."

Ainsley squeezed her sister's hand as if it would have any impact whatsoever on squeezing back her emotions.

Daddy's faith had always inspired her, but sometimes holding on to that faith felt as hard as holding on to him.

"I don't want to give up on them, but I'm honestly not sure where to go from here," she admitted.

"You can always start with yoga," Daphne interjected in her typical fashion of cueing the end of all things emotional. "My mom got another Yanni CD to add to her collection."

Ainsley laughed. "Of course she did. Where does she find these things?"

"Girl, don't get me started." Daphne strode to the window and sat on the sill. "She swears music is the healer of all things. She even brought Spock to class today, as if that CD stands half a chance at lulling that crazy buck."

"Spock? You're kidding." Yoga class was the last place on earth for a goat like him.

"I will say, he's actually not doing too bad." Fighting a grin, Daphne peered across the yard. "That guy he's partnered up with must be working some serious magic."

A guy crazy enough to take on Spock? "Okay, this I gotta see." She joined her cousin at the window. One peek toward the pasture, and every inch of her froze. She clutched the sill, her heart unsure whether to stop or soar. She squinted harder, swallowed. "Is that…?"

Chapter Twenty-Eight

Ainsley nearly collided with the fence. "Connor?"

He turned his head from his plank position. One look was all it took. His dimples sank in, and her voice felt like it was trapped under his yoga mat.

"What are you doing here?" she managed.

Another smile. "I seemed to have left without my flash cards. And apparently, I still have a lot to learn."

Spock rammed his forehead into Connor's hip to knock him over and relentlessly tried to climb on top of him. Clearly, Ainsley wasn't the only one who'd missed her cowboy.

She pinched her bottom lip to keep from laughing. "I thought you said I'd never see the day you do yoga."

"I guess even things we stubbornly resist are meant to be sometimes." Connor's green eyes held her right there in the messy, complicated, illogical embrace of a love that could neither be earned nor restrained.

Spock knocked over one of the other class members, and Aunt Penny's eyelids flew open from the front of the pasture.

Ainsley knew that look. They needed to stop disrupting her class... and fast.

Daphne came up from behind as if her mom had summoned her telepathically, maneuvered through the fence to grab Spock, and escorted him back to his pen.

While the rest of the class resumed their quest for inner peace, Connor hopped to his feet and jogged to the fence. Sunlight glistened across the eyes that Ainsley had missed so much. He covered her hand with his, and she had to lean into the rail for balance.

Everything she'd felt in the barn when she'd asked him to leave resurfaced and tore at her heart again.

"Connor—"

"Listen—"

Their simultaneous attempt to broach the silence ended in a soft smile from both of them.

"Sorry," she said.

"Me too, but not for interrupting you," he added with the playful inflection that drove her crazy and more in love with him than made sense. "I'm sorry for leaving."

"But I—"

"Was doing what you thought was best for me."

"Your father…" She looked up with every ounce of empathy in her. "I'd give anything for another day with my dad, Connor. Anything. I can't let you stay and miss being there for yours while you still have the chance."

"I know. And I love you for that."

Conflicted tears mounted at the single word. "If I had told you, you wouldn't have gone home, and I couldn't live with—"

"Ainsley." His thumb smoothed over her cheek. "I know," he reiterated. "But my dad's fine. Flynn jumped to the wrong conclusions."

"What?" She studied him. "But… he said…"

"Probably a lot of things he shouldn't have. One of the hazards of being a New Yorker." Connor rubbed the back of his neck and laughed softly until sobriety returned to his eyes. "My grandpa's the one who's dying, not my dad."

"Oh, Connor. I'm so sorry."

"I didn't know him at all. I didn't even know my dad was in touch with him still." He picked at a knot in the wood. "Turns out I had no right to talk to you and your mom about extending grace to each other when I've been misjudging my own family for decades."

Regret laced a heavy exhale. "My grandpa ended up with a lot of health problems working in a coal factory when my dad was growing up. But blast the pride in my family, he never admitted he was sick. Never explained why he was gone for weeks at a time in the hospital. Pop assumed he was out running around. That he didn't care that they were struggling to make ends meet. All while my grandpa was sacrificing his health to provide for them."

Connor clenched the rail. "I want to be angry with both of them for letting pride and assumptions shut them out of each other's lives—out of mine and Reed's. But how can I be when I'm as guilty of doing the same?"

Ainsley didn't miss the edge in his voice, still raw from things he was only now finding out. Her heart ached for him—for the relationships he'd missed out on, the forgiveness that might be even harder to give now.

"I get why Pop always turned to business. He was trying to be a better father by ensuring we were taken care of in ways he felt like he wasn't. But all we ever saw was his absence. Same way he saw my grandpa's." Connor raked his hand through his hair and smiled sadly. "Generations of getting it all wrong... All these years..."

Ainsley could identify with that mistake better than he thought. "Guilt and grief can be pretty strong blinders. Trust me, your family's not alone in that."

"I wish it didn't take someone dying to see that." He looked skyward. "This past year makes so much more sense now. The pressure my dad's been putting on me. The urgency. He didn't learn the truth about the past until he found out my grandpa's health had taken a turn for the worse. When he did, I guess you could say things kinda came to head for him. Guilt, fear, regret, you name it."

Connor gripped the fence post again. "He and Reed are already practically estranged. Makes sense he'd throw all his energy into making sure I didn't leave too. Tack on developing pneumonia earlier this month, and no wonder he decided to name me his successor."

"Wait, what?"

"Don't worry. I'm not taking the job."

"Connor." Ainsley reached for his hand. She knew how he felt about working under his dad, but surely things were different now. Even if his father's health wasn't in jeopardy, they should still be together.

"I know what you're gonna say, but—"

"I love you." She hadn't exactly meant to blurt it out like that, but it honestly didn't matter. It was true, and she needed him to know. She raised a shoulder. "I do. I'm in love with you, and I'd be lying if I said I didn't want you to stay, but not at the cost of coming between you and your family. You shouldn't be estranged from them any more than Reed should."

"I won't be." Connor ducked through the rails to stand beside her without any barriers. "There are a lot of things I need to work out with them. I know that, and I'm committed to seeing it through. But staying in New York, taking over Pop's practice…" He shook his head. "That's not the way. He and I both know it. I'm as certain about that as I am that this is where I'm supposed to be. Here, with you and Josiah."

He took her hands in his. "Listen, I'm the first to admit how complicated life is. And yeah, I ran when I was trying to sort it all out, but I didn't end up here by chance, Ainsley. Cancellations from other clients, Dr. Southerland's invitation, the leak in my condo… Call it what you want, but I don't have any doubt I was meant to come here, to find you." He rested his forehead against hers. "You've always been what I've been missing, even when I didn't know what I was looking for."

Tears fell at his words and the realization they evoked. She leaned back without looking away. "I've always struggled with the idea that everything that happens is meant to be. As if there's some cosmic, indifferent fate running our lives instead of a loving plan working things together for our good. Truthfully, it burned my biscuits to accept that." She laughed softly when he made a face at her southern expression. "Well, it did. And now I understand why."

His brow furrowed. Heaven only knew where he thought she was going with this.

Ainsley curled her fingertips under his. "What I mean is, I believe love led you here, not fate." She looked back at the barn loft where she'd been with Kate and Daphne moments earlier and smiled. "I believe it pursues our hearts instead of the other way around. When it's hard. When it makes no sense. Through the things that hurt. Even after loss, it's still fighting for us. But the choice is always ours, and I choose to trust in love again." She inhaled deeply and found his eyes. "I choose you."

She could've drowned in the emotion moving his shoulders up and down, and his feet a step closer.

Of all moments, his cheeks warred with his dimples. "Anyone ever tell you what a forward girl you are, Ainsley Grace?"

She tossed her head back. "Only the presumptuous doctor types."

"You gotta watch out for *those* types."

"I would if I could, but…" Grin to the side, she toyed with a button on his flannel. "Even an honest country girl has her limits."

He lassoed an arm around her waist. "I think I have you beat on that one, Miss Competitive. I have since you accused me of turning my coffee into a Candy Land board game."

Ainsley laughed again. But as minutes drifted in the breeze, all humor gradually faded, and time stalled as it always did when he held her this close.

Connor swept back the hair caught in her lashes. "From the moment I met you, I've wished I could skip to the end of your story and assure you of the happily-ever-after you deserve. I wish I could tell you what's waiting on every page, but all I know is this." The assurance in his eyes curled around her. "I want to write every single *romantical* sentence with you. Through the middle, beyond the back cover. I want to write our own love story." His lips hovered above hers. "Starting right now."

Epilogue

One Year Later

Connor dropped his bag, hustled across the carport pavement, and sprang for the van. "Not my suitcase, man. Not the suitcase!" He backed Spock away from the open trunk and dared a sniff in their luggage's general direction. Amazingly undefiled.

Spock eyed him like he was offended for not being packed along for the trip.

Laughing in spite of himself, Connor scratched a non-stained section of the goat's neck with the very tip of his finger. "Sorry, bro. Not this time." Or any time. Ever. "I need you to watch out for Kate this week, 'kay?"

Matty soared around the corner of the farmhouse and landed two muddy paws on Connor's thighs.

"Don't worry, boy." He ruffled the dog's ears. "You're the real one in charge."

"Until Daphne gets here," Ainsley said on her way through the front door.

Connor grabbed the two bags she was shouldering. "I thought she had some festival to go to with Penny."

"Change of plans. Kate took on a home care job this week."

Connor closed the trunk. "Since when did she start picking up in-home nursing jobs?" Had things been that tight for her since moving out?

"Since the patient is her ex-boyfriend's father."

"What?"

"Long story." Ainsley slid Josiah's sippy cup into his car seat's cup holder. "Suffice it to say, we might need to bring her back a gallon of real eggnog."

More like a barrel of it. At this rate, he might need one himself. He pulled out his cell to double-check his email one more time.

"I think Dr. Southerland can handle holding down the fort for a week without you."

Connor looked from his phone to the sassy grin that hadn't lost its ability to cripple his resistance. "You think so, huh?"

"I mean, he *did* kind of run the practice for, oh, twenty years before hiring you, so... I think he's good." She circled her arms around his waist. "You, on the other hand, look like you could stand to get an adjustment on our way out." Layers of intuition searched his eyes. "You wanna tell me what has your shoulders tight enough to springboard us all the way to New York? This isn't our first rodeo visiting your parents."

He laughed, half wondering if a bucking event would be safer than going home. "I know, but it's different this time."

"Why?"

"For starters, it'll be our first time visiting as a married couple." He laced his fingers around his wife's back and tipped a smile at her. "Just think. We'll actually get to stay in the same room."

"Doesn't sound so bad to me." She lifted on her toes to kiss him, and every other coherent thought blew off in the breeze not coming anywhere close to cooling him down.

"Is that all?" she said too soon.

He hoped not, because he definitely wasn't done with just one kiss.

She angled her head at him. "You were saying our visit will be different this time…"

"Right, sorry. Got a little sidetracked." Connor willed himself to focus but regretted it as soon as he did. He squeezed his neck. "Reed's gonna be there."

Ainsley's whole face lit up. "You talked him into coming?"

"I think his wife had more of a hand in that than I did, but yeah. He and Callie are actually coming. The girls too." It'd been so long since he'd seen his brother's family, he couldn't separate his nerves from the hope that getting to spend the holiday together this year might change things between them for good.

Ainsley curled into his side. "It's going to be great, Connor. I promise."

With her there beside him, he couldn't help believing it would be.

The teal front door that had welcomed him home every night for the past year opened again. Kate stepped out with Josiah.

"Dada!"

Connor hardly had time to squat before Josiah flew straight into his arms with a running start. Of the countless things about Whispering Pines that still undid his heart, nothing reached deeper than the privilege of getting to be a father to Josiah.

"There's my big guy." He whirled him in the air. "You ready to see Grandma and Grandpa? Me too, buddy, and wait 'til you meet your cousins." His voice broke a little at the end.

A warm look in Ainsley's eyes rivaled the winter breeze trickling up the driveway. She tucked her shoulder under his at the same time Josiah nestled his head under Connor's neck.

His throat tightened as it did every time the gift of grace caught him off guard. He kissed his son's sweet forehead, kissed his wife's soft temple. And there on the farm with the family he never imagined he'd be blessed enough to find, Connor savored the life that love had never once stopped fighting for.

From The Author

Ainsley's right about fiction. A thread of reality is always woven into it. Real-life experiences inevitably find their way into my stories. In this book, there are at least three (on top of all the baby fun), which only goes to confirm it. My life is a walking rom-com. Okay, not really, but I do have my share of embarrassing moments. So, take a girl's advice and avoid wearing your hair down at the chiropractor's, watch out for those fly-away dresses, and, most of all, embrace the spit-up. :)

I hope you enjoyed reading *Her Stand-in Cowboy.* Please know how much power and influence your words carry. They just might be what another reader needs to hear. Leaving a constructive review on Amazon and Goodreads is a tremendous help. I can't do it without you!

If you enjoyed Connor's charm, be sure to check out his brother's story in *Romancing the Conflicted Cowboy*, available on Amazon.

Also, grab a free copy of *Your Story Matters* at www.crystal-walton.com/new-release-mailing-list and be the first to hear about the next release.

Acknowledgements

Ryder, you hold my heart, sweet boy. Every ounce of spit-up down my bra, every shirt stretched out from you walking up my chest until I was flashing the world, every fever scare and diaper blowout were all 100% worth getting to hold you in my arms each day and take in the precious smile that changed my life forever. Thank you for the gift of getting to be your mama. Love you to Neverland and back. Always.

Dave, thank you for working hard to provide for our family so I can be home with our little ones and occasionally fit in this writing thing.

Mom, what in the world would I do without your help? Truly, I would not be able to survive the pandemonium that is motherhood if I had to navigate these years alone. Thank you for the countless ways you bless our family. This book would not be finished without your support.

Erynn, here's to yet another edited book. As always, thank you for coming alongside me to help strengthen this story with your thoughts, suggestions, and corrections.

Josephine, thanks for sharing your talent in creating a cover that fits the story so well.

Jaycee, thank you for making time to read an early copy of this book, for offering feedback and encouragement, and for letting me blather on about changes my mess-of-a-mama brain couldn't decide on.

Yaritza and Sherrinda, thank you for the name suggestions for Spock and Mr. Tumnus. They were perfect.

To each member of my launch team, thank you for your ongoing support, for journeying with me through different subgenres, and for hanging with me during these slower writing seasons. I appreciate you so much.

CPSIA information can be obtained
at www.ICGtesting.com
Printed in the USA
LVHW020730111119
636959LV00001B/199